Let the Shadows Fall Behind You

Let the Shadows Fall Behind You

A NOVEL

Kathy-Diane Leveille

CLEARWATER | FL | USA

LET THE SHADOWS FALL BEHIND YOU
Copyright © 2009 by Kathy-Diane Leveille.

All Rights Reserved. Published and printed in the United States of America by Kunati Inc. (USA)
and simultaneously printed and published in Canada by Kunati Inc. (Canada)
No part of this book may be reproduced, copied or used in any form
or manner whatsoever without written permission,
except in the case of brief quotations in reviews and critical articles.

For information, contact Kunati Inc., Book Publishers in Canada.
USA: 13575 58th Street North, Suite 200, Clearwater, FL 33760-3721 USA
Canada: 75 First Street, Suite 128, Orangeville, ON L9W 5B6 CANADA.
E-mail: info@kunati.com.

FIRST EDITION

Designed by Kam Wai Yu
Persona Corp. | www.personaco.com

ISBN 978-1-60164-167-0   EAN 9781601641670
Fiction

Published by Kunati Inc. (USA) and Kunati Inc. (Canada).
Provocative. Bold. Controversial.™

http://www.kunati.com

TM—Kunati and Kunati Trailer are trademarks owned by Kunati Inc.
Persona is a trademark owned by Persona Corp.
All other trademarks are the property of their respective owners.

Disclaimer: This is a work of fiction. All events described herein are imaginary, including settings and characters. Any similarity to real persons, entities, or companies is purely coincidental and not intended to represent real places or living persons. Real brand names, company names, names of public personalities or real people may be employed for credibility because they are part of our culture and everyday lives. Regardless of context, their use is meant neither as endorsement nor criticism: such names are used fictitiously without intent to describe their actual conduct or value. All other names, products or brands are inventions of the author's imagination. Kunati Inc. and its directors, employees, distributors, retailers, wholesalers and assigns disclaims any liability or responsibility for the author's statements, words, ideas, criticisms or observations. Kunati assumes no responsibility for errors, inaccuracies, or omissions.

Library of Congress Cataloging-in-Publication Data

Leveille, Kathy-Diane.
  Let the shadows fall behind you : a novel based on a true story /
Kathy-Diane Leveille. -- 1st ed.
       p. cm.
  Summary: "A woman whose life has been plagued by the disappearances of
loved ones reluctantly confronts her family's troubled past in this
enigmatic story of loss, forgiveness and the power of friendship"--Provided
by publisher.
  ISBN 978-1-60164-167-0
  1. Domestic fiction. 2. Psychological fiction. I. Title.
  PR9199.4.L477L47 2009
  813'.6--dc22
                                         2008050616

DEDICATION

To Pierre, Chris and Ben,
who always believed.

And to my mom and dad,
who set me free to roam
the fields on the farm.

ACKNOWLEDGEMENTS

Thanks to the New Brunswick Arts Board for the Creative Writing Grant.
Thanks to author M. J. Vassanji and his faithful mentoring through the
Humber Creative Writing Program.
Thanks to historian David Goss; naturalist Jim Wilson; and the archivists at
the Saint John Regional Library for their time and expertise.
Any oversights in the research are solely mine and not theirs.
Special thanks to publisher Derek Armstrong
and editor in chief James McKinnon
for their unflagging commitment.

Chapter One

No ... don't leave me!
Brannagh Maloney awoke in darkness. "Nikki?" she mumbled. Something pinched her eyelids shut. Brannagh popped two fingers into her mouth before laying them across each eye. She felt the ice crystals sealing her upper and lower lashes dissolving.
She opened her eyes. The down sleeping bag had slid off the mattress and onto the floor.
Don't go.
She rarely remembered dreams. If a rare echo carried over to the waking day, she ignored it.
Brannagh glanced at Nikki's dark, curly head on the pillow next to hers. He looked deceptively vulnerable with his six-foot frame curled inward. His right arm, browned by the hot summer sun, was flung across his forehead.
Brannagh yanked the cover upwards. She tucked one corner around his shoulder then sat up, pulling her knees into her chest.
In the muddy half-light seeping beneath the window curtain, whiskers of hoarfrost glinted on the timbered walls where the joints met below the red-shingled roof. Autumn was a mere blip in the changing of the seasons in northern Ontario.
Nikki was leaving today. Brannagh looked forward to a week of solitude and time to regain her perspective. She would sketch the surrounding hills now that the waves of scarlet and plum had disappeared, leaving behind skeletal branches; a bleak blend of brown and grey.
Alex Turner, Nikolai Mirsky's assistant, had found the cabin

after they had returned from their first expedition into Lake of the Woods to survey birds in the boreal forest. Their offices, housed in a pair of abandoned MNR trailers ten kilometres west of Ignace, didn't offer living quarters. Most of the staff stayed at Bob's Motel. Nikki had insisted he needed a retreat from the rest of the crew. What he hadn't revealed initially, even to Brannagh, was that he wanted her to share the retreat with him.

The cabin was at the end of a rumpled dirt road, perched on a cliff overlooking Davey Lake. It was rodent-infested and every spare inch that wasn't already littered with rusting coffee cans or tobacco tins had been filled with animal droppings.

"It's haunted," Alex had claimed one night, as they sat around a fire on a curve of shale that overlooked the water.

"What is?" Brannagh had been lying on her back trying to locate Ursa Major.

"This place."

According to Alex, who had grown up in Lake of the Woods, the cabin had been built at the turn of the century by a prospector for his mail-order bride. Child bride, the town folk called her. Thirteen years old. Ten months after she arrived from a small town in Minnesota, the prospector disappeared. She claimed he'd rowed out to the island to fish, that she'd found the lunch she'd prepared for him, yellow-jackets crawling over the jam cake, still wrapped in a handkerchief.

"Let's row out there." Nikki had jumped to his feet. "Fry a catch of northern pike."

Brannagh had peered intently into the fire, a shiver snaking her spine.

"Don't tell me you believe in ghosts?" Nikki paused at the edge of the cliff.

"People who disappear aren't ghosts," Brannagh answered

softly.

"What are they then?"

But she had already turned away.

There was only one piece of furniture in the room where Brannagh and Nikki slept; an old-fashioned bureau with a glass bowl and water jug. The floor was covered with stacks of paper, file folders and texts; all the research that they, and the team of university students, had carried out over the past year. Nikki was a wilderness preservationist. He organized the first count of birds in the boreal forest, which would set a baseline for the ecosystem before the building of dams and hydro plants (which big business and government insisted would not change the environment). The ten-year study would help measure the effect of sulphur dioxide on two million acres of lakes and rivers.

Nikki had fought long and hard to bring it together. Brannagh, by a pure stroke of luck (and white lies), had been hired as cataloguer. When she left Toronto and headed north last spring, she anticipated starting a whole new career, one that would change her life. Her life had changed, all right.

Brannagh leaned toward Nikki on one elbow until her face was inches from his. The mask worn by the man who fought battles all day was gone. Something rose to the surface in sleep that she only caught fleeting glimpses of when he was awake. When Nikki pondered an ornithological puzzle, his dark eyes flashed. It was this sense of child-like wonder experienced on the brink of the spectacular that left Brannagh weak. It was the enticement that beckoned and would not let her go. Still, she didn't know what possessed her to let down her guard and move into the cabin with him. The exhaustion at the expedition's close had skewed her better judgement. Luckily, their work would wrap soon, and they would go their separate ways.

Brannagh fell back onto her pillow. On mornings like this, when she was unable to drift back to sleep, Brannagh sensed the presence of that child bride. After she and Nikki had moved in and scrubbed the cabin from top to bottom, she would awaken in the half-light of dawn to a vague distant swishing crackle. She found clumps of faded newsprint on the floor. Old-fashioned insulation, Nikki explained, tumbling out from between timbers. Ghosts, Alex insisted with a wicked grin. Brannagh saved every one.

Advertisements: Dan Schinsky's Hair Dye.

Random pages from a pulp novel: *The Five Cent Wide Awake Library*.

The Bible: Joseph's brothers saw him coming from far away. Let's kill him and throw his body into one of the wells and tell our father that a wild animal killed him. Then we shall see what becomes of his dreams.

On days like today Brannagh sensed the presence of the child bride pacing the floor when the wind rose, or sighing when a log tumbled into the fire.

Brannagh added messages of her own to the cracks between the timbers. She pulled articles from Nikki's files: Canada Accepts Nuclear Warheads. Man Walks on The Moon. "I Have a Dream," says Martin Luther King.

This is who I am, she silently informed the chinks between the timbers. It's 1970. This is my world. Women don't need men to survive. I love being on my own. And then, just in case she was giving the impression that she was too serious, Brannagh scribbled: Bob Dylan writes "Like a Rolling Stone."

Brannagh pictured the child bride reading to the hermit every night from pulp novels, the bible. Did the grizzled old man grow dreamy-eyed and wrap his arm around her, or did he grumble over time better spent carving up a moose carcass?

Brannagh rose to her knees and parted the curtain on the window. Her warm breath fogged the pane, but she could see bits of feathery white drifting downward; the first snowflakes of the season. The rugged earth, pungent with the decay of rotting leaves, solid under her feet just yesterday, had disappeared.

Brannagh rolled off the mattress and fished around for the bush socks she had abandoned during the night. By 8:30 she was sitting cross-legged on the kitchen floor waiting for water to boil on the camp stove. When it did she tossed in a scoop of aromatic coffee grounds, followed by a handful of crushed eggshells.

Nikki was not a morning person, and lately it had been harder and harder to get him out of bed. Something seemed off, but then, how well did Brannagh know him? By the time Nikki emptied a dresser drawer into a rucksack and pulled a wool sweater over his head, it was 9:30.

"I'm late." He lumbered into the kitchen and pulled Brannagh close to him. He smelt of wood smoke and the flowery motel soaps they pilfered whenever they went into town for a night of beer and burgers at the Evergreen Motel.

"How late?" Brannagh opened her bathrobe and pressed against him. His breath was warm on her forehead.

"The vamp in the woollen underwear." He smiled.

She picked up the suitcase by the door and followed him outside, jolted awake by the morning air. The lake lay still and sullen beneath the falling snow.

Nikki tossed the rucksack into the front of the truck and leaned on the door. (Later Brannagh would recall a distant, haunted look in his dark eyes, the purple shadows beneath them.)

Brannagh wrapped her arms around her chest, shivering, and hopped from one foot to the other. "I'm sure it will be fascinating, your conference on ... whatever."

"Trends towards shorter turnover cycles in forestry, and their effect on boreal birds' seasonal movements between biomes in the course of annual migration."

"How terribly exciting. Whenever I tell people I'm a Natural Science Illustrator, they think I survey hydro lines in Labrador."

Nikki reached out and grabbed her hand. He kissed it, and then slid it beneath the neck of his sweater. "Brannagh ..."

"Yes?"

"I ..."

"What is it?"

And then he shrugged. "Don't forget to check the mail."

Brannagh gazed into his dark eyes. She saw crag and burbling streams and tamarack. They had spent so much time in the bush that she was unable to define him, he could not come into focus, without it. Suddenly, inexplicably she did not want him to leave her. The snow made a faint shush, shush sound as it fell to the ground. Brannagh tilted back her head. The flakes were icy on her cheeks.

"Coffee for the road?"

He shook his head. "I put new batteries in the torch."

Brannagh experienced a pang. Just when she least expected it, the big oaf did something sweet.

"Take it to bed with you if ..." He squeezed her arm gently before turning away.

Brannagh had an irrational fear of the dark and could not sleep without a light, or Nikki's foot hooked around her shin, and his masculine sea-scent interlacing her dreams.

"Nikki."

"What?" Nikki kept walking.

She swallowed. "Don't forget to eat."

Brannagh stood on the porch and watched the truck tires slide along the rutted road leading to the Trans-Canada highway.

Three days later, when Brannagh called the hotel in Winnipeg where the conference was being held, the desk clerk told her that Nikolai Mirsky was not listed on the hotel registration.

The tips of her fingers, clutching the phone, tingled.

Perhaps, the desk clerk's voice droned on, she would like to inquire elsewhere?

Brannagh hung up the phone and went outside to stand on the road. She stared down at the end, willing a dark figure to appear; first as a movement within the tall evergreens, then taking shape on its own. She told herself that the wetness on her cheeks was snowflakes. By the time darkness fell, Brannagh had abandoned the lookout. She already understood that, like the earth covered by the first snow of the season, Nikki had vanished from her life.

Brannagh Maloney had lived with disappearances all her life. They were as familiar to her as the changing of the Fundy tides.

People who disappeared left cast-off shadows of themselves, murky tremblings that slunk out of corners on drizzly autumn afternoons. They lurked offstage, silent or sighing or reaching out to run a finger across her arm. They were the curtains fluttering in the window on a breezeless morning, the musty scent that arose when opening an abandoned cellar door.

When Brannagh was three years old, her father, Ben, a shy man, not given to volunteering his thoughts, hopped a Russian freighter.

"When will you return to the mainland?" Pamela, Brannagh's mother, had asked as she squinted into a hand-held compact.

He shrugged his broad shoulders and laid one hand on

Brannagh's head. "Depends."

Brannagh remembered the stillness that surrounded her mother when he did not return, the way that sunlight springing from behind a parted curtain made her flinch. Eighteen months later, at eight-thirty on a Wednesday morning, Brannagh's mother packed a weather-beaten portmanteau and slipped out the door without a glimpse back. When Brannagh began to have nightmares, Aunt Thelma bundled her up in a quilt and recited an invented fairytale. After her mother's tragic death, Brannagh became determined to leave and find her own happy ending.

Her childhood home had been a four-story dwelling on Argyle, on the west side of Saint John, New Brunswick, two blocks south of the Provincial Asylum where her grandfather saw patients two days a week. Long before halfway houses and support systems became part of the neighbourhood, her grandfather had run what was known as the Nervous Clinic in their home. Selected patients, too healthy for the asylum but too sick for families to cope with, were released into his custody for respite care. They settled on the third floor, where he kept an office, studied and slept. He made fleeting appearances downstairs, ensuring Gran's comfort while treating Aunt Thelma more like hired help than family.

Brannagh had finally escaped to university ten years ago. With each mile on the train drawing her further and further away, personal scenarios had shifted, edges had blurred, sending secrets scuttling into corners. By the time classes started at the University of Toronto, she had taken to wearing black, and when she was asked about her roots, gave no telling revelations. After Nikki's disappearance, Brannagh experienced a queer sense of knowing. It was as if, after wandering aimlessly for years, trying to feel her way in a dark room, she had ended up in the very spot where she'd begun.

Sergeant Orser, the rakish ponytailed OPP detective who had arrived at the office after she filed the Missing Person's Report, asked her point blank, "Where do you think he is? Gut reaction?"

"Injured?"

Orser's dark eyes, behind the Lennon-style granny glasses, remained inscrutable. One bony finger tapped on the desktop. Finally he spoke. "You mean a robbery gone wrong?"

She nodded. Did he think she was wasting his time? Overreacting? That this was a co-workers' spat? The detective looked like he had dressed inside a paper bag and spent his paycheque on roach clips and floor-to-ceiling black lights.

"What else?" His finger tapping did not miss a beat.

"Maybe he was working on a top-secret project, and dropped out, like he has before, to throw big industry off his trail. Maybe someone wanted to get rid of him. Or he could turn up on a logging road, chained to a tree."

"Orchestrate a media event?"

He patted his pockets, pulled out a pack of cigarettes, glanced inside it then tossed it into the garbage. "Only nobody's tipped off any reporters."

"Not yet."

"Let's stick to the facts." His eyes narrowed as they scanned Brannagh.

"I have no idea where he is, that's why I called you."

"What's your relationship with him?"

Brannagh opened her purse, scrounged for a piece of gum. "He's my boss."

Sergeant Orser placed his palms flat on the desk and leaned forward until his face was inches from hers. She could smell sugar-laced caffeine and nicotine. "Are there any other relatives, besides his Uncle Zhuk, that you are aware of?"

She shook her head.

"He hasn't heard from Nikki, doesn't seem concerned."

She waited.

"Sometimes spending so much time in the bush, people get a little stir crazy."

"Your point?" Brannagh rose from her chair.

The detective held up his hands in a conciliatory gesture. The corners of his mouth shifted upward. "I'm just saying, they lose their perspective and get involved in things they later regret. Don't see any way of backing out but to—"

"Disappear?"

He fished a business card out of his vintage suit-jacket pocket and handed it to her. "If you remember any facts you think could be relevant, call me."

Brannagh nodded and felt her last remnants of hope exit with the detective. The aging hippy had probably been shuttled north for a reason; but even if screw-up was his middle name, he was right on one point. She had worked with Nikki long enough to understand the "facts," the implications of a solid scientific hypothesis. The cold hard truth was that, like everyone else in her life that she loved, Nikki had disappeared.

Brannagh felt as if the winter would never end. A hot nugget of fury lodged in the center of her chest and refused to budge.

At first, Alex had been concerned about Nikki's disappearance, but as time went on, and there were no reports of foul play from the police, Alex and the rest of the staff began to shrug it off as just one more of Nikolai Mirsky's eccentricities. They became annoyed when Brannagh started sitting in Nikki's office for days with the door locked. The office received complaints that inquiries from journalists and scientific bodies regarding the progress of the study were going unanswered. (Brannagh couldn't stand the sight of the bundle of mail stuffed into her box each day, knowing perfectly well each held a request for an update on the marvellous career of the infamous Nikolai Mirsky. When no one was looking, she opened the lid on the abandoned Port-a-Potty stored at the end of the hall and dropped each bundle in.)

In March, Brannagh stopped calling Sergeant Orser once a week. He never had any news, and the tenderness that had crept into his voice was irritating. She forced herself to summon up the energy to collate the data they had compiled up north: juggling percentages of tree heights, canopy and ground cover.

In April, Brannagh made a unilateral decision to clear out Nikki's desk. She and the detective had gone through it months ago, looking for any clues that might provide answers, but had come up empty. She was tossing things into the garbage without a second glance when the telephone rang.

"Any news?" Annie demanded, as if she needed no introduction. She didn't.

"I told you not to call any more."

"So, no news?"

"No." Brannagh glared at the receiver.

"Sorry."

Why did Brannagh think Annie's response always carried a swell of relief?

"Anyway. This is the last time I'm going to invite you."

"Jesus, Annie. Give it up already." Brannagh leaned back in the chair, phone tucked under her chin. Annie, Brannagh's childhood friend from Saint John, had begun telephoning her once a week to hound her about the reunion of the Tuatha-de-Dananns (the "girls only" club they had formed in grade eight).

"I need a smoke."

Brannagh heard Annie's sharp inhalation. She pictured Annie in the attic of the house on Argyle in Saint John; Annie as she had been, her long lean form sprawled across the dusty wooden floor, with a cigarette in one hand while the other impatiently gathered her long auburn hair into a pony tail and tucked it into the neck of her T-shirt. She would assess each of the four members of Tuatha-de-Dananns with her impenetrable brown eyes, and would proceed to methodically list what they each needed to do to save themselves.

"You swore you'd never set foot back here again," Annie grumbled.

"Exactly."

"Shit. Someone's at the door."

"People make different choices. You stayed. I left."

"Hey, I'm a doctor, I'm not supposed to smoke. Battleaxe McGillvery will—oh shit!"

"Goodbye."

"No! Don't hang up."

There was a clunk as Annie dropped the phone. Brannagh heard muffled voices in the background. Mrs. McGillvery was a nurse who had worked for Brannagh's grandfather until he retired, and then moved on to work for Annie's father, Dr. Baird. Brannagh almost smiled, relishing the idea of the Scottish spinster thwarting Annie. No one else could.

Brannagh contemplated hanging up the phone, but something held her back. Annie meant well, she always meant well. She sat in the wobbly chair behind Nikki's desk and glanced down at the trash can.

Minutes before Annie's telephone call, Brannagh's hand had

wriggled out a stained recipe card from the back of the drawer. On one side, in Nikki's scrawl, was written: -soak beans overnight -add molasses, brown sugar, mustard, lard. She remembered how, on their first night out, he had been sitting on a log by the fire, hunched in concentration, puffing on a pipe while writing furiously into a leather-bound notebook that never left his side. She had been nervous and intimidated, worried that her lack of experience would trip her up. Brannagh was convinced he was cataloguing some earth-shattering observation he had noted on the journey up river, one that she should studiously be making preliminary sketches of. Miserable, she shoved her pencil-less hands deep into the pockets of her down vest. Then he sprang off the log, dropped the recipe card into her lap, and after a brief smile, disappeared into one of the tents.

Alex, Nikki's assistant, rose to his feet. "Tomorrow's supper," he said, by way of explanation. "That's one of the cataloguer's duties, cooking supper. You gotta soak the beans."

Brannagh gaped. Now she understood why the six of them had sat around the fire for such a long time after setting up camp, eventually passing around a loaf of bread and jar of peanut butter. She choked on the stench of the cooling fire, fighting an urge to dive through the door of Nikki's tent and throttle him. Coward, she thought. Why didn't he say something?

The next night, Brannagh waited until they'd all been fortified with a shot of rum and Nikki was showing off a "proper demonstration" of the J-stroke to Cindy, one of the googly-eyed undergrads. Brannagh yelled, "Supper!" When she had Nikki's full attention, she whipped the jar of peanut butter at him football-style. It landed in the dirt. His dark eyes fixed her with a puzzled look as he bent down. He rubbed it clean with one blue flannel shirttail. Brannagh walked over, unscrewed the lid, and pulled out the gooey recipe card. "Yeah, it's done," she announced, slapping him on the back. The recipe card stuck to his shoulder before dropping to land on his foot.

"You still there?" Annie asked impatiently.

Brannagh shoved the card deep into the garbage can. "So, tell me, what's it like?" she challenged. "The Dr. Annie business?"

There was a long pause. When Dr. Baird had passed away, Annie had been forced to turn down a position at a hospital in Calgary until she could find someone else to take over the family practice. "The first time I sat behind Dad's desk it just felt ... bizarre. But my biggest headache? Battleaxe McGillvery."

Brannagh closed her eyes and could see it all. Stout Mrs. McGillvery in her hound's-tooth suit, the office, Annie's childhood Victorian home with the white gingerbread trim.

"As if I don't have enough to worry about, I've got this kid, Wilfred Adamson, a med student my dad promised an internship, in the office, and McGillvery is ordering him about like the paper boy."

Brannagh pictured Annie sitting behind the desk that Dr. Baird had sat behind for so many years. He was a plump, rosy-cheeked man who, before the death of his son, had a contagious laugh that came from deep within his chest, and gentle dark eyes. Annie would coax him into letting them listen to the dull ka-thunk, ka-thunk of their hearts through his stethoscope. Brannagh's heart would begin to pound, just because he was a man, up close and foreign. When he asked her questions about herself, she felt as if her feet had been nailed to the floor and that the blush rising in her cheeks was going to lift her scalp clean off. Dr. Baird would hug Annie and call her "my amazing child." Brannagh would stare out the window at the leaves on the maple that flipped in the wind like beggars' hands, and experience an inexplicable urge to bolt.

"I've got it all figured out." Annie was clearly losing patience. "You don't have to set foot in Saint John if you don't want to. Who would blame you if you didn't? After your mom, the murder, all that dumb gossip—"

"You haven't listened to a single word I've said."

"Here's what we do. We hold the reunion in your cottage. What is it? Ten, twenty miles up river from Saint John? No busybodies nosing around. All we need is a key."

Annie knew perfectly well Brannagh had keys. They had been sent to her years ago, along with a copy of Gran's will.

"Maybe it's time to forget about him."

"Are you finished?"

"Did it ever occur to you that you might be better off without him? Forget about bringing him back."

"I don't have a clue where he is. How could I bring him back?" Last November she had rented a car and driven to Winnipeg, stopping at every gas station along the route. Not one person had recognized Nikki or his truck from the picture she had shown them. Brannagh rose from the chair and started pacing.

"That's good," Annie insisted.

"Eh?"

"That you don't know where he is."

There was something in Annie's tone that made Brannagh's stomach clench. They had been best friends for years, but she had never forgotten how dangerous spending time with Annie could be. When Annie began sending letters this winter, Brannagh had mailed them all back with a bold "no such address" scrawled across the front. But as the weeks dragged on and her loneliness grew, she had relented and started accepting the phone calls.

"I mean, if you don't know," Annie back-pedalled, "you might as well stop thinking about him. Start thinking about yourself for a change."

"I'm not obsessing over him. I have work to do. The truth is, we barely knew each other."

"Good! Then you'll come home."

"They need me here. No one gives a rat's ass about sulfur dioxide contaminating canoe country. Bird counts aren't sexy. They're trying to cut our funding, and I can't let that happen." She still said our and us, even though winter had passed without one word from Nikki. Drama in the Canadian North was nothing like *Dragnet*.

"Dianne said you wouldn't come," Annie muttered.

Brannagh felt a stab of regret, imagining Dianne's big blue eyes, framed by platinum bangs, her slow, shy smile.

"Say hi to her and Tish for me?" "Tish" was short for Patricia, but Brannagh couldn't remember anyone ever actually using her full name. "How's the new baby?"

"Walks. Talks." It was a blatant reprimand. "Gotta go. Think about it. That's all I ask."

"Sure." But they both knew perfectly well that going home was the last thing Brannagh would ever do.

When Brannagh was a child, she suffered from nightmares and terrible growing pains. Her Aunt Thelma tried everything she could think of to make her feel better. Hot water bottles wrapped in flannel, Watson's liniment, a cherry sucker with a cup of warm milk before bed. But nothing alleviated the ache that started behind Brannagh's knees and radiated to her toes and hips. Brannagh would wake in the night, and stuff the corner of the quilt into her mouth.

Finally, at her wit's end, Aunt Thelma turned to her mother. Brannagh's Gran, Rye, was a wild-eyed, crinkly-haired woman, who religiously traced a path, back and forth, from Simm's Corner to Reversing Falls every Sunday afternoon after church without fail, an action that got every tongue in the neighbourhood wagging. Usually Grandfather was able to persuade his wife to keep her eccentricities under wrap, but after the tragic murder of a local boy had shocked the quiet neighbourhood and left them reeling, even Grandfather was powerless to calm Gran down.

"Brannagh's still having pains," Aunt Thelma had informed Gran, when they were alone in the kitchen shelling peas.

Brannagh's Gran, like the eldest child in every generation in her family clear back to the Druids (according to those who relished the telling of a good tale on the steps of Sanderson's Store) had been born with a tried and true knowledge of healing power. Only Mrs. Cunningham, the fastest back stabber on the block, had the guts to quibble.

"Pagan superstitious nonsense," she would say, with an air of crisp authority that left everyone feeling uneasy. "She's crazy and that's all there is to it." Though most didn't have a clue what the word pagan meant, there was no mistaking Mrs. Cunningham's implications. They were, in their open-faced gullibility, committing a sin.

The following day, after Grandfather left the house, Gran came to Brannagh's bedroom. Her silvery-blue eyes burned intensely as she asked a litany of questions.

"Where exactly is the pain? When did it start?"

Rye ordered Aunt Thelma to drive them to the family cottage up the Kennebecasis River.

"We can't." Aunt Thelma's jaw tightened.

"And why not?"

"I'm not supposed to leave the house. Grandfather's orders."

"But why?"

Aunt Thelma chewed her bottom lip. "It's been locked up ever since that boy ... I really don't want to go there."

"You asked me what to do and I'm telling you," Rye said. Brannagh rode in the back seat, trying to ignore the rising tension by counting the slanting farmers' fences that slipped past between luminous stretches of the river. Years ago, it had carried the steamships which the shipbuilders in Saint John had travelled upon to their summer homes. The old estates remained with tall Palladian windows and exquisite hand-carved woodwork. They had become permanent year-round residences for those who could afford the upkeep. The Maloney cottage was no bigger than one of the outbuildings on their grounds. Situated further upstream, close to the ferry, it was built of weather-blackened granite. The rooms were small and cramped, crowded with reminders of the old country, Ireland. The roof had a tendency to leak, and the cellar flooded every spring, but the northern windows offered a shadowy view of the Kingston Peninsula, a finger of land twenty miles wide and five miles long on the opposite shore.

When they arrived at the cottage, Rye wasted no time. She took a quart basket off one of the nails on the wall outside. "Brannagh, darlin', skim the leaves and bugs off the top of the rain barrel," she ordered. Then she marched into the woods that separated their property from the neighbouring abandoned cottage with the red roof, loudly singing, "All things bright and beautiful, all creatures great and small ..."

"Ordering me not to leave the house. What gives him the right?" Aunt Thelma muttered chewing one of the pills she kept squirreled in her pockets. She hurried indoors, and returned with a couple of wool blankets, and a bottle of Moosehead. She sat on a wooden chair, wrapping a blanket tightly around her shoulders, and squinted through the cigarette smoke towards the woods.

Brannagh peered nervously towards the bush. Aunt Thelma had been at the cottage the morning the berry picker spotted the boy's body a year ago. Upon hearing a scream, Aunt Thelma had run into the woods. For days afterward, she walked around whispering under her breath. A crazed lunatic had stabbed the boy in the chest and left him spread-eagled on the peak of the red-roofed cottage to bleed to death. Patricia, a girl at school whose father was the Chief of Police, whispered updates in gym class. She insisted that the police were hot on the killer's trail. They'd probably already caught him, Brannagh decided now, maybe just this morning or an hour ago or the very minute they had piled into the car.

Brannagh shivered as she stood on an overturned bucket and cleaned the rain barrel. The water was cold. The tips of her fingers ached. The water gave off the smell of moss in a blueberry patch after it's been peed on. When she was done, she picked the twiggy flower stems that remained in the garden and sat on a blanket, weaving them into a lump, pausing every once in a while to stare at the river.

The tide was high. Brannagh watched as the waves gradually gave up their restlessness. Dusk approached, blurring the edges of the clouds. Aunt Thelma's eyes grew heavy. Her grip on the arms of the chair loosened. Brannagh lay on her back with her hands under her head. The sky seemed bigger up river, away from the paper mill stacks, and the Provincial Asylum's hulk. She watched a group of clouds trailing one another like ghosts on a slow eastward journey. They seemed to take the holy thoughts she held to protect her grandmother, and tug them away, one by one.

In the distance, a shout arose, followed by the high-pitched barking of a dog. Aunt Thelma stirred in her chair on the dock. "What time is it?"

"Dunno." Brannagh followed Aunt Thelma indoors. When

Brannagh's grandfather and Rye had first married, they had decided to transform Rye's childhood home into a summer cottage. But Grandfather had always been too busy to spend time there. The cottage, in Brannagh's mind, defined the separation between Grandfather and them. Here, the women answered to no one but themselves and underwent a transformation of sorts. Brannagh's grandmother became almost beautiful in a wild, startling way that seemed to flash beneath the surface of her skin in the cold Fundy breeze.

"As usual it's left to me to pull the meal together. Would you all starve if I just up and left?" Aunt Thelma found a jar of jam and some soggy crackers. They sat at the kitchen table and washed the makeshift meal down with metallic-tasting water from the pump.

"Can she really do magic?" Brannagh asked, licking raspberry seeds off her thumb. "I mean, can she cure me?"

Aunt Thelma fished a cigarette out of her jacket pocket. "Don't depend on anything but this." She tapped her forehead.

"My brain?"

"Never mind, don't waste your time. Lot of good it's done me."

"But ... " Brannagh faltered under the scrutiny of her gaze.

"We should go after her." Aunt Thelma pushed her chair back, but instead of heading out the door and into the woods, she filled the kettle with water, then took the old-fashioned letter box that had belonged to Gran's mother, Brigid, off the shelf. She leaned down and opened it with a key from her pocket.

"What happened to your necklace?" Brannagh asked. Aunt Thelma always wore a gold medallion with an engraving of a starfish around her neck. Brannagh's fascination with it grew in direct proportion to the degree of Aunt Thelma's refusal to let her play with it. She never took it off. Ever.

"It musta broke! You lost it. We gotta find it." Brannagh started scrabbling across the floor on all fours.

Aunt Thelma sat down in the rocker, setting the stack of recipes she kept in the letter box onto her lap. Sometimes Aunt Thelma looked right through Brannagh, as if she wasn't even there.

"Gran said it was a gift from a boy."

Aunt Thelma's head rose. She glanced toward the window. "We should go after her."

"I'm ... I'm scared."

Aunt Thelma stared at her blankly. "Then we'll wait."

Brannagh tracked down a dog-eared copy of *Wuthering Heights*. She had already read it twice, but she curled into a corner of the couch, convinced that a third read would illuminate the true mystery behind Heathcliff.

She awoke, hours later, to a "shushing" in her ear.

"It's only me," Gran whispered.

Brannagh sat up, relief washing over her as she rubbed her eyes. Aunt Thelma, who never seemed to need to sleep, was snoring in the rocker, head thrust back. A line of spit ran from the corner of her mouth, forming a dark oval on the collar of her blouse. A wind had arisen. The dark branches of the oak churned outside the window.

"Look at these." Rye sat beside Brannagh and pressed something cool into her palm. One, two, three stones: rough-edged lumps that, on closer inspection, she could see were flecked, here and there, with spots of green, some as warm as the sun shining through leaves at the end of the day, and some as dark as the bottom of a well.

"Lie down now," Rye ordered. She rolled the legs of Brannagh's shorts up. In the dampness, her frizzy hair had risen round her head, creating a silver aureole. "We need to stop the struggle," she explained gruffly, "for the spell to take hold, I mean to *really* set." Her face radiated an invisible light, some shining, humble knowledge that Brannagh could only wonder, and scoff at, and envy. "If you don't surrender to the pain, it won't matter what I do, or how long I do it …" Her voice drifted off as her gaze fell on the stones in Brannagh's palm. Sometimes Brannagh imagined that God looked like Sister Mary Margaret at Saint Patrick's School, sitting behind a huge desk in the clouds. She knew God had his pets. She wasn't one of them.

Rye picked up the stones, and rolled them in her fingers. "No, it must be three green stones, gathered from a running brook, between midnight and morning, while not one word is said."

Brannagh watched silently while her grandmother rubbed the stones up and down her legs. Her large-knuckled fingers traced a path. First thigh, then dip and rise over the bump of the knee, then smooth slide down the shins. A light rain began to patter on the roof overhead. The air in the room grew damp, stuffy, and the smell of the ashes overpowering.

"Wear away, wear away … there you shall not stay … Cruel pain, away, away."

Brannagh closed her eyes, hiding her misery. Her Gran rubbed her skin raw with a bunch of rocks. What if someone found out? Mrs. Cunningham already called Rye a crackpot the minute she turned her back. Didn't everyone, sooner or later, depending on which direction the wind was blowing?

"There you shall not stay."

Brannagh opened her eyes. What if, when she wasn't feeling well, Rye brought her an aspirin, carbonated soda, and the funny papers? She would have a heart attack, from the shock of it, that's what.

Rye laid shaky fingers on Brannagh's brow. "You look different," she concluded with a self-satisfied nod.

"I feel different," Brannagh lied. "I really, really do."

Gran asked Brannagh to roll over onto her stomach. "Cruel pain, away, away."

How long her Grandmother kept it up, Brannagh had no idea. She fell asleep. Later, she was thankful, and even gloated over the fact that God had finally answered one of her prayers. Rye never offered to perform the ritual again.

The odd thing was that the growing pains seemed to drift away after that. Not all at once. Just a gradual lessening, until Thanksgiving in the house on Argyle came and went, and Brannagh realized that they had disappeared altogether.

"Of course," Rye said, as if there was never any doubt, while she poured cream into her morning tea.

"You outgrew them," Aunt Thelma interjected, flipping pancakes onto a plate.

"But look! Your necklace. You found it. The magic helped you too." Brannagh pointed to the familiar star medallion dangling from Aunt Thelma's neck.

"It fell in the flour bin, and you outgrew the pains." She klunked the frying pan sharply for emphasis.

"Rats," grumbled Annie. She yanked the corn syrup bottle out of Brannagh's hand. "I was hoping you had Polio. Then I could have your pink and blue hopscotch chalk."

And then Grandfather had come into the dining room, and they all quieted and concentrated on cutting their pancakes into tidy, fork-manageable squares.

After Nikki disappeared Brannagh would awaken in the two-room cabin and hear a faint echo of familiar words drifting through the night:

Wear away, wear away ... There you shall not stay ... Cruel pain, away, away.

Brannagh would wrap the sleeping bag tightly around her and wonder where Gran was now. She would fall into a restless sleep and dream she was standing in the Kennebecasis during spring thaw, its swollen waters tumbling over gravel and scrub. Brannagh felt the gritty riverbed beneath the soles of her feet and the icy waters tugging at her shins. She watched, with growing trepidation, the path of the rising river as it spilled over the banks, wild and unfettered, sweeping toward the closed black woods.

Brannagh gazed at the empty drawers in Nikki's desk. Everything was bundled into trash bags, except for a few file folders and a Rolodex. The telephone rang. She scowled, realizing too late that she had neglected to take it off the hook.

"What now?"

Tish's husky voice held a hint of uncharacteristic hardness. "Don't come home."

"What?"

"I don't think you should come home. You'll regret it if you do."

"Uh, okay." Brannagh paused to digest this bit of news. "May I ask why?"

"Annie ... it's just not a good time."

"It isn't."

"No."

"Finally, someone's on my side." Brannagh waited for more. "So."

"So."

"How's the baby?"

"Belinda's teething. Everything goes in her mouth. Socks, leftovers, dust balls."

Brannagh pictured Patricia, with her curly red hair and wide-spaced emerald eyes.

"You feel like they're going to pin a medal on your chest the day they're born, but they don't tell you that you're never going to sleep again."

"You love it."

Tish laughed. "Guilty as charged."

Brannagh nodded. It was all Tish had ever wanted in life: to meet the man of her dreams. Of course, that drove liberated Annie crazy. She had argued for kidnapping Tish when she decided to drop out of high school and tie the knot. "It's such a waste!" Annie had railed. "Let's show her some mercy, perform a lobotomy. If she insists on going through with this barbaric charade, at least it will be painless." Annie took the work of the Tuatha-de-Dananns seriously. Ironically, Tish's father, the mayor of Saint John, had agreed with Annie, and wished he was still the chief of police with the power to threaten to put his teenage daughter under lock and key.

Brannagh heard Belinda gurgling in the background. "Hey, remember how we used to link pinkies and chant?" Tish asked.

"I try not to."

They had named themselves Tuatha-de-Dananns after an ancient Irish race. They snitched some pamphlets they found hidden under Aunt Thelma's bed, and snuck up to the attic one night to perform a secret ritual. They swore by candlelight to "honour, uphold, and protect my sisters' self-a-steam in the club, at any cost to life and limb, until death do us part. Amen."

Dianne added the "Amen" just in case God misconstrued what they were doing with the burning of the candles and the kissing of the Gaelic cross.

Not to be outdone, Brannagh, who was always filling their ears with ancient legends that she said were passed on by Rye (but in truth she had simply made up) ordered them to repeat Rye's charms for protection with their eyes closed.

"But," Tish protested, "we aren't all women of Erin."

"My Gran's magic," Brannagh whispered, gazing at the cross through slitted eyes, "is strong enough for us all."

And because Brannagh had always been the resident expert on witches and magic, no one argued the point.

Even when Dianne found a library book that said that the Tuatha were great necromancers, which meant they were *yuck* able to *puke* raise the dead, Brannagh didn't waver. She cautioned them not to miss the point altogether. *What about Jesus? What about Easter?*

"I couldn't possibly get away," Brannagh lied when Dianne called, sheepish and strained-sounding, an hour later, confirming Annie's hands pulling invisible strings behind the scenes.

"I miss you, Brannagh."

"Sorry about your Mom's funeral." Brannagh had been saddened to hear that Dianne's mom had passed away.

"She loved geraniums."

"I couldn't get time off."

"Thanks for sending them."

"And you're okay?"

"I'm—"

"Great, so, anyway, listen, as far as this reunion thing goes, you're a sweety for thinking of me, but please, convince Annie to drop it. I promise I'll think about it. Just get her to back off, please?'

And, surprisingly, thankfully, Annie did.

Brannagh forgot about the reunion. When one of the ornithology students, Glen, started flirting with her (it was silly, really, he had to be ten years younger than she was) and she felt a slow tingling rush down her spine when he placed his hand on her back, she told herself that maybe everything was going to be okay after all.

One night, after Glen convinced everyone in the office to go for a beer at the Legion, Puffin, Brannagh's cat disappeared. Someone had let the resident skunk out of its cage, which sent the poor feline scaling the curtains. Brannagh hunted everywhere to no avail. Glen gallantly put off quenching his thirst for five minutes, but then he, like everyone else, headed off. Brannagh was just zipping up her coat when she heard a faint mewing coming from under the window in Nikki's office. She coaxed Puffin out from underneath the sagging couch, where she was tangled inside a ratty woollen scarf. Brannagh sat, clutching the mass of fur, wool and dust in her lap. Wrapped within the scarf she found Nikki's beaded tobacco pouch. She opened it and inhaled the familiar sensuous biting tang. She remembered how, those first few nights in the woods, she would sniff this scent, then catch Nikki's warm dark eyes watching her intently from across the fire.

Every night during the trip up river, Nikki and his assistant, Alex, pitched their tents next to Brannagh's. Brannagh would never admit it, but she was grateful for their presence. She had discovered that there was no darkness as bottomless and chilling as the night that fell in the deep woods of the Canadian North.

Brannagh sneezed and Puffin leapt off her lap. She wrapped Nikki's scarf around her neck, tucked the tobacco pouch into her back pocket and headed toward the door. When the telephone rang, she decided to cut the line and drop it down the Port-a-Potty.

"What now?"

"Miss Maloney?"

"Uh, Sergeant Orser?"

"OPP found a body."

Brannagh felt an icy needle prick her sternum, and numbness spread across her chest. How desperately she had prayed for his phone call with news of Nikki, but she had never paused to contemplate the grisly reality the call might bring. Until now.

"On a deserted back road, ten miles west of Upsula," he continued.

"Is it ... ?"

"A hunter went missing not far from the location last spring. My hunch is it's him."

"Can you tell from the picture I gave you? Does it look like—?"

"Impossible. The body's been ravaged."

"Meaning?" An image flashed in her mind's eye. A body under a sheet. Cloud-shaped blood stains. She winced.

"Some animal ripped open the abdominal cavity. Entrails dragged off. The face is—"

"That's enough." She couldn't do this. She thought she could, but she couldn't.

"You asked. Look, I'll call you as soon as the autopsy results are in."

He paused. Brannagh swallowed. Is this how the summer would pass? Waiting with trepidation for the phone to ring to confirm the worst? "Miss Maloney?"

"I'm listening."

"The OPP in Kenora brought me up to speed."

She waited.

"Why didn't you tell me about the murder last summer on your expedition?"

Brannagh felt all the muscles in her body loosen suddenly as if an invisible string running the length of her spine had snapped.

She sank into the chair behind the desk. Bloody hell. But there was no escape hatch, was there? "No, there wasn't a murder. That's not true."

"There's an ongoing investigation into the death."

"The insurance company, one of the students, he overreacted."

A measured tapping came from the other end of the line.

"Remember when I said if you recalled any facts to contact me?"

Brannagh closed her eyes. "I didn't think—"

"The stench? It's fierce."

"I just ... didn't think ..."

"There's a reason why I've outlasted the techno-whiz cadets from suburbia. Constables who think it'll be a cake walk coming up north and pulling rank on the red-neck dick."

"I wasn't, I wouldn't ..."

"Solitude is good. The senses sharpen up north, every one of them. Cut through crap like a butter knife."

Brannagh shook her head.

"You do not want to jerk me around."

After he hung up, Brannagh buried her head in her hands. She pictured Nikki that last morning as he lay sleeping on the mattress, frowning. Her hands felt bloodless, wooden as she dialled the numbers on the phone. This was the lesser of the two evils? Wasn't it?

"I've changed my mind," Brannagh told Dianne. "I'm coming to the reunion."

"But I thought you said—"

"I need a change of scene. I can't sit here worrying day after day about Nikki, about what the police might turn up."

"I can't believe it." Even beneath her excitement, Dianne still managed to sound worried. Brannagh figured the earth would stop spinning on its axis if she didn't. "It's never felt right, without you here. Without you walking down Main Street, without you bent over a table in the library."

Brannagh's eyes smarted. She had always been Dianne's protector. Leaving her had been the hardest of all.

"Life just hasn't been right since you left."

No, Brannagh wanted to object. There never was a time when my life was right. But she didn't. Instead, she hung up the phone and set about trying to track down Max, her new supervisor, at the local Legion Hall, to see which two weeks in the summer she'd be able to take off, praying silently that she would remain clear-headed enough to argue against any protestations he raised to talk her out of it.

Annie opened the door slowly. The room was dark. She could hear his breathing. She could smell him. He had a scent, a distinct aroma that she was growing accustomed to, coming to like, to look forward to, that she thought about in the middle of the day when she was busy doing other things. It was, she liked to think, the smell of the forest, a deep, dark, unexplored forest and he was at the heart of its centre.

From the moment she left her office she had known that she would come to him tonight. Because for one startling moment, while eating supper, when she had imagined him lying in this room, she had thought, "It can't be. It isn't true." She had given her head a shake. It was someone else's life, not hers.

It seemed for a moment as if it had all been a daydream, slow, hazy, lazy, like the kind you experience on a summer day in the middle of the afternoon, after a swim and a meal and a nap in the shade of a weeping willow.

She stood beside the bed, watching his chest rise and fall, and re-experienced a familiar frisson of wonder. The thrill of fear that ran beneath it. It was true. She had done it. It was startling, really. She had never been an impulsive person. Not like some. And yet look what had happened when she followed a crazy dare that rose within.

He slept like a baby, curled on one side, knees drawn in towards his chest.

She was surprised about this; about men, that they too could appear so vulnerable at times. She hadn't known that. Hadn't imagined that to be true. Because she had known so few men. Really known them. Beneath the layers of bravado and bluffing and hard sheen of masculinity. She had always been too busy trying to prove she didn't need a man; always trying to prove to her best friends that they didn't need one either. She had viewed men as crutches only weak women required.

Annie pulled back the covers and slid into bed behind him, pressing her knees behind his, sliding her arm around his waist.

He stirred in his sleep, mumbling. She pressed a finger against his lips. They were soft and full. A girl's mouth. The kind of mouth that could tremble and cry when a heart was breaking. Who could have known that was possible?

"Shhhhh," she whispered in his ear, pushing dark curls off his forehead. She circled both arms around him, and pressed her cheek against his shoulder blade. He smelt of sweat and the forest and a baby's skin after a bath.

She was struck by the thought that this was all she wanted, all she had ever wanted. "Shhh," she whispered. "It's just me."

Chapter Two

Predictably, as soon as Brannagh crossed the border into New Brunswick it started to rain. It wasn't the sort of orderly, polite shower she'd grown used to in Upper Canada. One minute the sun was shining; the next, a dervish rocked the horizon.

Brannagh understood the ferocity of the east coast sky. She pulled the car onto the shoulder of the highway, and waited it out. She remembered one summer day when a fierce torrent had swept over the cottage. Gran had jumped up. "Grab the umbrella," she had ordered. They had headed out the door, wind pressing their clothes to their skin, and climbed up the shaky wooden ladder to the roof.

Gran tilted back her head, wet hair plastered to her skull. "This is better than any sermon for lifting the spirits," she yelled. Unlike Brannagh, Gran loved storms.

Teeth chattering, Brannagh peered through the needles of rain, the churning treetops and white-edged swells, and watched. If she raised an arm, she was convinced she could thrust a fist clean through the storm's belly. She felt smaller than small. Eventually Brannagh's heart eased its pounding high in her chest, but she didn't stop worrying that a swirl of darkness was going to descend and swallow her whole.

Brannagh rubbed her tired eyes. What was she doing here? She really should turn the car around and drive back through Quebec to Northern Ontario before it was too late. Gritting her teeth, she put the car into gear and turned south toward the Fundy coast.

Gran's cottage looked smaller than Brannagh remembered it. The pale blackened granite glowed in the early evening light. The surrounding bush was overgrown. Gran's gardens and the old-fashioned water pump on the eastern slope were smothered somewhere beneath the tangle. The wild apple trees on the opposite ridge rattled their branches in the wind.

Great-grandfather Erin O'Kelly had considered it a castle when he built it; a kitchen and dining area, and a parlour that doubled as a bedroom at night. He took a backbreaking job in a quarry in the nearby town of St. George and hauled a wagonload of pink stone home every ten days. Time and the elements had tarnished every inch. His pride and glory had been the large veranda, with the hand-carved mahogany railing built off the kitchen, which faced the river. It was his offering to Brigid, his cousin and bride, who had arrived via matchmaking relatives in the old country. After their first child, Gran, was born, he had added a second floor with two bedrooms, and had waited patiently, and in vain, for more children to come along to fill them up.

Brannagh dug garbage bags and boxes out of the trunk. The familiar raw scent of the sea clung to the dampening night air, and in the distance water lapped on the shingle. The cottage overlooked the Kingston peninsula, tucked between the Kennebecasis and the Saint John River. They joined below the southernmost tip to flow into the Bay of Fundy at Reversing Falls in Saint John. Twice daily the Fundy tide flooded the rivers. Brannagh had grown up marking her summer days by its rise and fall.

She struggled through the weeds and muck adjacent to the gravel drive until she found the path leading to the back veranda. Someone had cleared that out at least. There were several posts missing in the back porch railings and some of the boards underfoot were loose. It took a few minutes of jiggling the key in the lock before she managed to thrust the door open.

She set her bags down on the sloping, worn linoleum in the kitchen and, pulse jumping, slowly inched her way into the darkness, down the hall to the parlour, groping along the wall for a light switch. Finally her fingers encountered the familiar bump. She clicked it once. Nothing happened. Cursing, she jiggled the toggle again. Suddenly, the room flooded with light. Brannagh experienced relief, along with a pang of regret, as she noted that nothing, not one blasted thing, had changed.

The walls were covered with wooden shelves, the floor with an assortment of tables built from odds and ends or fashioned from travelling trunks. Every surface was replete with the tangibles collected by all who had passed under the roof: driftwood, rocks, shells, maps, mugs, dried flowers, loose buttons and an assortment of feathers: gull, duck, cormorant and goose.

Gran had told stories of ancestors who, over a hundred years ago, had packed their belongings and sailed from County Cork in the coffin ships, and survived the crowded journey, the cholera, the poverty, the anti-Catholic sentiment, to carve out a place for themselves in New Ireland, as New Brunswick had been called back then. Gran liked to talk about her journey back to the Emerald Isle, and the tiny village on Mizen Head near Roaring Water Bay where her father, and her father's father before him had been born.

"Dad led me up a rocky path to a hut on a hill. As soon as we stepped through the door, I understood for the first time why we lived in a cottage of stone on Canada's east coast with cramped, crooked rooms, and a hodgepodge of cupboards." Gran would dip a knuckle into the corner of one eye. "As I watched my father step forward, cap in hand, to hug an old woman with fingers like tree roots, I understood that the cottage on the Kennebecasis River would never come close to the real thing, but that it was all we had for the O'Kelly clan on the other side."

Brannagh ran her hands over the spines of the books on the shelves above the fireplace: *Wild Geese*, E. J. Pratt's *Newfoundland Verse*, *Dr. Miles Weather Almanac and Handbook of Valuable Information*.

The walls were covered with old-fashioned Victorian wallpaper, flowers with twisting vines. It rumpled in the middle and had oblong stains, in the shape of people's heads, above the back of the couch. A worn velvet wing chair was angled at one end of an antiquated piano. Gran's wooden rocker sat opposite.

In the kitchen, the wood stove stood in the centre of the room, with its nickel-plated handles, oven plates and skirting gleaming. Brannagh could almost smell the raisin scones browning. Someone had filled the match box hanging on the wall, and the kindling box directly below it.

Brannagh swung open the tin-lined oven door and stacked kindling in the fire box. Annie? The fridge had been cleaned recently and hummed steadily. There was a loaf of bread, milk and eggs on one shelf. In the darkened pantry she found a sac of sugar, canned soup and a tin of tea.

Brannagh lifted the kettle and spotted the rumpled piece of paper anchored beneath the toaster. Words were hastily scrawled across it in smudged black ink.

I'm off to Fredericton to teach summer session at St. Thomas. Fortuitous as you, no doubt, have no desire to see me any more than I you. If you remove anything from the cottage, a cup, a tea bag, a spoon, there will be legal repercussions.

There was no signature. None was necessary.

Brannagh swung open the stove door and tossed the note into the fire. It darkened in the corners, crumpled, and burst into flames. One moment her grandfather was there, and the next he was gone.

―※― ―※―

When Brannagh was eight years old, one of the neighbourhood girls on Argyle Street set up a lemonade stand on the corner. She was a girl who Brannagh especially disliked, not only because she liked to flaunt ringlets that her mother rolled every night, but because she was always the first to point out to the teacher the wastefulness, the uselessness of Brannagh creating a card for Mother's Day in school when her mother had left town.

Her name was Hilda Outhouse.

For two weeks, Hilda sat behind the lemonade stand like a queen upon a throne.

"Cold drinks for sale!" she cried.

The girls at school crowded round Hilda at recess, each yearning to be chosen to assist because Hilda used real lemons, bottled cherries and tissue parasols.

Brannagh ignored them all. She knew that even if she wanted to help, which she most certainly did not, Hilda would take great pleasure in turning her down.

One Sunday afternoon, when the house on Argyle was quiet, Brannagh went up to Gran's bedroom. She pulled a wooden chair over to the closet and reached up to the heavy box on the top shelf. She dragged it to her room and closed the door. She unwrapped a layer of crinkly thin paper and gazed at the object buried in its nest. She clutched a creamy teacup, shiny as baby's teeth, thin as a flower petal, to her chest. For a moment, it seemed to be a living thing holding a heart beat of its own.

She had discovered the box only one week ago. When Brannagh had come down the lane from school, she saw Aunt Thelma pouring cream into a saucer on the back stoop for the stray cats. She had a round silver tin in her hand and shook its contents into the dish. "Hey!" Brannagh shouted. Aunt Thelma jumped. That's when she brought Brannagh upstairs and shared a secret, the box hidden high in the cupboard that held great-grandmother Brigid's tea set. Brannagh held the teacup to her lips imagining her mother's mouth, warm and soft, taking a sip.

On Monday morning, Brannagh delivered smudged, creased notes to a select number of desks at school: You are cordially invited to a tea party at the request ...

On Monday afternoon at recess, Hilda Outhouse stood by the double doors and picked her nose while all the girls crowded around Brannagh. On Monday evening, Brannagh came home to find her grandfather waiting for her in the parlour, the box resting by his feet. He stood absolutely still.

"There are areas in this house that are out of bounds."

"But I only wanted—"

He brought his face down close to hers. His breath was hot. It smelt of nickels clutched too long in a sweaty fist. "She should have taken you with her."

"But ..."

"She had no business dumping you here."

"I didn't mean ..."

"She did it to spite me, stir the muck."

"I will never touch it again."

"You are the worst of it. The family curse. The dam breaker."

The whites of Grandfather's eyes seemed to float before Brannagh's face.

"Aunt Thelma!"

He scooped her up and tucked her under one arm like a rolled carpet.

"Please!"

He clamped one hand hard over her mouth. Through the hall they went, her feet toppling a fern, tangling briefly in drapery, then into the kitchen, where her elbow knocked every corner.

"If I had my way, you'd be off to the orphanage tomorrow."

Bang, bang, bang; Grandfather's feet went down the stairs.

A low grunt and the creaking of hinges. The cold dirt floor of the cellar knocked the wind clear out of Brannagh. She was enveloped by the frightening and familiar darkness.

Slowly, Brannagh's eyes opened. "Nikki?" she muttered, running her fingers through her hair. Her eyes darted from the highboy to the suitcases on the floor by the bedroom door, where she had dropped them on the braided rug the night before.

There was an early morning chill. Brannagh wrapped the knit afghan covers around her shoulders and, rising from the bed, paused to inspect the contents on Gran's dresser: A statue of the Virgin Mary from which hung various war medals; one round green stone; a copy of *Canadian Home Journal* dated September 1928: Where is this modern society going? Pressed between the pages, sheets of butcher paper folded upon locks of baby hair. Brannagh held the green stone in her palm briefly before slipping it into the pocket of her pyjamas.

She opened the rucksack beside the suitcases. As she pulled out a sweater, Nikki's blue and white beaded tobacco pouch flipped onto the floor. The pattern resembled dark birds circling the sky. Why had she brought it along? Brannagh opened it and inhaled deeply. "I'm pathetic," she muttered. As she tugged the draw-string closed she saw a flash of white. She inserted her fingers and tugged. She withdrew a crumpled business card and read:

>LAURENTIAN COURT
>Fine Dining and First Class Accommodations
>Bathing huts and groomed scenic walking trails.
>Boat and canoe rentals.
>Our No.1 priority is your privacy & discretion.
>For reservations call 1-819-223-4546

The information was repeated on the reverse side in French. Below that was a name scribbled in pencil: Detective Arto Pietila.

Nikki had mentioned something about the Laurentians once. What was it? Brannagh strained to recall the conversation. Something about his grandmother?

Why did Nikki leave? she wondered for the umpteeth time. Was it something she'd done or, more likely, hadn't done? She could have made more of an effort early on to be warm, loving and fun. Instead she'd wasted so much time suspecting his motives, fighting his attempts to get close. Or maybe that had been smart and it was switching gears, letting down her guard that had been the mistake.

A distant thud prompted Brannagh to go to the window. Pressing her forehead to the pane, she glanced down to see the roof of a navy Ford in the drive. The back door opened, and an auburn head bent over the back seat.

Annie? She glanced at the clock on the dresser. It was 8:00 AM.

Brannagh slipped the card back into the tobacco pouch and put it inside the rucksack. She hopped down the stairs, two at a time, wool socks sliding on the wooden steps. She was in the hallway leading to the kitchen when the back door opened. Brannagh paused. She watched Annie push three paper grocery bags indoors. They were topped with bread, hamburger, bananas, and were followed by a navy canvas bag, and a basket of apples. She looked shorter than Brannagh remembered. Her long hair was tucked into the neck of her T-shirt. She kept poking the bridge of the rimless glasses that slid down her nose whenever she bent down. Annie wore an Indian print skirt, with navy cotton socks, and brown sandals that made her feet look like they were strapped into the lids of cardboard boxes. She unloaded the groceries with an air of efficiency.

Brannagh felt shy suddenly, standing in the shadows, in her rumpled flannel pyjamas. It was just like when they were kids, and she was tormented by an awkward flush of embarrassment that rose out of nowhere, making her acutely aware of the fact that she was different from everyone else, so different from Annie, Tish and Dianne, that the desire for life to embrace her in its arms and carry her off was as real and intense as an unquenchable thirst during a heat wave.

"Need some help?"

Annie started.

Brannagh registered a flicker of something indefinable in Annie's eyes. She caught sight of her own reflection in the square of mirror hanging over the sink: eyes puffy from sleep, hair a mish-mash.

"Oh, Brannagh." Annie's hands dropped to her side. She used the same tone a mother would use towards a disobedient child, exasperation mixed with relief. Later, Brannagh would recall the hint of satisfaction in her voice.

Suddenly, Annie was crossing the room. The distance between them shrank and Annie's arms were around Brannagh, pulling her into a forceful embrace. Her hair smelt like lemons and cigarette smoke.

Annie pulled back and gave her the once-over. "I knew I could make you come back. I just knew it."

"I can't believe you agreed to come to the reunion," Annie enthused. She tore open a croissant, and stuffed half of it into her mouth.

"Don't gloat." Brannagh plucked at the croissant on the plate.

Annie smiled, showing the gap between her front teeth. Her stepmother had argued that she needed to get braces, but Annie had bucked her all the way.

"I can do my research anywhere."

Annie poured cream into Brannagh's cup. "Remember how your Gran used to plug the holes in the condensed milk tin with wooden match sticks?"

They exchanged grins, but the giddiness born from childhood recollection skipped a beat and fizzled. Brannagh looked away, tugged at her bush socks. She hadn't expected this, hadn't expected that she and Annie would feel awkward with one another, but it had been a long time, and there seemed to be something different about Annie, something forced and unnatural. Or was Brannagh imagining things?

"C'mon." Annie sprang off the chair.

"I've just driven over a thousand—"

"Up." Annie yanked Brannagh's arm.

"Cripes, I forgot what a pain you are."

In a cupboard, built into the wall adjacent to the back door, they found a couple of pairs of Wellingtons.

Against the muddy bracken and craggy limbs of newly-budded trees, the river shimmered. The last tendrils of morning mist rose from its surface and floated toward the dark hills on the Kingston peninsula. The dampness held the earthy scent of spring and an occasional waft of the river: dead minnows, rotting bracken and the tang of the Atlantic.

Brannagh headed down the narrow path, through knee-high grass heavy with dew, toward the dock where Annie had already set up lawn chairs.

Annie glanced across the river, inhaling deeply. "God, I envy you. Getting to work from here." She pointed to a pair of loons bobbing in the distance.

"God, you sound cheerier than Anne of Green Gables."

"Sorry." Annie grimaced. "We hated that book."

They sipped their tea, settling into the silence until it wasn't silence anymore. The twitter and chirp of birds (robins, swallows, warblers) rose from the brush; Brannagh could identify them now after months spent observing them with Nikki in Northern Ontario. She wondered briefly about the business card in his tobacco pouch.

"I often see him, you know," Annie announced matter-of-factly.

Brannagh slipped off her rubbers and tucked her feet under her hips.

"Your grandfather." Annie poked at her glasses.

Brannagh watched a grey-winged bird circling high in the air. Was it soaring, coasting or flapping? Was its neck extended, folded or kinked?

"I went by the house on Argyle, told him you were coming, I wanted to make sure that the cottage was, you know, half decent. I asked him for a key, but he said he'd come out himself."

"You don't need to explain." So that's why he'd come nosing

around. "How is the old fart?"

"Good."

"Did he throw you out?"

Annie flashed a familiar, crooked smile. "On the contrary, he insisted I stay for tea."

Brannagh felt a flare of anger. "Of course he did."

Annie glanced away. "But then we've always gotten along," she finished lamely.

And why not? Brannagh groused silently. They were birds of a feather. Loyal Loyalists, through and through. Dr. Baird, Annie's father and Dr. Maloney, her grandfather, were part of the good ol' boys who supported Tish's father's run for mayor, celebrating when Chief Eden, an honest, god-fearing man, unexpectedly defeated the popular "fork-tongued papist" who had previously held office.

Brannagh had grown up with the mysteries that arose from these unspoken tensions. There had always been a rift between the Protestants like her grandfather, who posted want ads reading "Only God-fearing Christians need apply" and the Catholic shamrock wavers like her grandmother.

Brannagh had understood early on that she had to choose sides and she did, much to her grandfather's consternation.

Brannagh sided with Gran and went to Saint Patrick's School, and the Holy Catholic Church on Dufferin Row with its regal Byzantine arches and domes. But often during mass, novenas or candle lighting, instead of contemplating God or the fourteen Stations of the Cross, Brannagh would ponder the mystery of how her Gran and grandfather had ever gotten together. In the eyes of the Holy Catholic Church they weren't married. It was only young Father Angus's visits, dropping by the house on Argyle for a bracing cup of whiskey-laced tea before family hour with his aunt in the Provincial Asylum that gave Gran the courage to hold her chin high.

The insinuation that the marriage had been against Gran's will rose to the foreground of every scenario Brannagh fabricated about the old couple's union. The dramas that played out in her head originated in the plots of dimestore novels and usually revolved around her rich grandfather saving her poor grandmother's family from financial ruin and being rewarded with her hand in marriage. She never knew the real story. None of her Gran's family was alive by the time she was born, and if her grandfather had any living relatives in the world, they had never come to visit.

"He says he's gotten rid of everything," Annie interrupted Brannagh's thoughts. "Of your Gran's." She gathered her hair in her fingers and tucked her ponytail into the neck of her T-shirt. To the right of the dock, through thinning brush, Brannagh could make out the red roof of the cottage next door.

"I wish I could forget the day they discovered your little brother there," she said softly, holding one hand over her eyes to shield them from the sun. A police constable had pounded on the door of the house on Argyle. Chief Eden had come to bring Grandfather a pair of stolen gold cufflinks that had been retrieved from a disgruntled orderly at the hospital. As the constable rushed into the parlour, gasping for breath, spilling the horrible news, it was the first time Brannagh ever saw her grandfather at a loss for words. He simply sat, his mouth opening and closing, the gold winking in the open palm that rested on his knee.

Annie remained silent, her eyes widening.

"Oh, Jesus, Annie, I'm sorry." Brannagh flushed. What an idiotic and tactless subject to bring up. "I'm too tired to think straight. It's been on my mind ... my mother, they were both found the same way, on the roof, stabbed in the chest, all that." This was exactly why she'd sworn she'd never come back.

Annie's expression softened. "Yeah, well."

"I don't know how the hell you've stayed here."

Annie swallowed. "I don't remember anything. It ... I wish I did, but I don't." She glanced over her shoulder at the cottage. "That place is still deserted. No wonder. It's in worse shape then ever. Loose boards and nails. A realtor, a friend of mine, has been trying to sell it for years. No luck so far."

Brannagh nodded.

Annie stared out at the water. "Just checking things out." She sipped her tea. Her final words were so soft that Brannagh barely heard them. "You're safe here. I've made certain of that."

Brannagh paused. "What's that supposed to mean?"

"Safe from interruption. From intrusions."

Brannagh stiffened, pushing her hands into the pockets of her sweater. The tide was pulling out, leaving a ripple of dirty foam on shore. "Look, Annie, I don't need a babysitter."

Annie sighed. "Of course you don't."

An awkward silence settled between them.

"Tell me about him," Annie said quietly. She gnawed at the tip of her middle finger. It was what she used to do when they were kids, whenever the rare occasion arose that she was nervous, uncertain of herself.

Brannagh felt light-headed suddenly, as if the dock had become detached from the land and was being slowly sucked out by the tide. Her jaw tightened. She knew who Annie meant. And she wanted to slug her.

Annie's thin fingers slipped into Brannagh's pocket and interlocked her own.

"Everything," Annie said, more firmly. "I want to know everything about Nikki. Every little detail."

"Why?" Suddenly Brannagh was filled with a wave of mistrust.

What was Annie really up to?

"Why not?"

"There's nothing to tell."

"Don't be silly."

"There isn't."

"Of course there is."

"I can't." She wanted more than anything to eject Annie's hand from the pocket of her sweater.

"Yes, you can."

"You don't understand." Her eyes welled with tears and she swiped at them furiously.

"Yes, I do," Annie said firmly. "Just pretend. Pretend, Brannagh. It's Saturday night, my friend's come to visit and you've given me a hot water bottle, and we're curled up on the couch in the parlour with one of the cats, the fancy one with the back that curves like a woman's hip, by the fire. You're going to pop some popcorn, and we can smell the apples your Gran is boiling on the stove for jelly."

Brannagh stared at a lone cloud on the horizon. Her voice cracked. "The clock above the mantle is ticking, and I'm wishing the dumb old radio hadn't blown a tube because Grandfather's out and Aunt Thelma would let us turn it up loud and dance and swoon to that sh-boom, sh-boom song, which is what I want to do, what I need to do, because I'm head over heels in love."

"For the first time," Annie put in.

"Always for the first time," Brannagh agreed. The corners of her mouth didn't know whether they wanted to turn up or down. She wrenched her hand free from Annie's and clasped her fingers in her lap.

"Yes." Annie's words were spoken so low that later Brannagh was certain she misunderstood what she heard. "And I'm so jealous I could cry."

Brannagh's first impression upon meeting Nikki was confusion. She arrived in Ignace on the Greyhound bus at ten o'clock at night; tired and wired. Past Sault Ste. Marie, the train had snaked along Lake Superior offering long stretches of spruce and water, and the odd hump of granite that resembled the fossilized bones of some prehistoric beast jutting out of the earth. But as soon as Brannagh boarded the bus in Port Arthur for the last leg of the journey, she started to sweat. She kept going over and over what she would say upon meeting the great Nikki Mirsky whom she had heard so much about in the Naturalists' Club.

The journey had begun two years beforehand. Brannagh had graduated and was working at Osten-Med. She took evening classes towards a Fine Arts Degree, hanging around the Royal Ontario Museum on lunch breaks, latching onto school and bus tours. She soaked up the ambience like a weed in a spring flood. One day she wandered into a room filled with people attending to a tall, blond man at the front of the room.

"Welcome to the monthly meeting of the Toronto Field Naturalists' Club," he had announced.

Two weeks later, on a bright Saturday morning, Brannagh was amongst a group of birders waiting to board the Toronto Island Ferry.

"I'm Rudy," said the fellow who had been up at the front of the room that first day. He was tall and florid-cheeked, with a scorched fringe of blond hair that rose off his skull.

By the time they finished their hike along the shoreline from Centre Island to Hanlan's point, Brannagh had already filled half a sketch pad with rough drawings of gulls, terns and various shore birds.

"Hey, you're good," Rudy observed.

"Passes the time." Brannagh felt a surge of energy, unlike anything she had experienced for a long time.

"So is this what you do for a living?"

Brannagh folded up her sketch pad. "Not quite." She went on to explain how for three years she had been working as a research technician for a lab whose speciality was designing microscopes for scientists who were on the cutting edge of neuroscience in invertebrates. Brannagh spent her days experimenting with optical sectioning techniques on the phylum *Platyhelminthes*, the flat worm, famous for its ability to split and create two new planaria out of one. (Annie immediately touted it as a wonderful example of true independence, during a phone call between cramming for exams at McMaster.)

Brannagh had not given up her childhood hobby of "scribbling" in her spare time, doing portraits in her basement apartment near the beaches on weekends to earn extra money; but she had vetoed artsy courses when earning her science degree because they weren't practical. It was only after graduating, that she had decided she could afford to indulge a whim. By the time of the outing to Toronto Island, Brannagh was admitting to herself that she loved drawing. It was the only time she ever experienced true release and freedom, but from what exactly she could not say.

"You gotta meet this guy," Rudy interrupted Brannagh's thoughts, as they followed a path leading to Sanford's Pond. "He's at the forefront of the environmental movement here."

"Oh yeah?" Brannagh peered at the choppy water.

"Nikki Mirsky."

"Who?"

"You don't know him?" Rudy was horrified by Brannagh's ignorance. "The most exciting thing to happen to the winged world since Roger Peterson? The wilderness preservationist?"

Brannagh realized then that she had heard the name, usually peppered through arguments in dark corners in student pubs or debates on campus radio. Nikki, Rudy insisted, simply broke the stereotype people had of birders.

"People like to think we're these lisping knicker-clad egg-heads skipping through the woods with binoculars strung around our necks." Rudy did a clumsy skip down the path in demonstration. "But Nikki won't let them get away with pigeon-holing us, pun pun."

Nikki had heard rumours that in the next decade Ontario Hydro would propose building an electrical generating plant in Atikokan, and so he was stepping up efforts to organize a long sought for survey of birds in the boreal forests. Rudy would sell his mother, his landlady and his goldfish up the river to be part of the expedition. When positions for the study were posted in the classified ads in the conservation magazine *Audubon*, it was all he could talk about for weeks on end.

"This is what I'm applying for," he kept reminding Brannagh, and himself it seemed, pointing to the word Cataloguer in bold, black print on page 102. "It's a great way for a nobody like me to break into research."

"Yeah, yeah, yeah." Brannagh patted his shoulder indulgently. "So you'll learn to shit in the woods."

But later that week, she found herself continually wandering to the magazine aisle in one of the specialty bookstores on Bloor. Finally she bought a copy of *Audubon*, and read over the job description of cataloguer. At first, it seemed a ridiculous, unlikely consideration, but, as time passed, the proposition forming in her mind began to appear perfectly logical.

She didn't have the required Master's degree in biology, but why not fill out the application as an experiment? Just to see if it really was viable to plan to pursue it eventually? Brannagh grabbed a pen. On the application, she made squiggles (left open to interpretation) in the blanks, like Master's Thesis, where she had no qualifications to fill in. Brannagh went to the library and read everything she could find on acid rain. Which wasn't much.

The day of the interview Brannagh changed her clothes five times, got off at the wrong stop on the subway, and was late. An elderly woman with a long, pointy noise sniffed at her tardiness. "You are familiar with the issue of acid rain," she said in a tone that implied the opposite.

Brannagh babbled. "Didn't the wife of King Henry III complain in twelve something or other that the fumes from burning coal made her eyes burn?" The panel of interviewers studied her blankly. "That's when it all started."

The woman's eyes bore into Brannagh's. "You do have your Master's in biology?"

"The documentation is being forwarded." *Like in five years!* Brannagh turned red then pulled out her sketch pads and handed them over. "I brought along a sample of my work."

The panel studied the sketches intently.

"Are you aware of what the job of cataloguer entails?" asked the only man on the panel; a dark-skinned gentleman with blood-shot eyes.

Brannagh repeated Rudy's words verbatim. "I think," she added, "that being able to draw the birds would be a bonus."

The woman with the long pointy nose hung onto the sketch pads and kept flipping back to the drawing of the male nude (Gerald Boone, a dance major who lived next door to Brannagh).

Brannagh was convinced the panel snickered at her naivety as soon as she walked out the door. Then, six weeks later, a letter arrived in the mail, announcing that she was the successful applicant. She had been stunned. Had called Rudy. They met at a coffee shop in little Italy.

"I hate you," Rudy seethed, tossing the letter onto the table. "Why you and not me?"

Brannagh avoided asking herself that question, but she figured it had something to do with Canada Post workers going on strike. The panel probably made assumptions, and had given her the benefit of the doubt. Now was the time to tell the truth, admit she didn't have the qualifications. Call the whole thing off. Instead, Brannagh splurged on a copy of the *Elephant Folio* in a second hand bookstore and studied Audubon's original drawings and the works of Kenneth Carlson and Rex Brasher until she saw them in her sleep. It wasn't only the birds that excited her, but also the subtle placement and depiction of trees, sky and water.

Brannagh had received a package of material describing the methodology they would use, and had discussed the tailoring of these options with a freelance statistitician hired by Nikki, but she had yet to meet him in person. She couldn't help wondering if when she did, and he determined her lack of ornithological knowledge and nonexistent skills at roughing it in the bush (she'd barely passed the required two-week canoeing course on Lake Muskoka), he'd send her back to Toronto in two seconds flat.

Brannagh's stomach tightened with apprehension when the bus pulled off the highway into Ignace. She got off, studying the parking lot for someone who looked like he was from a research group. After ten minutes, while the other passengers wandered off down Main Street or climbed into trucks with enormous tires, the likes of which Brannagh had never witnessed before (there didn't seem to be any *cars* in this neck of the woods), Brannagh wasn't sure what to do. She gazed up and down the stretch of highway that served as Main Street for the small mining town: gas station,

OPP, hockey arena.

Finally, starving and exhausted, she dug a piece of paper out of her rucksack and wrote: Mr. Mirsky, arrived safely. At the Esso Voyageur across the street. Brannagh Maloney. She taped it to the bus depot door.

She lugged the boxes two at a time across the street. There were four of them, along with three suitcases, two backpacks, four green garbage bags, and her cat, Puffin's, travelling cage. Brannagh had needed to bring her own research texts, along with everything on the thick list of camping gear they had mailed to her: the huge down-filled jacket and sleeping bag, a wet suit, long underwear, bush socks, waterproof matches, petroleum jelly (good for waterproofing just about anything).

Brannagh piled everything against the wall behind the gas pumps, below a sign that read Home of the Bottomless Coffee Cup. A short, muscular man in grease-stained overalls kept scratching his chest while he watched her. On her last trip in, he muttered, "Uh, you can't, uh, you're blocking the fire exit."

Brannagh straightened up from scooping Puffin out of her cage. It was, she knew, totally impractical, bringing a cat along. But she hadn't had the heart to give her away. "Professor Mirsky said the owner—I'm sure that must be you—wouldn't mind," she said, gazing up at him wide-eyed. "I'm with his research team." She attempted her most winning smile.

The man straightened, flushing as he wiped his hands on a rag. "Sure. Don't worry about nuthin'. I'll help Nikki load up, soon as he's done. " A bit of silver flashed in his mouth as he nodded toward the restaurant.

"Done?" Slowly the words registered in Brannagh's tired brain.

The gas pump attendant stepped back, bumping into the counter.

Brannagh tucked Puffin into the inside of her jacket, zipped it halfway up, and headed indoors.

It took her a few minutes to orient herself. He had to be the dark curly-haired guy sitting in the last booth, behind a plate heaped with fried eggs, back bacon and hash browns, wearing a filthy canvas hat and a dilapidated multi-pocketed red vest. His mouth was going a mile a minute. He jabbed a heel of toast into runny egg yolk for emphasis, as he argued with the young fellow sporting a crew cut, who sat across from him. Brannagh marched towards them.

"Two spare motors, Alex. No more, no less."

"But we can't—"

"We have no choice."

"Excuse me, Professor Mirsky?" Brannagh asked.

Nikki paused, eyes narrowing as he gave her the once over. "Well, well. Nice of you to drop by." He turned back to his companion. "We keep busting the blades, there's no way around it on that river." Nikki folded a piece of toast in half and shoved the whole thing into his mouth.

Brannagh had never seen anyone eat the way he did, as if he were devouring the plate whole, as if the food would leap off the table and needed to be captured before it did. The dark curly hair under his hat was matted and greasy. His face was streaked with dirt, and hunks of egg white and toast crumbs hung in his beard. His eyes were bloodshot, the corners crusted with yellow.

"Well, *you* can carry them then," the young man grumbled, folding knobby elbows tight into his chest. Nikki's companion didn't look a day older than fourteen. "We've got too much gear as it is."

"I'll figure out something." Nikki pushed his plate away.

"Professor Mirsky," Brannagh tried again, but Nikki rose to his feet and brushed past her, keeping up a running dialogue with Alex all the way to the cash register on the proper way to waterproof and double bag everything from powdered eggs to tent pegs.

Brannagh grabbed a slice of toast and trailed after them.

"Look, Professor Mirsky, if you don't mind."

People in the restaurant turned to stare at Brannagh. Two young teenage girls, puffing cigarettes with forced casualness, eyed her up and down.

"Fishing tackle." Nikki handed the waitress behind the cash register a five-dollar bill and tucked his wallet into his back pocket. He turned towards Alex, scrubbing his chin. "And twice as many tarps. Insulation mats, a smaller stove, night vision binoculars."

Alex blinked.

"Professor Mirsky, if you don't mind I've just travelled all the way from—"

Suddenly Nikki beamed. He grabbed Alex's hand and shook it. "Welcome aboard, son. You'll do your dad proud."

For a brief instant Alex looked terrified, then his face broke into a grin. "So, I've got the job, you're going to let me, you know, be your guide, help out, I mean, and everything, and get paid too?"

Nikki was halfway out the door when he turned around and tossed something through the air to Brannagh. "Tomorrow morning, four o'clock," he announced. "On the nose or you're shit out of luck." He glanced at Puffin's head, sticking out of her jacket. "And get rid of that." Then he was gone.

Brannagh picked the book of matches up off the floor and walked outside the restaurant. Both sides were covered in bold red letters: ANDY'S MOTEL. Either he was propositioning her or this was where the crew was staying. The trailers that would house their offices were being set up on a piece of abandoned Ministry of Fisheries and the Environment land north of Davey Lake.

Obviously, they weren't ready yet.

Brannagh didn't know how long she stood outside the restaurant, turning the pack of matches over in her fingers, while transports whizzed past on the highway sending a wall of wind that rocked her onto her heels. She was ready to hop onto the next bus heading out of town, while Alex, who had started loading her boxes onto the back of his truck, was in a state of bliss that nothing could ruin.

"Nikki and I just returned from a ten-day trip up river. It was my test." Alex went on to explain that his father had been a respected guide in the area, but had had a heart attack and died last winter leaving a wife, who had never worked outside the home a day in her life, and five kids. Most of the locals scoffed that Alex was too young and inexperienced to carry on the business alone, but, Alex informed Brannagh, he was seventeen, the man in the family now, and Nikki had been willing to let him prove himself by organizing a preliminary trip up river to the point where they would have to portage into Lake of the Woods. Only Alex had been so nervous, so certain he was going to blow it, that he hadn't slept the night before, and had forgotten to double bag their food and matches, and they had lost it all when they dumped in some rapids. They hadn't eaten or slept in three days, and he had been sure that Nikki was going to chew him up and spit him out once they had this much needed meal under their belts. Instead, Nikki had done the unthinkable and hired him.

"I think he did it on purpose," Alex said, as he carried her suitcases to the waiting truck. "He let me screw it up big time. There's no way that'll happen again."

"So," Brannagh said wryly. "Does your mom like cats?"

The next morning when Brannagh showed up at Andy's Hotel, Nikki immediately approached her wearing a sheepish expression.

He wore a freshly-laundered flannel shirt and jeans. His face was scrubbed and beard newly trimmed. He hesitated, a purple flush rising up his neck. He extended one large hand. "Brannagh Maloney?"

She nodded, briefly returning the handshake.

Nikki grinned. "I owe you an apology. This'll probably sound like something straight out of a sit com, but I thought you were Kim Burke. One of our team members, in charge of packing supplies? She was supposed to be here five days ago. I was pretty upset when she didn't show up."

Through the pre-dawn darkness, Brannagh could make out Alex and a tall native boy, as they struggled to load a canoe onto a truck.

"Apparently, Kim got waylaid by a boyfriend." Nikki inspected the frayed lace dangling from one of his boots. "At least that's my opinion. She swears there was a death in the family, but I've heard that excuse more times than you can imagine."

"But I left a message with your answering service that I'd be arriving."

"I got it last night after I left the restaurant, along with Kim's call." Nikki turned to smile and wave at a petite young woman with glossy black hair and huge green eyes. She was dragging a bulging pack-sack behind her. "On the school bus, Cindy! Assuming it isn't your private stash of Oh Henry! bars."

Cindy grinned mischievously. "Nah. Just Kotex pads."

Nikki's face reddened and turned back to Brannagh. "I, uh, we're having a load flown in to base camp. There are airtight containers if you have any non-perishables, to lighten your portage."

"I'm fine."

"It's a week going in. Unless you're built like—"

"I said I'm fine."

"Well, then." Nikki studied her, nodding. "Departure day is

Sunday. Do you have questions, issues, anything that needs sorting out before we head off?"

"The methodology is set up. I double-checked it with your statistician. He had no concerns."

Nikki gazed at her steadily. "This is your first expedition?"

"Yep." Her chin rose.

"It's tough going." His eyes, large and dark, probed hers. "The honeymoon ends on day three. Most people want to throw in the towel at that point."

"Well, I'm here."

"I'm just saying you're going to get frustrated and feel like shit and wonder why in the world you signed on. Just come and talk to me, okay? The kids are going to have enough struggles of their own. I've got a secret stash of vodka I'll let you in on." He grinned.

Brannagh squinted past his right ear.

Nikki rubbed his temples. "Okay, we better figure out what we're doing here. How about you and I and Alex share one canoe?" He nodded toward the native boy. "Tom and Cindy will share the other with Kim's replacement, Gordon." A short, chubby boy, whose face was covered in pimples, stood sullenly holding a torch over Alex and Tom as they lashed the canoes to the back of the truck.

"Fine."

"Well, if you have any questions—"

"I know where to find you." Brannagh picked up her rucksack and headed toward the truck. She sensed his gaze following her and squared her shoulders.

Two days up river, she understood what Nikki was talking about.

After gruelling twenty-mile portages, carrying fifty-pound packs (that weighed twice as much in the rain), and nerve-grinding paddles through rapids that bubbled and hissed and spat, and days that started at three AM with the hoots of owls, and ended long after midnight, Brannagh's hair was greasy and knotted, her eyes red-rimmed. She had no energy to talk to anyone, let alone look at them. She gobbled whatever food was put on her plate quickly before mosquitoes and black flies and whatever else in the woods was hungry took a notion to steal it. She acquired the habit of ignoring everything, except what was absolutely necessary, in order to conserve energy.

One day when Alex sliced his forearm by slipping on algae-covered rocks while pulling in a canoe, and Nikki sat up with him all night, feeding him vodka, and deftly stitching the gash, Brannagh decided she might just ask him to share that secret stash after all.

"He was taking one hell of a gamble with all of us. He knew how tough the journey up river would be." Brannagh drank the dregs of cold tea remaining in the bottom of her cup. "But I made it even harder for him. I don't know why."

Annie sat quietly, chin in hand. "He doesn't sound right."

"What do you mean?" Brannagh rose to her feet, pulling her sweater around her tightly. She shivered, even though the sun, rising higher in the sky, was warming the damp grey boards underfoot.

"He doesn't sound like the sort of guy I pictured you with." Annie rubbed her chin. "Not that I pictured you with anyone."

"Why should you?" Brannagh grasped the railing and stared at the river. It was smooth on the surface, so smooth that in spots it reflected the clouds and sky, and it was hard to tell where the river ended and sky began. But the tranquillity was deceptive. There were dangerous currents threading its depth.

"I have an idea," Annie said softly.

Brannagh turned around and stared as recognition slowly dawned.

"Forget Nikki."

"There's nothing to forget."

"What I mean is, quit—"

"Stop." Brannagh held up one hand. "Don't you get it? I barely know the guy. All we shared was birds and orgasms."

"You'll feel better if—"

"No." Brannagh bristled. "This is exactly what I didn't want to happen. Exactly why I didn't want to come. But I should have known what this was really all about."

Annie's hands gripped the arms of her chair.

"The *plan*. Oh God, yes, we must have a *plan*, right Annie? So what's the plan this time, eh?"

"There's no plan." Annie's mouth tightened.

"Then what is this?" Brannagh's arm swept through the air. "Don't kid me. The cottage, the reunion. It's all just part of the plan to get poor Brannagh back where she belongs, where she can be looked after, where she won't be disturbed, because heaven forbid that she should follow in her crazy mother's footsteps!"

Annie slowly rose to her feet. "What the hell are you talking about?" Her voice was low, her words clipped.

"The plan! When we were kids you always had one. You were always telling us how to run our lives. Me. Tish. Dianne. Tish wasn't supposed to get married and have kids, I wasn't supposed to go to University in snotty old Toronto, Dianne had to get a nursing degree, just had to. And none of us were ever supposed to fall in love, period. Don't you remember Annie? None of us were ever supposed to need a man to justify our existence."

"I've always been one who likes to organize—"

"What's the plan, Annie, eh? What's the plan? Now that Nikki's

...." She choked around the sudden swelling in her throat. "Now that Nikki's fucked off. What's the plan to save poor pathetic Brannagh from her miserable lot in life?"

Annie grabbed Brannagh by the elbows. "You've got it all wrong."

"The hell I do!" Brannagh shook her off, wrapping her sweater tightly around her. "Well, you can take your plan and shove it where the sun don't set, Annie. There's nothing in me that needs to be fixed. Try focusing on yourself for a change. We both know who the real sicko is around here, don't we?" Brannagh felt a brief flicker of regret, as echoes of long ago buried anguish flitted briefly across Annie's face.

Brannagh ran towards the cottage blindly, losing a boot along the way. Inside, she peeled off her wet socks, and climbed the stairs. She fell onto Gran's bed, pulling the covers over her head. But not even this could block out the image of the bruised expression on Annie's face.

"Son of a bitch," Brannagh muttered, as the tears began to flow. "You bastard, Nikki. Why did you have to leave?"

When Brannagh awoke, she heard sounds drifting up from the first floor: snatches of music from the radio, pots and pans banging. She smelled tomato, garlic, basil. Her stomach rumbled.

She pulled on a pair of jeans and a sweatshirt and paused at the top of the stairs, one hand on the railing. Annie sat in the wing chair by the fireplace reading a book. It appeared she had attempted to light a fire, but having never been a dedicated Girl Guide like Tish, the results were pathetic.

"Hey," Brannagh said.

Annie turned away, but not fast enough to hide her red, puffy eyes. She snatched a pile of crumpled tissues by her elbow with one hand, and shoved the whole mess down behind the cushions.

Brannagh brought out the brightly wrapped package that she had been hiding behind her back and held it out. "For you."

"Don't." Annie stared at her hands.

"C'mon." Brannagh waved the package awkwardly.

"You don't need a peace offering." Annie's chin rose defiantly.

"It's true. I've always been bossy." She took off her glasses and cleaned them with the hem of her skirt. "The irony is that the qualities that make me such a good doctor, are the very things that …" She cleared her throat. "Make a lousy friend."

"Shut up and open it." Brannagh dropped the package into Annie's lap. But Annie was preoccupied with getting the lenses of her glasses absolutely spotless.

"Oh, for the love of …" Brannagh picked up the box, tore off the flowered wrapping paper, and turned the box upside down. A tattered stuffed toy, a cat that looked like it had seen better days, dropped into Annie's lap.

Annie turned the animal over in her hands. "Is this …?" She lifted the cat's tail and inspected it closely.

"Puffin. The original," Brannagh confirmed. "Gran found him on the third floor, sent him to me when I was in university."

Annie's eyes crinkled. "I used to sleep with this thing every night. I used to love all the stray cats Aunt Thelma adopted. My stepmother hated cats."

"Look, I'm totally wiped." Brannagh clasped Annie's shoulders in an awkward embrace. Annie turned her face away. Brannagh stepped back. "My brain is fried."

"No." Annie waved one hand dismissively. "You were right. I did have a plan, to bring you here, fatten you up, and make you smile again."

"Because you're my friend. You mean well. You always mean well."

"Because I'm a control freak. I admit it. And I've gotten worse over the years." There was a pained expression in Annie's eyes.

"Don't." Brannagh dropped down onto the ottoman. "See, the thing is, I'm pissed off at Nikki. Not you. Furious at him for doing this to me. How dare he leave! How dare he vanish into thin air without one bloody word." Tears rolled down her cheeks. She backhanded them with her thumb. "In the middle of the project. You have no idea how much work is involved."

"Wait," Annie ordered. She disappeared into the kitchen. The fridge opened, then closed. Annie returned with two glasses of white wine. She handed one to Brannagh.

The first sip was cold and sweet on Brannagh's tongue. "But it wasn't a romantic thing. You're off the mark. We shared a passion for feathers." She grinned. "Ornithologically speaking. Nothing kinky."

Annie didn't smile.

Brannagh paused, gulped some wine. "We were just keeping each other warm at night, relieving the monotony in the woods. That's it. I was *the* summer fling, probably the first of many to come over the ten year study." That's what she had told herself during the long winter.

Annie traced one finger around the rim of the wine glass, eyes downcast. "Have you ever been intensely happy, but at the same time filled with this strange sadness, this fear, like you know it isn't going to last, that something is going to happen to ruin it all?"

Brannagh ran her fingers through her hair. "Cripes, Annie. When did you turn into Leonard Cohen?" She got up to resuscitate the dying fire, make a salad and refill their wine glasses.

They ate by the fire, and slowly, gently, shifted to neutral topics: the last time they'd eaten a drive-in cheeseburger, cheap vacation spots, their favourite radio shows when they were kids. Brannagh couldn't remember having tasted anything as satisfying as Annie's lasagne. She had two helpings, which put some of the spark back in Annie's eyes.

As they carried the dishes to the sink, Brannagh couldn't resist teasing her. "Gee, I just love your selection of reading material. Is this something new or is it an acquired taste?"

Annie rolled her eyes. She squirted dish liquid into the sink.

Brannagh disappeared down the hall, and returned brandishing a paperback historical romance, the one that she had seen Annie sliding behind the cushions of the wing chair, along with the soggy tissues. It was the sort of dime-store novel she and Tish had read when they were kids, never Annie, only back then they were always about nurses or secretaries, who were in a dilemma about whether or not to kiss on a first date. "Since when did you start reading this stuff?" she demanded.

Annie gave a dismissive shrug. "It was a gift."

"Sure, sure. Why Annie Baird I never knew you had it in you." Brannagh scampered to the corner of the kitchen and stood on a chair. "You'd think she'd feel a draft," she quipped. The woman on the cover was in period costume. Her bodice was split practically to her belly button. A wide-shouldered, swarthy looking man pressed her against his bare chest. Brannagh held the book open and read with an exaggerated breathless tone. "He would come to her at night—"

"One of my patients figures I work too hard, that I need some romance in my life, so she's always bringing me books and—"

"He would come to her chamber when she was asleep, and slip into bed beside her."

"So just to shut her up promised I'd read it. Okay? Enough already." Annie tried to grab it out of her hand, but Brannagh held it out of reach.

"No, no, I'm just getting to the good part. 'His hand slid round her waist, slowly inching higher. "Shhhh," he whispered in her ear, "Don't be afraid. I'm here now." But he knew she was helpless, his captive, his slave.' "

Annie growled and picked up the broom. Brannagh jumped off the chair. Annie's broom went curling rink wild. Brannagh escaped into the parlour, grabbed a couple of oranges out of the fruit bowl and stuck them under her sweatshirt. She paused in front of the fireplace, thrusting out her chest. "Help me, I'm being ravished. I is soooooo helpless, and horny, me oh my, what do I do?"

She dodged Annie's flailing broom, snorting with laughter.

"If you ever breathe a word to the others," Annie threatened.

Brannagh stopped in front of the picture window, dead in her tracks. The oranges tumbled to the floor.

Annie whacked her across the butt, snatched the book out of her hand and dashed back to the kitchen.

Brannagh stared at the window. An invisible fist tightened around her throat. There had been a face peering in the window. A man's face. For one brief second, a flash of dark hair, dark eyes. Then it was gone.

Trembling, Brannagh returned to the kitchen, picked up the dish towel and started drying dishes. Thankfully, Annie launched into a long story about a patient who had shoved an aspirin up her nose and had hidden in the office washroom until all the other patients had left.

Long after Annie had said good night and gone upstairs, Brannagh sat in Gran's wooden rocker staring out the picture window. Annie had said that the cottage next door was still deserted, abandoned, and that their only neighbour was an eighty-year-old retired grocer five miles down the road.

So how could she explain the face that Brannagh had seen

peering in the window?

The man's face.

For a second, a brief, insane flicker of time, Brannagh had recognized the face.

She would have sworn, would swear still, that it had been Nikki's.

Chapter Three

Despite Brannagh's best intentions to outrun it, exhaustion finally caught up with her. During the first few weeks alone in the cottage, all she could do was sleep. She couldn't open her eyes until at least noon and wandered around in pyjamas, only donning a shirt and jeans when she went onto the front porch to write a letter to Alex. She penned letters that were breezy, brimming with efficiency and reassuring references to the tables, graphs and reports she was compiling. Then she crawled back into bed.

Brannagh usually ate a late lunch and settled on the couch with Nikki's papers and textbooks spread around her. She told herself that today was the day she would go for a walk to the cottage with the red roof while the sky was a bright blinding blue. As the late afternoon sun slanted through the window, her eyes grew heavy, and the book in her hands tumbled to the floor. She awakened with a start to discover that another day had disappeared into the twilight.

The third week of Brannagh's stay, the day before Annie, Dianne, and Tish were all driving up for the reunion, she set the alarm for ten AM. She forced herself to get out of bed, and to dig out her sketchpads. She pulled on a pair of jeans and dragged a rickety table from the hall onto the porch. She set out all her papers, weighting them down with rocks, brewed a fresh pot of coffee, opened a new pack of HB pencils. Then she stared at the mist rising off the river.

Finally, she pulled the preliminary sketches of the warblers out of the carryall: a myrtle warbler with its yellow rump, a blackpoll warbler in a bayberry patch. Nikki had given up trying to teach her to imitate the song: Zi-zi-zi-zi-zi-zi-zi. At the bottom of the pile, lay a smudged set of pencil drawings: two enormous birds, wings forming shallow Vs. She remembered Nikki's air of excitement as he tilted his head back to observe them.

They had been travelling up river. After the incident with the baked beans, Alex came up with a system, a schedule that he kept in a baggie, and hung on a tree wherever they camped. It worked on a rotational basis, whereby everyone took turns. When Brannagh's number came up, and everyone was off stringing packs into treetops, or oiling their boots, Nikki would saunter over and pick up a knife. Though he was often the centre of attention, the hub around which the wheel of the expedition revolved, there was something out of place, a quiver in his bravado, that she couldn't quite put a finger on. Or maybe it was Brannagh who had the quiver. While he peeled potatoes, she sought safety through small talk, attempting to distract him from the bird count and asking questions she might not be able to answer.

One night, as they roasted the last of the real potatoes over the fire, Alex passed around his prized bottle of Jack Daniel's.

"Tell us about your grandmother," Cindy prodded Nikki. She had informed Brannagh that she had saved every newspaper and magazine article about their fearless leader, that she worshipped the environmentally sound ground he walked on.

Nikki held the bottle to his mouth.

"Your *Russian* Grandmother."

Nikki passed the whiskey to Brannagh, and cast a sheepish look.

"She was a seamstress with a ballet school in Petersburg."

"And mistress to the tsar's third cousin. Just like Dr. Zhivago!" Cindy leaned in close to Tom. "The last tsar. Cool, eh?" Her hair swung like a shiny curtain in the firelight. Tom was bewitched. "I think it's thrilling that she came to Canada during the revolution."

Nikki pulled off his hat and tried to run his fingers through the knots in his hair. "She opened a dress shop in Montreal. Guess that's glamorous, literally. But she taught me to thread a needle, and if I bugged her enough would tell me tales of grand dukes and imperial castles. Heady stuff for a boy whose biggest thrill was shooting a puck and making it land in the neighbour's storm cellar."

Gordon took the bottle from Alex, sniffed it, pulled a face. "You know," he announced peevishly, kneading a zit on his forehead, "when I had my interview they said there was to be no fraternizing between members of the team. No, er, romance, i.e. dating is prohibited." He glanced meaningfully at Cindy and Tom.

Alex gulped the whisky. "Yeah? So? Should I be worried?" He wiped his mouth on the back of his hand. "Why Gordo, I didn't know you cared so much."

They all laughed. Gordon blinked, mouth twitching. "Just pointing it out, that's all. Just so you don't forget."

"Excellent idea, Gordon, very astute of you." Nikki's tone was suddenly serious, his eyes firmly glued to his boots. "That rule is there for a reason. So we all stay sharp without any distractions to interfere with completing our mission."

When Brannagh glanced up from the fire, she was disconcerted to find Nikki's eyes resting on her.

One day, as they hiked through the woods, Brannagh fell behind the others and stood perfectly still, sleeping on her feet, truth be told, which she had only recently mastered, when the flash of orange-pink dream images behind her closed eyelids abruptly stopped, and she was startled awake by the thump of a hand on her shoulder. She turned and there was Nikki, pressing a finger to her lips, warning her to remain silent. Brannagh let her pack slip from her shoulders and craned her neck upward. Above the tree tops, two black Vs circled.

"Turkey vultures." Nikki's eyes sparkled. "Hunters of dead flesh. Fascinating creatures."

He handed her the binoculars. They climbed for what felt like hours, finally coming to a clearing, and a flat spruce-pocked cliff of igneous rock.

She sat on a patch of warm, crinkly lichen, and supported the sketch pad on her knees. The breeze whipped the paper around her wrist. Nikki circled her, one hand planted on her shoulder. He stopped, hunched before her, a human barrier against the wind. They watched the birds, listening to the creak of tree boughs and the scratch of the conte stick. She was conscious of Nikki's smell: wood smoke and sweat and citronella.

"Incredible." She glanced at him, and frowned. "Dumb word. Doesn't do it justice." She shrugged. "I mean, I feel foolish to think this has existed all this time, and yet I never ..." She gestured at the surrounding copse of birch and poplar.

Nikki smiled. "Don't feel foolish."

She fumbled to dispel her awkwardness. Why had she said anything in the first place? "I mean, were you just born paying attention?"

He laughed, rocked back on his heels, and turned his face skyward. He was silent for so long she decided that he was going to ignore her. Then he spoke, so softly that she had to strain to catch the words. "When I was ten, my father died."

"I'm sorry."

"You know how when you're young there's that kind of careless, one-day-is-a-lifetime world? Summers last forever."

"Yeah, they did."

"Well all of that, everything I took for granted came to an end when my dad died. My mother spent every day in bed and then suddenly she'd appear, this ball of nervous energy, rearranging furniture, pulling weeds, shining window panes. It was my job to watch over my little sister, Marina."

A breeze picked up. Brannagh welcomed the coolness on her face.

A wistful smile loosened the curve of Nikki's mouth. "Marina loved to sneak extra vitamin pills at breakfast. I was supposed to make sure she got dressed for school with socks that matched. Once when I couldn't find any, I got her to pull rubber canning rings half-way up her calves, and stained her skin with a wad of toilet paper dipped in beet juice."

Brannagh laughed despite herself. "That's ingenious."

"To me it looked like she was wearing maroon dress socks, the kind my dad used to wear to a wedding or a funeral."

He turned and met Brannagh's gaze. She turned back to the drawing pad, nervous suddenly. She held her breath, listening.

"When the school principal phoned home, my mother shook me so hard I thought my head was going to snap off. She slumped to the floor, crying silently into a dishtowel and told me I should call the police, the firemen, the school. Tell everyone to come and take her children away from her because she just wasn't looking after us the way she was supposed to."

He dropped down onto the ground beside Brannagh, and she felt the heaviness of his limbs as he pressed against her. He took the pad out of her hands and studied it intently. There was surprise in his eyes and a hint of envy. He handed it back and nodded. "This is good."

"Thanks." A flush of pleasure warmed Brannagh's cheeks.

"It was about that time that I decided that I wanted, more than anything else in the world, to learn to fly."

"To fly?"

"I would catch the subway and then walk and walk until I came to the Old Belt Line ravine. From that perch I studied the birds, and learned to tell the difference between a Great Horned Owl and Long-eared Owl, Redpolls, Evening Grosbeaks, and Prairie Warblers. There was an opening in the brush that ran the length of the ravine. I'd clear a cubby and lie flat on my back, and watch the shapes that travelled across the blue. Circle, dip, glide." Nikki gestured with one hand, as if conducting an invisible orchestra, his eyes gleaming. "The simplicity of the act was absorbing."

For a brief moment, Brannagh imagined Nikki as a boy, his thin frame stretched out on a bed of cedar, hands behind his head, bony elbows and eyes directed upwards.

Nikki sighed. His hands dropped by his side. "Circle, dip, glide. It was like a poem in one of my mother's books about Kitche Manitou. Wind, sky, air. Effortless grace. Old bones loosening and falling from the sky. I don't remember it all now. Or maybe I just made it all up."

That day, as Brannagh's eyes darted from sky to pad and back again, in between the split seconds of time, she had registered a tear on the sleeve of Nikki's flannel shirt. It had been mended with tiny black, even stitches that you would never spot unless you inspected it closely. Yet his hands, so large, pine-gum-stained, nails dirt-caked quarter moons, and fingers blunt-tipped, were surely incapable of picking up a needle, let alone threading it.

Sitting on the porch of Gran's cottage, looking at the sketches, Brannagh saw bits of regret for actions left undone on every page, between the lines, the smudges, the minute eraser shavings that still clung to the heavyweight paper: Nikki's fingers grasping a paddle; his mouth clamped around the stem of a pipe; his eyes filled with puzzlement as they studied her across the fire.

Dismayed, Brannagh gathered everything into the carryall, took it inside the cottage, and shoved it into the back of the bedroom closet. She regretted turning down Annie's offer to close the office and drive up early. Annie was the only one who understood what it was like to have a hole in your heart like a piece of a puzzle gone missing. Deep down, no matter how much you tried to pretend otherwise, you knew that what was gone, the part that had disappeared, would always prevent the pretty picture, the glorious seamless whole, from ever coming to be.

The day Brannagh met Annie was a drizzly Saturday. Brannagh was eight years old. Whenever it rained, the house on Argyle grew damp and chilly and emitted the rank odour of mildew. The Victorian English home, with its fancy finials and cornices atop the steep gabled windows and balconied widow's walk, was heated by an ancient system of chimneys and flues that emanated from a furnace in the five-foot-deep cellar. Much to Grandfather's consternation, it gobbled coal like candy no matter how much it was tinkered with. If he was in a generous mood, most likely when families of patients were paying a visit, he would order Aunt Thelma to light fires throughout the house. Usually, however, everyone made do with bulky wool fishermen cardigans, the sort that could suck up an Atlantic roller and still keep the wearer dry, which Gran, luckily, could knit in her sleep.

Brannagh came out of her room that morning and wandered down the hall. Aunt Thelma was sitting, eyes red rimmed, below the window, fully dressed, scrubbing the gray fur on the latest stray cat that had turned up outside the kitchen door. When it got enough to eat, it would slip away just like the others and she would adopt a new one.

"No sleep?" Brannagh asked, bending down to stroke the feline's soft fur. "He's sweet."

"Dustball, that's what I named him." Aunt Thelma rose to her feet scooping the cat onto one shoulder. She was tall and large-boned slim. As she swept down the hall, tightening the belt of her sweater, she called out, "Somebody new came in last night."

Brannagh's stomach tightened.

"He wants you to go up this morning."

Brannagh nodded. No need to qualify who "he" was.

Grandfather was tall and lean, with a wide jaw, a pinched nose, and deep lines that bracketed his mouth like thirsty furrows in a farmer's field. He wore mutton chop sideburns, and his eyes were bright blue and penetrating. Everyone in the house had a habit of tiptoeing around him, as if a mere hiccup might send him into a fit. Brannagh had decided long ago that the underlying tension that wove through the house was there for good reason. It kept them all on red alert. Brannagh seemed to have a knack for doing the very thing that rubbed him the wrong way, the moment he walked through the door.

Whenever Grandfather locked Brannagh in the cellar, his face grew white and pinched and his nostrils flared. In the darkness, Brannagh tried hard not to think about the horror stories that Hilda Outhouse told in the schoolyard ever since the murder of the little boy.

In the cellar darkness, Brannagh had never been so afraid. Eventually she learned a trick to survive. She discovered that if she worked hard enough she could imagine a blank page in her mind's eye, then a hand, then a pencil. The hand would sketch on the page. Soon the cellar would be filled with rolling boats or cats or clouds. By filling the blank page in her mind with drawings, Brannagh was able to hold the ooglie-booglies at bay. Only much later, when she lay in her own bed, safe and sound, the nightmares began. Luckily, she would find Aunt Thelma wandering the halls and they would spend the night trying to train the current resident cat to go after the mice that scuttled between the walls.

After learning that Brannagh had taught herself to type, Grandfather decided that she should help in the Nervous Clinic when his secretary, Mrs. McGillvery, and Aunt Thelma were too busy to complete his paper work.

"I would help you in the office this morning, but he wants me in the kitchen," Aunt Thelma muttered before disappearing behind her bedroom door.

Instead of heading into the bathroom, Brannagh moved quietly towards the staircase that led up to the Nervous Clinic. No one was allowed up to the third floor until the patients were awake. Grandfather had strictly forbidden it. But Brannagh needed to sneak a quick peek just to see if there was a light under his door. If not, she would have time to wolf down some toast.

Slowly, Brannagh tiptoed up the staircase. It was dark, but she didn't dare turn on a light. The rail beneath her fingers was cold. Suddenly, from up above, came the sound of a slamming door. Brannagh jumped and scurried back down the stairs. A flame of pain shot up her inner arm and she yelped. A sliver of loose wainscoting had broken free and pierced her wrist. Up above, footsteps pattered across the floor.

Brannagh drew back into the shadows of the stairwell. Her heart pounded in her throat as she listened. If she had woken Grandfather ... but the only sound that filled her ears was her own laboured breathing. Brannagh rose to her feet and moved closer to the hall light, inspecting her arm. A sliver of wood, a quarter of an inch wide, three inches long, stuck out of the cotton sleeve of her nightgown, just above the wrist.

Brannagh touched the splinter and winced. Her arm jerked. Her head began to spin.

"Here." An unfamiliar voice drifted down the stairs.

Brannagh froze, eyes turning towards the upper landing.

A tall, thin, pale girl with long brown stringy hair, stood at the top of the stairs. "Let me do it," she said matter-of-factly. She descended the stairs sedately, chin in the air. She grabbed Brannagh's arm and, before Brannagh could struggle or protest, pulled the sliver out, in one swift motion.

"Got it," she said triumphantly, holding it up to the light.

The girl stared at Brannagh's astonished face for a moment, then spun around, flipping up her nightgown to reveal her rear end in a pair of white ruffled underwear.

"My name's Annie," she grinned wickedly over her shoulder, eyes registering Brannagh's repulsion with a glint of satisfaction. "And I'm crazy."

❧ ☙

"Le Château Laurentien, bonjour. Puis-je vous aider?" The woman's voice was bright and chipper.

"Uh," Brannagh stared at the business card in her hand. The tobacco pouch lay on the table in the kitchen of the cottage. She had dialled the number on impulse, assuming the number was defunct. She hadn't expected someone to actually answer.

" 'ello? 'ello?" The woman's voice rose in pitch.

"Yes, sorry, je parle Anglais." Brannagh shoved the business card back into the tobacco pouch.

"Oh, oui, Madam, S'cuse. May I help you?"

"I wanted to speak to one of your patrons. Nikolai Mirsky."

"Room number?"

"Uh, see that's the thing, he told me, but I forget."

"One moment, while I check the register."

Brannagh leaned against the windowsill. She heard muffled voices in the background.

"Oui?" A man barked.

"Yes? I'm looking for one of your patrons, Nikolai Mirsky, I understand he has a room …"

"Who is dis?" She heard the apprehension in his voice.

"A friend."

"Name?"

"I …"

"What do you want?" he demanded.

"I'm just trying to find Nikki."

"Leave us alone."

"Please if you could just tell me where he might …"

"We don't know anyone by that name." He hung up.

Brannagh stared out the window. Rain clouds rolled in, darkening the sky. The thought of being alone in the cabin during a downpour made her feel claustrophobic.

She scurried through the rooms, randomly grabbing things and throwing them into a canvas tote bag: plums, an umbrella, her purse, a jacket, a magazine and the car keys. Brannagh hurried outdoors and tossed the bag into the back seat of the car. A few light drops of rain fell. She had no idea where she was going. Didn't care. She only knew that she couldn't stay another minute alone with her thoughts.

She started the car. Something moved through the bushes in the distance, near the cottage with the red roof. She shut off the wipers and stared hard through the window. The patter of the rain on the car roof grew louder.

Brannagh pulled onto the highway, welcoming the reassuring motion of the car, as she drove along the river road. Trees bordering the road were lashed by the wind, and whitecaps rolled across the bay.

~~~

The third floor of Grandfather's house in Saint John smelt different from the rest of the house, lemon-lime dry, gag-in-the-throat germ-free. There were two bedrooms in the east wing and one in the west wing. They had each been converted into three narrow rooms, and thick iron locks had been fastened to all the doors. The Nervous Clinic was able to accommodate nine patients at a time. The sitting room at the end of the hall had been converted into Grandfather's office. The old Nursery Room was the patients' lounge, though sometimes Grandfather took it over with Aunt Thelma, locking everyone out and pulling down the shades, when the billing notices fell too far behind. It contained two old-fashioned settees, a shelf of books, an aquarium and a locked closet with a telephone inside.

Brannagh had grown up with the patients. Before the little boy had been murdered, she had often played school in the lounge with any patients who were willing to play along. When Grandfather was busy at the hospital, Brannagh would take it upon herself to give them free drawing lessons, using old Mr. Rupert, who slipped into spells of catatonia, as a model. Gran insisted the patients were harmless to anyone but themselves. Often they were allowed to wander freely about the house and invited to eat with the family down below.

But now, whenever there was a new admission, Brannagh's imagination kicked into high gear. This morning, Brannagh had waited to climb the stairs until it was absolutely silent. She didn't want to run into the girl with the auburn hair. She couldn't say why. She didn't drool, or gnash her teeth; none of the patients did any of the ridiculous things that Hilda Outhouse claimed they did. But there was something unsettling about the girl with the ruffled underwear nevertheless.

Brannagh slipped into the office and shut the door. She was home free. Today the pile of notes beside the typewriter on the high oak desk, with its nest of drawers, was thicker than usual. Brannagh found it a challenge to decipher the hasty notes her Grandfather had scribbled on the paper: Axis 1: Schizophrenia. Axis II, Axis III.

"Morning," Mrs. McGillvery said softly, wheeling a metal trolley through the door. She spoke with a faint Scottish burr that thickened when she became emotionally heated. She had plump fingers, and varicose veins, and lumbering black sensible shoes. She was as glum as a toad, yet she was the first person people in the neighbourhood turned to when they needed help.

"My knees are predicting rain." She took two clove mints out of a jar, tossed one to Brannagh and popped the other into her mouth. She had a weakness for sweets (and a good peat fire–dried malt it was rumoured), and kept horrible tasting bitters squirreled away in various pockets, change purses, and hankies on her being.

Mrs. McGillvery shook her head. She disapproved of Brannagh working in the clinic as much as Aunt Thelma did. When Aunt Thelma declared that it was ridiculous to expect an eight-year-old to take on that responsibility, Grandfather had brushed her off.

"You did it. Started running this house the day you were born," he had gruffed. "Didn't harm you any."

"Didn't it?" Aunt Thelma echoed so softly, after Grandfather left the room, that Brannagh barely heard her.

Mrs. McGillvery groaned as she pushed a trolley out the door toward the dumbwaiter filled with trays from Aunt Thelma's kitchen.

Brannagh's arm still throbbed where the sliver had been pulled out. The roller bar made a clicking sound as she inserted a fresh blank admission form. She started to type:

NAME: Annie Baird.
REASON FOR ADMISSION: (see chart notes,
General Hospital attached and police interview).

Brannagh flipped to a yellow carbon copy report and read it. It described an eight-year-old girl whose family had moved from Fredericton to Saint John several months ago. Being intensely jealous of her younger stepbrother, her stepmother claimed, had been her stepdaughter's biggest struggle. At least it had been until the day of the tragedy. Annie Baird had been found lying in a ditch, covered in cuts and scrapes, half a mile from where her little brother was murdered.

Brannagh paused lifting her hands off the keys. This girl's brother was the little boy who had been murdered? She rubbed her cold fingers together and with trembling fingers pulled the notes closer.

Annie remembered nothing of the event. The last thing she recalled was cycling to the corner where she usually escorted her brother across a busy intersection after his piano lesson. He was too young to cross the street alone. After that, she remembered nothing. Her bicycle was found lying not too far away. The chief of police, Mr. Eden, felt that Annie had been traumatized by the event, that perhaps she had witnessed something. It was he who suggested she stay in the Nervous Clinic for a while after completing several interviews with the family. He felt the stepmother's emotionalism and accusations of Annie's jealousy towards her brother, and the insinuations that the girl was somehow to blame, weren't helping matters.

According to Annie's stepmother, Mrs. Baird, Annie had a problem with urinary incontinence that started three years ago when her stepbrother was born, and had recently worsened when the family moved from Fredericton to Saint John. She claimed that Annie was slow, a mental misfit, not right in the head, that she needed to go to a special institution for her sort, and that she had begun having odd daydreaming spells. Mrs. Baird had found Annie straddling the railing of the widow's walk on the third floor of their home, holding her baby brother in her arms. Mrs. Baird had grown frustrated after being unable to convince her husband, a physician himself, that there was cause for alarm. A week before the murder, she had taken it upon herself to seek help. Annie was admitted to the General Hospital for a workup. All the test results were negative. When it came time to discharge the patient, Annie refused to go home because "my stepmother could care less what happens to me." The nurses, while sympathetic, had completed the doctor's discharge notes. Now, Dr. Baird agreed with Chief Eden, and encouraged his daughter to stay at the Nervous Clinic to facilitate healing of the family dynamic, further assessment and diagnoses.

Mouth dry, Brannagh undid the staple behind the sheets of paper and pressed them flat on the desktop. Typing the remainder of the form, she discovered that Annie didn't live very far from the house on Argyle. Her father was a doctor. Her stepmother grew prized orchids. (Is that what Annie had peed on?) Annie's younger brother's name had been Brian.

Brannagh had been shocked when she heard a boy had been

murdered in the woods. It seemed like the kind of poisonous affliction that could only befall a foreign land far far away. Aunt Thelma would only divulge that the boy had been a stranger, no one that Brannagh had grown up with. In some odd way, that fact seemed to make it less frightening to all the school children, and suddenly they clamoured, as if it were a game, for Patricia, Chief Eden's daughter, to tell every detail of the investigation.

Brannagh felt lightheaded typing the notes, and experienced an enormous pang of empathy for Annie. The words "my stepmother could care less what happens to me" kept rolling around inside her head. A vision of the wildness in Annie's expression, after she had flashed her underwear, kept reasserting itself.

Every year on her birthday, Brannagh allowed herself a slim bud of fantasy. A corner of her mind would reserve a burning hope: what if her mother mailed a card from away? It would, she knew, be gilt-edged and covered with cabbage roses, just like the ones she saw wrapped in plastic in Sanderson's store, and when she opened it up, it would read, "My precious darling daughter, I think of you every moment of every day."

Only, the card never arrived.

Brannagh stopped typing, and wiped her sweaty palms on her thighs. She knew why Annie's defiant bravado bothered her so much. It reminded her of the face she saw in the mirror, gazing back at herself, on her birthday every year.

It had only been a sun shower. Brannagh was pleased to see that already the ominous clouds above Gran's cottage were a thing of the past. An airy feather-grey sky seemed to dominate the day now, giving it a whole new look.

She circled round the back of the cottage with a grocery bag in each arm and set them on the porch. It had been good to get out and have a change of scene. The drive along the river to Sussex had been tranquil: grazing cows on a patchwork of hills and valleys. At the mall, she'd bought steaks and a hibachi, and even remembered to stop at the hardware store to purchase a screw driver to assemble it with. There was something satisfying about being in a strange town, anonymous and mingling.

Brannagh hefted the hibachi out of the trunk of the car, balancing the bag of briquettes and a jug of wine on top, and whacked the trunk closed with one elbow. As she walked toward the cottage, she kept her gaze focused on the ground for any obstacles that might trip her. Just below the large picture window in the parlour, she stopped, lowered her bundle, and dropped to her knees.

In the muddy flower bed, unmistakably, pressed deep into the wild pansies, was a set of footprints.

Large footprints. Wide footprints. The sort that would be made by a man's shoe.

Abandoning the hibachi, Brannagh ran to the back of the cottage, fumbling with the key in the lock. Once inside she slammed the door shut and flicked the bolt. She dropped into a kitchen chair and sat, willing the shaking hands folded in her lap to be still.

Brannagh's first memory of her mother, Pamela, was of an image viewed through white fronds dangling from the hem of the bedspread. She had liked to crawl under her mother's bed, where it was fusty and warm, to play peek-a-boo. Brannagh remembered the crimson fingernails on the hands that scooped her up and swung her high, the whites of her mother's black-lashed eyes, the scarlet mouth breaking into a wide smile. When she pressed Brannagh to her chest, her shiny slip was cool and slippery on Brannagh's belly. The scalloped lace prickled her cheek.

Pamela sat with Brannagh propped on her knee while she did her makeup, and Brannagh waved plump fingers at the multi-images cast back from the three mirrors above the boudoir. Her mother drew delicate lines on her brows, and eyelids, then playfully dabbed her powder puff onto Brannagh's nose.

These were the memories that Brannagh held of the ritual they performed every morning before her mother went to work at the hotel where she was a receptionist at the front desk. Brannagh liked to think that she could remember one morning in particular, one that stood out from all the others, when her mother's hugs were tighter than usual. A morning when her mother's hand shook so that she couldn't draw the red line on her mouth. A morning that, when she went to put on her coat at the front door, had offered an array of suitcases to manoeuvre around.

But the truth was Brannagh simply remembered that for a string of mornings her mother was there, and then, for a long stretch that became the norm, she wasn't.

Brannagh had had no idea that the goodbye kiss she received one morning was different from any other.

So she romanticized her mother's disappearance as the months passed, creating various scenarios. Didn't Gran promise out of Grandfather's earshot, when she cuddled Brannagh in the big chair by the fire, that her mother would return someday?

"She had to go and seek her fortune in the big bad world, darlin'. This place was just too small for the likes of her. She needed something grand and fancy and full of life and promise." Gran would smile and shake her head. "She'll be back one day. You'll see."

Brannagh imagined her mother in China, or Africa, or having tea with the queen. "Once I've travelled the world and made my fortune, I must get back to my daughter," she'd say, tilting her head to one side and gazing coyly through dark lashes at the prince.

It wasn't until Brannagh's sixth birthday that anyone noticed her reluctance to leave the yard on that particular day of the year. Hilda Outhouse wondered out loud why Brannagh was sitting like a lump on the front steps when everyone else was practising their double-dutch. When Brannagh haughtily informed her that she was waiting for the mailman, that she was certain he was bringing a card from her mother, Hilda bellowed, "Geez, your mother could just as easy drive down as send a letter."

And that was how Brannagh found out that her mother had only gone to Moncton, an hour and a half away. That she worked behind the makeup counter in the Eaton's Store.

It would have been as easy as pie to whip down to Saint John any time she felt like seeing her dear darlin' daughter.

Clearly, she didn't want to.

Brannagh spent the entire morning after Annie's admission to the Nervous Clinic typing reports for her grandfather in the office. When she got to the bottom of the pile, she headed downstairs for lunch. She stayed holed up in her room for a good long while and then, when she was certain that it was safe to do so, she climbed the stairs back up to the third floor. Slowly, she walked down the hallway. Hands shaking, she pushed opened the door of the bedroom with the big number 3 on it. Annie was scrunched down in the bed, dwarfed by the huge pillow that she hugged to her chest.

"Hey." Brannagh's greeting came out squeaky.

"What do you want?" In bed, in the narrow room, Annie's air of unyielding daring seemed to have shrunk. She turned her pale face towards the window.

"I just wanted to thank you." Brannagh tentatively approached the bed. "Thank you for pulling out my sliver." She held out her arm and rolled up her sleeve. The gauze was lumpy where Brannagh had hastily rolled it round, and was bound by a mish-mash of black electrical tape (the only tape she could find in the kitchen drawer). "I thought you might want to see it. The wound I mean."

"Is it gross?" Her eyes lit up.

Brannagh sat on the edge of the bed. "Kinda. I guess. I never looked at it since, since ..."

Annie plucked at the edge of the tape. "My stepmother doesn't like me. She says I'm stupid and slow. She wants to send me away. She makes up stories."

"Oh," Brannagh said.

"Did you wash it?" Annie pulled off the last of the tape.

"Wash it?" Brannagh instinctively drew back her arm.

"Jeepers." Annie threw back the covers. She pulled the trolley that Mrs. McGillvery had filled with a jug of water, soap and clean towels closer to the bed. "You have to make sure it doesn't get infected."

"And I brought you this." Brannagh thrust a lumpy package out from behind her back.

Annie stared at the wrinkled pink paper, coloured with swirls of purple and orange crayon. There was a picture of a house, a sun and an enormous buttercup reaching to the sky. Annie stared at Brannagh hard. Her lower lip trembled and for a moment it looked as if her face was going to crumple.

"You didn't have to," Annie said, sounding thoroughly annoyed, "go to any trouble." And then she tore the paper off and pulled out a stuffed animal, and held it at arm's length.

"It's a cat. Puffin. Her tail fell off." Brannagh felt her cheeks flush. It seemed stupid now, this whole idea. "I thought maybe …" Annie didn't blink.

"M-maybe you could fix her too."

"Sure," Annie said, sliding her hand closer to Brannagh. She linked her baby finger with Brannagh's baby finger.

"We have a new cat in the kitchen too named Dustball."

"I can fix anything," Annie said. "Just watch me."

By the time Brannagh had finished her second cup of tea, she had come to her senses. Obviously the shoe print was her grandfather's. Hadn't he come nosing around before she'd arrived, intent on leaving his note and getting the first word in?

This is what came from having too much time on your hands, she concluded.

Brannagh went back outside, leaving the back door wide open, and the radio playing loudly. She lugged her purchases indoors. She had just finished putting the steaks in the fridge when she heard a faint unfamiliar buzzing sound.

It took her a moment to recognize the hum of a boat's motor. She went out onto the dock and stood at the end, shielding her eyes from the sun with one hand as she followed the boat's path downriver. She didn't immediately spot the woman standing behind the waist-high brush on the riverbank, about a quarter of a mile away. When she did, she waved. But Brannagh realized that she herself probably appeared to be a grey blob, on a grey dock, on a grey day. The woman slipped out of sight behind some trees. A few minutes later, the woman's blue scarf caught Brannagh's eye further along the shoreline.

The birds seemed to hold the woman's attention. Seagulls reeled and squawked as the woman tossed bread onto the water.

Brannagh was caught up in watching them too. Her first thought was, *Why didn't I think of that?*

She and her Gran had stood on so many shores tossing crumbs, and their cares, into the wind.

Her second thought was, *So I'm not alone, after all.* Behind the woman, through the trees, she could make out the red roof of the cottage.

Her third thought, as the woman tilted her head back, and her kerchief fell to the ground, revealing a wind-whipped whirl of long auburn hair, was, *Annie?*

Brannagh's stomach tightened, as she stood woodenly and watched Annie turn on her heel and disappear into the cabin with the red roof.

Chapter Four

"I saw you."

"What?" Annie's expression froze.

"I saw you go into the cabin with the red roof. I thought you said it was abandoned, a wreck, falling apart."

These words ran through Brannagh's mind as she sat on the dock and watched Annie brush barbecue sauce on the steaks. It was what she wanted to say, what she willed herself to say, while they were still alone and, Tish was preoccupied fixing drinks inside the cottage.

"You're deep in thought," Annie observed. She wore a jean skirt with an orange T-shirt and green socks. A blob of barbecue sauce hung on the right lens of her glasses.

"Hmmmm?" Brannagh pretended to be distracted by a houseboat pulsing downriver.

She had been watching Annie covertly ever since she had arrived at the cottage a few hours ago. Watching for a hint of anything out of the ordinary. It unnerved her that Annie appeared so utterly calm.

What the hell is going on, Annie?

"Are you okay?" Annie asked abruptly. She came and stood next to Brannagh's chair. Brannagh could smell the tang of lemons on her hair.

"Is everything all right?" The concern in Annie's eyes was grating. "You look lost."

"Betrayed, you mean? Like I don't know who the hell to trust anymore?" The fury slicing through each word startled them both.

The steaks sputtered, dripping fat, and a flame shot upwards. Annie turned abruptly and raised the grill. "I just thought maybe the party was too much, too soon. We haven't given you time to rest up properly," she clarified.

Brannagh finished the wine in her glass. "Yes, it's overkill," she said evenly. "I wish I'd never come."

Annie turned around, mouth opening and closing and opening again.

Brannagh turned to glance back at the cottage as the back door slammed. Tish's shout of "I hope you two are behaving yourselves!" and the high-pitched sound of Annie's beeper prevented her from saying another word.

※ ※

· "When is Dianne going to get here?" Tish grumbled. She crossed her legs and swung one plump calf.

Brannagh shrugged. "Tomorrow. She phoned Annie yesterday and said she'd be delayed."

Outside, the sun lowered in the sky. They sat at the table in the kitchen, going through the motions of having fun. Annie said her beeper had signalled an emergency with a patient. She had to return to Saint John. "The big reunion," Brannagh observed wryly, "is underway, folks."

"Dianne's whole life was tending her sick mother." Tish resumed slicing the inch-thick T-bone on her plate. "Now she's gone, Dianne's lost. It'll do her good to get away."

Brannagh, who had zero appetite, sipped wine and folded a napkin fan-style. She was slowly coming to terms with the fact that Annie must have rented the cabin with the red roof to keep an eye on her. Despite its morbid association for them both, Annie had always been able to intellectualize her emotions, burying them beneath words and theories. In fact, the more Brannagh thought about it, she was certain it had been part of Annie's plan all along. Good old Dr. Annie, coming to the rescue, not taking any chances with her unstable, unpredictable friend. *Brannagh's going through such a rough time; I hope she isn't thinking of doing anything desperate; like mother, like daughter.* Were Tish and Dianne in on this too?

Brannagh took a gulp of wine and tried to switch gears and concentrate on Tish. She hadn't changed much over the years. Tish's toenails and fingernails were painted peach to match her hair band and the bangle on her wrist. She was the only kid on the block when they were growing up who was colour co-ordinated.

Tish's mother, Wanda, felt it was extremely important that she and her children live up to the image expected from the town's chief of police. She was thrilled when her eldest son was accepted at dentistry school in Upper Canada and complained for weeks when the *Telegraph Journal* neglected to send a reporter to interview him despite her repeated telephone reminders. Tish, being a girl, thank God, didn't need to worry about that sort of thing, but she required certain necessities, a certain polish to maintain the family's social standing, like store-bought clothes and bread.

Tish always brought desserts to school in her lunch bag, modern works of art (fluffy baked-from-an-envelope cakes) which made the other kids want to hide their hideous homemade hockey puck–sized oatmeal cookies. To get back at Tish, especially after her father became mayor, they teased "fatty fatty, two by four, bum got stuck in the outhouse door."

It was Gran, in the end, who rescued Tish, so to speak, in grade five, by asking her if she could possibly see it in her heart to entertain Brannagh while she attended one of Wanda's fund-raising tea parties. Tish rose nobly to the occasion, sharing a piece of cherry cake that came with its own foil pan into which one stirred a dry mix with water before popping it into the oven. Once the sweet had broken the ice, the girls spent days inventing a code for reading tea leaves, and loftily determined Hilda Outhouse's and her loopy girlfriends' fortunes—complete fabrications plagiarized from the copies of *True Romance* Aunt Thelma kept hidden under her bed—and charged them a penny each.

When Brannagh eventually brought Tish along on a bike ride, wearing a look that dared Annie or Dianne to object, they all pretended hard that there was nothing out of the ordinary about Tish wearing a crinoline that had been stiffened with sugar water. Wanda agreed with Kate Post that slacks were only appropriate on a boat, or to play golf; no girl should be seen on city streets wearing shorts.

Some things never change, Brannagh reflected, as she toyed with her napkin. Earlier, when Tish had dug out a wallet bulging with pictures, Brannagh had been bemused to see Tish's daughter, Belinda or "Billy," wearing colour co-ordinated ribbons and frilly socks.

Tish popped a piece of bun into her mouth. "What I don't get is Annie going back to town. Isn't anyone else capable of looking after an emergency in that hospital?"

Brannagh picked up a clean plate, and speared one of the steaks. "Why did you tell me not to come here? When you telephoned up north?"

Tish eyed Brannagh guardedly. She toyed with the bracelets on her wrist. "She told you, didn't she? You guys were always like this." She crossed two fingers and held them up.

Brannagh was travelling back in time, back to sleepover fights on Saturday nights when it was long past midnight and everyone was coming down from the homemade fudge high, and Tish would have a hard time not letting her insecurities get the better of her.

"Annie did not tell me about whatever. So why don't you?"

Tish hesitated, turning her wine glass in her fingers and staring at the tiny bubbles that rose from the stem. "I went to Reggie's restaurant for breakfast one Saturday, and guess who I see? Annie coming off a stint in Emerge."

"Go on."

"Well, she wasn't alone."

"So?"

"So, she was with Eddie."

Brannagh had to work hard to disguise her surprise. "Eddie? Your husband, Eddie? So, is it a crime to have breakfast with your girlfriend's husband?"

Tish shrugged. "No. Of course not."

"So you joined them for breakfast and—"

Tish flushed. "No, I waited until Eddie left. Then I joined Annie."

Brannagh frowned. "Tish."

"I don't know why, okay? I just did."

Brannagh was silent. *Damn you, Annie.*

Tish's fingers were white against the wine glass. She frowned. "We hadn't seen each other in a while. I asked her if anything was new."

Brannagh picked at her salad. "And?"

Tish gulped. "Not one word about Eddie. I mean that's okay. Really. Not a big deal. Maybe she was worried I'd get jealous. Didn't want to upset me."

"You've always had a green streak."

"Well, it bugged me. I got kinda ticked. She started telling me all about her cases at the hospital, and I made the mistake of telling her that she worked too much. That if she wasn't careful she'd end up being an old maid, like your Aunt Thelma. Well." Tish topped up their wine glasses.

Brannagh winced.

"She went bonkers." Tish nibbled an olive. "Just shoved her plate aside and walked out without looking back. Ever since? Whenever I run into her, she ignores me."

Brannagh pushed her plate away.

"We're supposed to look out for one another. Protect one another. I reminded her of that. And she agreed."

"Protect one another?" This was a typical Tish conversation, zinging from one tangent to another.

"To protect one another's self-a-steam forever and ever amen," Tish recited impatiently. "Tuatha-de-Danaans? The pledge? Am I the only one who remembers? I thought that was important. I mean, how long did we sweat over writing that thing. The candles, the cross. I thought that meant something."

"We were just kids," Brannagh muttered.

"So?"

"Now we're grown up."

"And like, we have all the answers?"

Brannagh shrugged.

"So that's what I said to Annie, according to the pledge we're supposed to keep an eye on one another, forever and ever amen, and she agreed, so I told her that I thought her whole life was wrapped around work, that if you took it away, it'd be like pulling the rug out from under her feet, and you know what she said?" Tish's lower lip wobbled. Her hand darted out and she snatched a serviette.

"Hey."

The serviette trembled in Tish's open palm. "She said that it was easy for me to say that work isn't important, because I don't have any. And I said, 'But I have Eddie, I have love,' and she got all huffy. How would I know what love is, marrying straight out of high school? Never known anything else but this stupid little town and its stupid little ways."

"Oh boy." Brannagh rose, and hunched over Tish awkwardly, encircling her with her arms. She glanced at the empty wine bottles on the table. Time to put the kettle on, she decided. "Don't pay any attention."

"But … but," Tish gulped for air. "What if it's true? Oh, Lord, what if it's true. I mean Eddie is old-fashioned, his ideas, I mean, and sometimes I'd rather give in than start a fight, but then later, I feel so mad. And I think what would people think? We argue about such piddly things. Like the right way to chop tomatoes. They'd think I was stupid, that's what. And they'd be right. I was never smart in school. Not like you. Not like Annie."

"School smarts aren't everything." Brannagh paused. Outside the window the last streaks of the setting sun rimmed the clouds. "You knew that time that we should go weed Mrs. Sanderson's flowers when her cat was hit by the milk truck."

But Tish wasn't listening. "After a while my head starts to spin, so I go to the fridge and eat like nobody's business. And I think, is this all there is? Remember when we were kids? When we had the world at our feet? And now here I am, getting fatter and stupider by the minute."

Brannagh rubbed the small of Tish's back.

"What if she's right? Eddie hasn't changed one twit since we used to go necking in Martello Tower."

Brannagh did a second take. "You used to neck in Martello Tower?"

"Honestly, Brannagh." Tish pulled back to gaze at her with

red-rimmed eyes. "What did you think we were doing? Picking blueberries? It was the only place we could get away from my father."

"Well, you always had those paper bags and tweezers and that great big magnifying glass."

"Yeah, and I always won first prize in the Science Fair," Tish retorted. She sat in the chair and blew her nose.

Brannagh joined her at the table. "Necking in Martello Tower?"

Tish's mouth wobbled. She broke into a smile, then back to a frown. "Some days I worry, I just worry that there's supposed to be more. That maybe I'll realize when I'm sixty that I missed out on the most important thing in life, and then it'll be too late."

"What important thing?"

"How'm I supposed to know?" she muttered irritably.

"Look, Annie is wrong," Brannagh said firmly. "Do you hear me? Annie is wrong. There is more to life than having a job to hang your hat on every day." Brannagh got up, and piled dirty dishes in the sink.

"Bullshit," Tish eyed her accusingly. "I don't care what either one of you thinks. You're not me." Her chin rose defiantly. "And the trouble is, I don't know what I want. I love Eddie and Billy, but some days it's just not enough. It's always been this way, my crazy mind, like I'll think 'Oh if only such and such happens, I'll be happy forever and ever,' and then such and such happens and I'm not. Happy, that is. And I get so mad, because I think I should be. I should be content. But it's like I have this hungry snake twisting around inside my belly. No matter what I feed it, it always wants more." Tish drained her wine glass and folded her arms across her chest.

Brannagh collected the dirty cutlery.

"I keep remembering," Tish muttered, "how Eddie had a crush

on Annie when we were kids. How he tried to kiss her once, on the steps of Sanderson's store." Tish paused. The rest of her words came out so low, Brannagh could barely hear them. "What if Eddie has the hungry snake in the belly too? What then?"

It would be better, Brannagh decided, to drop this subject altogether.

"Do you—" Tish hesitated and then rushed on quickly. "Do you regret it?"

"Regret what?" Brannagh wiped her hands on a tea towel.

"Do you regret falling in love? I mean, really falling in love." Tish's expression was open and honest, washed clean of the pretence that came with their initial awkwardness together, born of the need to appear carefree and happy after all these years, and not a failure, never that, heaven forbid, no matter what the cost. Brannagh envied Tish's quick child-like flow of hot tears. She had always been able to boil over at the drop of a hat, spilling everything out in an illogical mish-mash, then basking in a clean glow afterwards. "It's kind of like jumping off a cliff, isn't it?" Tish ventured, eyes shining. "Without looking down."

Brannagh's ability to express her emotions was something else entirely. She had learned, from living in the house on Argyle, to compartmentalize everything. Her feelings were relegated to the distant third floor, behind closed doors, and thumps, and bumps, and meandering shadow-filled halls.

Brannagh attempted to smile then gave up. She reached into the top cupboard for the tin of tea bags. "No, I don't regret falling in love." She dropped two teabags into the pot, and filled it with hot water. "What I regret," she finished coldly, "is not falling out."

Nikki's estimates were off. It took the bird counting team eight days to get to the site of their home base. Along the way they lost one student (Gordon who had a habit of wandering off when Mother Nature called), one camp heater, and two boat motors (one from a busted propeller, and the other from sheer laziness when it fell off the back of a canoe mid-stream). Nikki confided that he figured Gordon loosened the screws on purpose because he couldn't be bothered carrying it any further.

The bird counting team arrived at their home base mid-afternoon on a cool, unspring-like day in May. Cindy, Tom and Alex clambered out of the canoes and into the clearing in the scrub, and immediately began whooping and hollering and giving one another jubilant slaps on the back. Gordon dropped spread-eagle onto the shingle and groaned. Nikki flashed Brannagh a satisfied grin before he dug around in his pocket for his pipe and issued orders to unload the gear. The lower half of the camp site crossed the Canadian border into Minnesota (a deliberate calculation on Nikki's part because a large chunk of their financial support came from concerned parties to the south). The base camp was located in the centre of the degree block, the portion of boreal forest they were covering in the count. Back in Toronto, Brannagh had divided the degree block into sixteen plots that radiated outward like spokes on a wheel. Each plot would be surveyed (according to her calculations) at least two hundred times by the three pairs of observers. For the moment, Brannagh had been simply relieved beyond words to know they'd finally be staying put long enough for her blisters to heal.

"Don't get too comfortable," Nikki warned, coming up behind Brannagh.

A faint alarm bell rang inside Brannagh's head.

"We've got work to do." Nikki glanced at his watch. "Here you go." He handed over her rucksack.

Brannagh rose slowly.

Nikki hoisted his own onto his shoulders and motioned for her to follow.

Shit, she thought. Shit, *shit*.

After they had walked for an hour, her head began to throb. The back of her neck felt as if someone pressed a hot iron against it. Ever muscle in her body whined. Over the last few weeks, she could have sworn that all the portages had been uphill. The only thing that had kept her going had been the knowledge that they were almost at base camp, and that once she got there, she'd be able to drop, sleep forever—at least past three AM—and nurse her wounds. It had taken every ounce of determination, and all the teeth-gritting she could muster, not to reveal a hint of how truly exhausted she was.

It had been a hellish odyssey. Broiling heat, the occasional hail storm and cold downpours that stopped only long enough to highlight the insanity producing kzzz-z-z-z-z of blackflies; not to mention encounters with angry hornets, poison ivy and porcupines. It was amazing what dampness did to the body; amazing what meagre encouragement fungus needed in order to grow. The group's concentration had become focused on how to rid themselves of rashes, scales, blisters and boils.

After they had lost a full day searching for Gordon, who had become turned around in the woods, Nikki decided to tighten up the buddy system. They were made responsible for one another's whereabouts at all times. Brannagh's partner was Cindy. Brannagh suspected that Nikki just wanted to separate Cindy and Tom. She had witnessed him shouting orders at Tom whenever he spotted the young man's hand on Cindy's arm, or the two of them sitting thigh by thigh in the canoe.

So, as if the weather and athlete's foot and the agony of waking from dreams of pizza with double cheese weren't enough, Brannagh had to put up with Cindy dragging her feet and spinning out the plot of *All My Children* from the very beginning, because she couldn't "buh-lieve" Brannagh never watched it. Brannagh learned to tune out Cindy's voice, her humming, her yelp if a mink or red fox scuttled through the undergrowth, her fingernails digging into Brannagh's forearm when dusk approached and a timberwolf howled.

By the time they had finally arrived at base camp, the place where they were actually going to eat fat juicy hamburgers with the works (okay, so they were only powdered protein patties with dried mustard and onion flakes) and share the last dregs of Alex's Jack Daniel's, Brannagh had been beyond exhaustion.

"Do you do this on purpose?" Brannagh asked now, as she followed Nikki away from base camp; concentrating on the retreating red rims of the wool socks that rose above the tops of his boots.

"Hmph?" His eyebrows rose.

"Do you purposely dream up ways to make life wretched for the rest of us? Is that how you kill time on portages?"

"So right," he chuckled. "You've discovered my secret." The bough of the spruce that snagged Nikki's shoulder suddenly became free and fwumped Brannagh's chin.

Brannagh surprised herself by giving in to a popular student practice: she gave Nikki the finger. Once, then twice, for good measure.

Brannagh couldn't remember if her pencils and pads were in her rucksack. If they were headed towards a site that needed to be sketched, Nikki was shit out of luck. He had lectured them time after time about keeping the bare necessities of survival directly on their person in case of emergency (while his pipe and pouch of tobacco hung haphazardly out of his hip pocket). Brannagh did a mental run through; she knew she had long pants and a sweat shirt, matches, water, compass, macaroni (she had finally acquired a taste for chewing it raw), a torch, bug spray, flares, a pocket knife.

The sun was lowering behind the tamarack by the time they began their descent into the bog and sedge that rimmed a small, oblong lake.

At the bottom of the slope, Brannagh pulled out her binoculars and scanned the trees. A kingfisher darted through the pine boughs and dived down to the water.

Vaguely, she became aware of an unfamiliar noise in the distance. It grew louder. A white bullet parted from the clouds, and descended from the sky. It landed on the lake, sending a flare of water rippling into the swaying reeds.

"Good timing." Nikki squinted into the distance

"We have company." Brannagh made out a figure, the pilot, opening the door of the plane and waving. "Wonder what he wants?"

Nikki pulled a thick wad of filthy yellow rubber out of his rucksack, and pulled a cord. In less than five seconds a dinghy floated in the water. He brandished two collapsible paddles and handed her one.

"Us," Nikki informed her, holding the dinghy steady. "Hope you don't get air sick."

By the time the plane was airborne once again, Brannagh had managed to find out where they were headed. Apparently, Nikki was checking in with one of the private financiers of the expedition, to give a progress report. He, in turn, would contact the other contributors, and if all went according to schedule, a cheque for the costs they'd incurred to date would be in the bank on Monday. Nikki explained that it was her job to present the sketches in a professional manner.

"I can't do it," she announced with great satisfaction. "You should have kept me informed. I don't have my charcoal or drawing pads."

The lines around Nikki's eyes fanned downwards. "Try to rest up." He dismissed her with a nod and went up front to talk to the pilot, a pot-bellied man with a crew-cut who kept a plastic coffee stir stick clenched between his teeth.

Brannagh opened her rucksack, and saw that her sketchpad was indeed inside, along with the thermal long underwear that she wore to bed, a clean pair of cords, T-shirt, mackinaw and socks.

Who the heck did this guy think he was? Merlin the Magician? She sat, frowning out the window, but it was hard to nourish prickly annoyance, gazing at the ever-changing curve of rock and water below. The lowering sun glinted off ribbons and pools rimmed by evergreens, sparse and spindly loners, then thick interesting clumps that never looked the same way twice. Barren, bleak rock, with no hint of a crevice capable of catching one weather-beaten grain of sand on the wind, would suddenly flaunt an act of defiance; a black mangled fir tree thrusting boldly skyward.

By the time they landed on the bay, dusk had descended. Lights floated like ghostly apparitions in the distance.

The plane glided towards a raft with a rowboat tied to it. They disembarked, and Nikki helped Brannagh to climb into the boat. He rowed, pausing to raise one hand in salute after the plane had lifted off the water and circled round.

Brannagh gazed at the surrounding stars emerging in the navy sky.

"My grandmother used to tell me that God had a needle, and that when it got dark, He poked the sky with it to let in just enough light to remind me He was there, but not so much that ..."

"It'd be too bright to fall asleep?" Brannagh guessed.

"That the sky would rip in two and fall on my head." He swung the oarlocks in her direction. "Your turn to row."

She grimaced. "How far?"

"Ten miles." His eyes twinkled.

Brannagh shook her head. "You're too much, Nikki Mirsky, just too too much." Brannagh fell into rhythm. The soft lapping of the water was the only sound anchoring them to the bottom of the dark blue bowl. She found her gaze moving back to Nikki's grey-whiskered chin, tilted upward.

"There's an island over there. My Uncle Zhuk built a hunting shelter on the southern shore." Nikki pointed. "I used to run away there when I was a kid, when I'd get pissed at his wife for trying to tell me what to do. I thought no one had any idea where I was. But he knew all along. Never said a word."

"Zhuk? Any connection to Zorro?"

"It pays to have a superhero uncle in your pocket when you're financing an expedition that big industry wants to kill."

A shout drifted from shore. A lantern bobbed in the distance. Soon Brannagh could make out a burly man with a dark beard standing at the end of an L-shaped dock.

"Finally! What kept you?" he shouted, lifting Nikki clear off the ground before his foot had time to steady itself on land.

Nikki's shoulders hunched as he submitted to a bone-crushing hug. The large man poked him in the stomach. "What's this?"

Nikki scuffed the dock with the toe of his boot.

"Getting too old for this stuff, eh?"

Nikki's head shot up.

"Think you can handle it?" The burly man teased. "If I'd known you were going soft on me, cavorting with those soft-jowled liberals, I might not have—"

"Where's Valova?" Nikki glanced toward shore.

"Heating up the sauna." The older man slung one arm over Nikki's shoulder. "Tell me, tell me, are the canoes featherweight battering rams, everything I told you they'd be ... eh ... eh?" He hip-checked Nikki playfully. "The truth now."

With that the two men walked down the dock, lantern swaying, gesturing and bellowing.

"No, no, don't worry about me, I'm fine, just fine," Brannagh muttered, slinging her rucksack over one shoulder and climbing onto the dock.

She thought about how, in years to come, when she was a famous artist launching her third coffee-table book, she would tell this story, with just the right amount of tongue-in-cheek humble charm to a group of admirers around the Chablis and caviar.

Brannagh trudged up the hill. She only hoped there was food, real food, behind the brightly lit windows in the distance.

Then at least the trip wouldn't be a total loss.

"Do you ever think about ...?" Tish dug into the bag at her feet and pulled out two marshmallows.

"About?" Brannagh skewered a marshmallow with the stick propped between her knees. After washing the dishes, her only desire had been to have a hot shower and crawl into bed, but Tish appeared determined to continue their heart-to-heart. It was her idea to light a fire down on the beach. Brannagh had to admit that, despite her trepidations about heading out into the pitch black, she was glad she had succumbed.

It was cold and damp by the water, but the warmth and light of the fire was soothing. The flickering flames brought to mind all the fires she had ever sat around, remnants of camp songs, shy, yearning glances from older boys, and goose bumps that came from staying too long in cold northern waters.

"Do you ever think about *that* summer?" Tish ventured.

"Which?"

"Before high school, '54." She gauged Brannagh's reaction.

Brannagh stared into the fire. *This is what she wanted to talk about?*

"When we formed Tuatha-de-Dananns."

Brannagh's marshmallow blazed and she waved the stick in the air. It flew off and landed in the water with a plop and a sizzle.

"Not a good year."

Brannagh sat back down on the log, and dug another marshmallow out of the bag.

"In fact, it was probably the worst, for all of us."

For some reason, Tish had the past stuck in her craw and was determined to shake it out. "I don't recall." Brannagh lowered her stick carefully over the flames. *Had Annie put her up to it?* But she quickly vetoed that notion as it appeared they weren't even talking.

"Just before summer ended, Dianne's mom had the stroke. It was so awful because Dianne was the one who went into the house and found her." Brannagh would never forget it. For weeks, Dianne wouldn't talk or leave the house, and sat minding her mother and father, both invalids, waiting for Dr. Baird to call.

"And that was the summer Annie flipped out. Pulled a one-eighty. Miss Einstein turned into Marilyn Monroe."

"Just a passing whim." Brannagh propped the stick between her knees, undid the lid on the thermos and poured tea into a mug. She handed it to Tish and fished another one out of the haversack lying on the ground between them. "What I remember is that that was the summer *you* just had to have a boyfriend. One week it was hide-and-seek till midnight; the next, you were carrying a bottle of Evening in Paris everywhere you went."

Tish absent-mindedly twiddled a curl with one finger.

Brannagh shrugged. "But I guess that's life, isn't it? People always changing. Just when you think, this is it, this moment, I love it, please let it last forever, people change, things drift, something calls someone away from you." She felt Tish's hand reach out for hers.

"I don't blame you for not wanting to come back," Tish said softly. "It was horrible, wasn't it?" She cleared her throat. "And I guess I always blamed myself. Felt like I could have done something."

Brannagh made a shushing motion with one hand. It had been a terrible summer, the summer of '54. Brannagh avoided thinking about it. But it had brought Annie, Tish, Dianne and Brannagh together for a brief vulnerable moment of solidarity to form Tuatha-de-Dananns. Then, when their first year in high school started, it was as if the burden of being who they were suddenly grew unbearable, and they became self-defensively aware of the need to harden and cool and distance themselves. They each did everything in their power to resist, deny and scatter. Dianne begged off every outing with the excuse that she had to stay home with her mother. Annie touted her newfound decision to be a doctor and the need to hole up in her father's medical library as a reason to isolate. And Tish got a job. (Had anything really changed then? Here they were on the day of the big club reunion minus two members.)

"I always wondered if it bothered you," Brannagh said finally. "When we were kids, when Annie's brother, Brian, was killed. When we hounded you to tell us about the investigation at school."

Tish's expression froze. She stared at Brannagh, speculating.

"I used to feel sorry for you. I could tell you didn't want to talk about it. That it made you feel uncomfortable when Hilda Outhouse badgered you to hide outside your Dad's office, to listen in on his phone conversations, and spill all the details you overheard."

Tish wiped her mouth on her sleeve. "Not everyone."

"What do you mean?"

"I wasn't uncomfortable with everyone." Tish stared at her feet. "Just you."

"Me?"

Tish chewed her lip. "I didn't tell the one-hundred percent truth."

"Big deal. Like I'm a saint?" Brannagh frowned. "So you exaggerated to make it more interesting, threw in a few white lies to get more attention, and then hated yourself for doing it. You were just a kid." Brannagh put her arm around Tish's shoulder. "We all knew that, deep down, but we couldn't stop being fascinated. That's why I brought it up. It was never a big deal. Not then and not now. We liked you regardless. It had nothing to do with whether or not you had a scoop of the day. That's the truth."

Tish's head rose. She gave Brannagh a long, hard look. She started to speak, but it was as if the words were caught in the back of her throat and wouldn't shake free.

"Hey!" Brannagh pointed skyward. A glowing green star sank like a dying ember towards the water. "Make a wish."

They both closed their eyes.

When Brannagh opened hers, Tish was still sitting with her eyes screwed shut, such an earnest expression on her face it brought a lump to Brannagh's throat.

Why was life so damned screwy? she wondered.

"I wanted to tell you the truth, that summer, back in '54," Tish's voice interrupted Brannagh's revery, "the summer your mother—"

"Came home." Brannagh jumped to her feet.

"And she—"

"Came home from Moncton with her boyfriend and shocked the heck out of everyone." Brannagh scooped up the bag of marshmallows and handed Tish the bucket. She was not going to talk about her mother's murder. Not now. Not ever. "Put out the fire. I'll get the garbage. The last thing we need is a skunk nosing around."

Tish hesitated then walked onto the dock and picked up the empty barbecue sauce bottle and half a bag of buns. The call of a loon carried across the water.

Brannagh took a deep breath, silently told her heart to stop its thumping high in her chest. "You know what I think?" she said quietly.

"What?" Tish's voice drifted up from the beach.

"You worry too much. You worry too much about Eddie, and everybody telling perfect one-hundred percent truth, and how to chop tomatoes, and his dating Annie once, all that. What's the big deal?"

"Thank you, Ann Landers."

"Never mind. You're the one he married, in the end." Brannagh gazed across the water, concentrating on the dots of light that reflected the windows of houses on the peninsula.

"Whoopdeedoooo." Tish replied. "Big whoopdeefuckingdoo."

At first glance, Nikki's Aunt Valova was about as appealing as a pile of mud. She was short and plump with sunken brown eyes and a nose the size of a truck driver's fist. But it was her ears, Brannagh decided, that were truly the epitome of gross. They were long-lobed and rumpled, like strudel dough, slowly giving way to gravity's pull.

She didn't, according to Nikki, like English, and had never bothered to master it, but he insisted she would enjoy Brannagh's company.

Seeing Valova nude, after she pulled open the steambath door, didn't change Brannagh's opinion one bit. Her body resembled one huge lump of dough. She had sagging, blue-veined breasts that swung above the flesh on her upper thighs as they spread to form a table over her knees. When she raised her arms to swat the air with the branch in her hand, the flesh on her upper arms hung as if it had become unhinged from the bone. Her pale skim milk feet seemed to be protesting their thrust into the light of day.

Brannagh made these observations covertly while she undressed. She placed her clothes in a neat pile beside the door and joined Valova on the top of the two-tiered wooden slatted steps. Valova handed her a branch and mimicked waving it through the air. She dipped a pot in a wooden barrel of water, and aimed a splash at the pile of hot rocks circling the wood stove in the corner. There was a hissing sound, followed by an emphysematous wheeze. Puffs of steam rose in the air.

Brannagh waved the branch. "Thank you," she said.

Valova smiled shyly. Her cheeks were as shiny and purple as waxed plums. She pulled a can of beer out of a bucket of cold water. When she popped the top, foam rose and ran down her arm. She shrieked and held it to her mouth, tilting her head back.

"Have a good trip?" she asked haltingly, handing the can to Brannagh.

"Yes," Brannagh nodded. The beer was icy cold, sending an ache into all the childhood fillings in her molars.

"You tired?"

Brannagh nodded again energetically, as if the motion of her head would somehow make her better understood.

"You sleep good after this."

Brannagh nodded.

"You like Nikki?" Valova's eyes probed Brannagh's.

"Hmmm. Right now I think he's a bossy, wet noodle, pain in the ass." Brannagh smiled her sweetest smile.

"Oh?" Valova murmured politely.

"For sure," Brannagh said.

A foghorn burp erupted from Valova's mouth, startling them both. She covered her lips with both hands and blushed to the tips of her ears.

"The guy doesn't let up for a second," Brannagh continued, handing her the rest of the beer. "Like we all trained for the Iron Man? One of these days when he starts barking orders I'm going to say, bug off you twit, do it yourself."

"Ah." Valova nodded, deep in thought, as if Brannagh had just uttered the most profound maxims she'd ever been privileged to hear.

"Hey!" A shout erupted, followed by a quick, thorough pounding on the door. "You guy's ready to come out yet?"

It was Nikki.

"Go away," Brannagh yelled. "We aren't done yet."

"Yeah!" Valova waved one fist in the air. "Bug off, you noodle tit!"

Brannagh grinned and decided that if Valova was a pile of mud, she was the most engaging pile of mud that she'd ever come across.

"Tell me about Cindy," Valova said. They were washing now, sharing a second can of beer.

"Cindy?"

"My niece." Valova held one finger to her lips. "Shhhttshhhtt."

"Niece?"

Valova nodded conspiratorially. "My littlelest sister she come from old country after me. Marry too."

Brannagh dipped the bucket in the barrel of water and poured it over her head. It tightened her scalp, unfurling in icy ribbons down the length of her body. Streams of soapy water swirled towards the drain in the centre of the floor. "Your niece," she repeated. She filled the bucket and handed it to Valova.

Valova held the bucket high, tilting her face upwards with a joyous expression, as if she were about to receive a benediction.

They hunkered down on the wooden slats, dripping.

"You think she stupid?" It was more statement than question. Valova's chin rose in the air.

Brannagh took a sip of beer, more or less to muffle the first response that leapt to her lips.

"No." She shook her head. "Confused. Naive. But not stupid."

"Confused," Valova repeated the word. She nodded.

"She's smart. Very smart."

Valova's laugh erupted. "I know this." Her eyes shone with self-satisfaction. "I tell them. She would show it. Just because she flunk a grade don't mean she not smart. And Nikki say, okay, we give a chance. She young, needs us. Give another chance to prove hiself. Thassit."

Brannagh nodded, willing her eyes to look innocent, as if she knew exactly what Valova was talking about.

"That's one thing," Valova said. "I glad for anyways." She wiped her mouth with the back of her hand.

"Eh?" Brannagh's eyebrows rose.

"He love her anyways."

Brannagh nodded.

"Told her, ship up or ship down, and don't tell nobody he's Uncle Nikki. She call him dat since she could walkit. She follow him, like puppy, everywheres. Her hero." Valova patted Brannagh's hand. Her voice dropped to a whisper. "Nikki's a good boy." Valova pointed to her heart. "Here. Where it matters, eh?"

Hah, Brannagh thought. Someone certainly had the old girl bamboozled.

"Do you ever think about how, in the land of our childhood, it was the women who ruled?" Brannagh changed the subject, hoping to divert the direction of Tish's reminiscing as they headed up the hill towards the cottage. "I mean, how they dominated our lives, ran the show?" Brannagh held a torch in one hand. It shook as she fanned it across the path, over the surrounding brush.

"Women ruled?" Tish murmured distractedly.

"Well, you know, you saw the fathers at the beginning of the day and the end of the day. In between they disappeared into the land of the Great Providers, which you assumed was a place where great battles were fought and won. Meanwhile, at home the whole feeling in the air changed as soon as the men left, as if the women suddenly shed their skins and released some kind of underground hidden energy, and grew larger, stronger, more vibrant. As soon as the men disappeared on the street car, the women bustled through the neighbourhood, calling across fences, running to put on the tea kettle." Brannagh knew she was talking faster and faster in her nervousness as the darkness pressed upon them.

"All I remember is 'the look.' My mom could detect a lie a mile away."

With one look, Gran would know what I was feeling, and

thinking and what my day had really been like." Brannagh paused peering upwards. Something dark whirled overhead blotting out the stars. A bat? "It was almost as if, in a weird way, my Gran had to work hard to lessen herself, to keep herself from getting in the way of that power, the big shiny thing that gave her that knowledge. Know what I'm saying? This big shiny river of intuition that just flowed through her, the minute I stepped in the door after school, that allowed her to see right through me, like an x-ray, to know exactly where I was at."

Tish frowned. "But men would never give into the big shiny thing and let it be, they would have to *be* the big shiny thing."

"Will you listen to us? We sound like a couple of—"

"My dad would saunter in from the police station, just show up at supper time, and suddenly everything in the house would reverse itself. My mother faded back into the woodwork."

"The men were head of the house, but in a different way. With no invisible link to the guts of your day. You wanted them to be." Brannagh pictured her grandfather. Yes, there had been a time when she had wanted him to be. She hurried up the stairs, flung open the kitchen door and elbowed Tish inside before slamming it firmly shut and sliding the bolt across.

Tish didn't seem to notice Brannagh's fear. She yawned and wearily pulled off her sweatshirt. Halfway up the staircase, she paused.

"Brannagh," she began hesitantly, "you don't think, I mean, do you ever wonder, well, if Annie's capable of ... going too far?"

"Too far?" Brannagh gazed at a flying ant batting the windowpane.

Tish rubbed her forehead with one thumb. "Sometimes I worry."

"About?"

"Annie going overboard with things." Her words came out in a rush.

"Things?" Brannagh felt a flash of impatience and something else that she couldn't define.

"She'd do anything if she thought we needed her."

"It's true. She would."

"I guess, I just wondered, you know, about Eddie, and about Annie. Well, how far would Annie go, you know, if she thought I was ruining my life, how far would she go to protect me?" She paused. "Or you? From Nikki? Or Dianne?"

"Dianne?"

Tish flushed. "Oh, it's dumb, really. Gossip. Annie was Dianne's mother's doctor. The death was so sudden. She had been fine. Mrs. Sanderson said it was a toxic reaction to the new medication that Annie prescribed. Dianne insisted it was nonsense but—"

"What are you saying?" A hard edge had crept into Brannagh's voice. *There were a lot of things Annie had neglected to tell her in all those phone calls.*

Tish frowned. "It's just, never mind. Nothing. You're right, I think too much."

Brannagh closed her eyes and pressed her fingers to her temples. "Tish, go to bed," she ordered softly.

"Right." Tish backed up to the bedroom. "Bed." She disappeared behind the door.

⁂

The cold lake water shocked Brannagh's body from head to toe. Every cell in her body tingled. Valova surfaced next to her. "Ahhhhhhh," she moaned, rolling onto her back. Nothing more needed to be said.

They floated contentedly, side by side, gazing at the flickering lanterns hanging from a line of poles on shore. The night air smelt clean, with faint traces of pine and wood smoke.

When Valova had first told Brannagh that this was how they ended their sauna, by jumping into the lake, Brannagh had said, "No thank you." But after sharing another beer, her curiosity got the better of her.

"With no clothes on?" she asked. "But what about the guys?" She jerked her thumb towards the door.

"They close their eyes," Valova declared solemnly. "For hundreds of years, sauna in old country hassit three rooms. One for taking clothes off, one for eating, one for washing. Den we all jump in lake."

And now Brannagh understood why jumping in the lake was part of the ritual. It was the final stage after the cleansing: the rude awakening, the slap on the butt of a newborn babe.

"Heaven," she murmured.

"Mmmmmm." Valova disappeared under water.

"Hello-o-o-oooo." A voice rose out of the darkness. Brannagh made out a form zigzagging through the lanterns, climbing onto the dock. She began treading water, letting her lower torso drop perpendicular to the surface. Nikki?

"Go away," she muttered.

She saw him drop something white on the dock and turn towards shore. "Valova!"

"Yoooohooo," Valova's voice floated from a distance.

"Towels and robes are here! On the dock!"

"Good, good!"

"Goodbye, adios, good riddance, " Brannagh sang.

"Hey, Maloney, didn't think you had it in you," Nikki quipped. He walked away. He mumbled something she couldn't catch.

"What'd you say?"

"I said, 'nice buns.' You'd think you'd been hiking ten miles every day."

Brannagh sank underwater and stayed there for a good long while.

✺ ✺

By the time Valova convinced Brannagh that she would have to come indoors, her body had turned into a giant prune. She ran after Valova to the cabin and welcomed the warmth of the wood stove that hit as soon as they entered. She dropped onto the couch and studied the room while Valova busied herself in the kitchen. It was farmhouse plain, filled with dark wooden furniture and light lacy curtains on all the windows. Propped above the windows were framed sepia photographs that were difficult to make out in the pale lighting. The chairs grouped around a low, square coffee table had been chosen for comfort rather than for effect. One wall was filled with bookshelves; a desk faced a large window that looked out onto the water. A hand-woven wall hanging, filled with an exquisite pattern of geometric shapes and flowers, hung above the stone fireplace.

Brannagh started awake when the door slammed.

Nikki's head appeared around the doorframe. "Oh, so the rumours aren't true."

"Rumours?"

"That you swam away."

"Escaped, you mean?" she retorted. "Like Papillon."

Valova plodded into the living room, as if all the grace and sensuality granted during the ritual they had shared in the lake had been a mirage. She carried a steaming tray piled with aromatic rolls. Nikki followed bearing a pickle dish and a wooden platter with a knife and a large square of pale cheese. He gestured over his shoulder towards the man with the beard who had met them at the dock. "Brannagh, this is Zhuk, my uncle."

Zhuk took her hands in his with an old-fashioned courtly air. "He has been telling me how smart you are. How lucky he was to nab you."

Nikki, chin in chest, made a beeline for the cupboard in the centre of the room. He handed out shot glasses and plates. Zhuk settled into an easy chair and methodically tamped tobacco into his pipe with the same absent-minded gestures that Brannagh had come to recognize in Nikki's ritual. Soon a wreath of spindly grey smoke rose above his head. Zhuk appeared content to contemplate life in the depths of its meandering.

"So," Zhuk addressed Brannagh, once the vodka was poured and everyone seated comfortably. "Is he driving you crazy with the bird thing?"

Brannagh smiled.

"He has always been that way. No one else would have him."

"Ah," Nikki teased. "What does an old man know? Come. Drink up. A toast to family, Valova and Zhuk, and to—" He aimed his shot glass in Brannagh's direction. "Brilliant and beautiful colleagues." The three of them flung back their heads and raised their hands in one fluid motion.

Brannagh stuck her tongue into the vodka and grimaced. *What, no orange juice?*

"No," Zhuk tut-tutted, "like this." He showed her how to lift the shot glass to her lips, tilt her head back and toss it down in one quick motion. "It is a ballet, a dance. With grace. As soon as you feel the fire on your lips, open the throat, and let it go down."

A trail of heat rolled down Brannagh's throat, landed deep in her belly, and spread to her limbs. She choked.

"Ah, ha!" Valova trumpeted. "Very good." She was busy wrapping napkins around buns and plopping fat sausages into their cleavage. She handed a warm fragrant offering to Brannagh. Brannagh took one bite and rolled her eyes.

"Oh my God," she groaned.

"Help me," Nikki joined in.

They looked at each other and then registered the befuddled, abashed expressions on their hosts' faces and started to laugh.

"Real food," they spoke in muffled unison, mouths full. "Honest to God real food."

They gobbled down three sausages on buns each, and cheese, and homemade garlic pickles that made Brannagh's mouth water more than the vodka. She found herself leisurely beginning to melt into the chair. Every once in a while Nikki's dark eyes caught hers and he broke into a deep belly laugh as if unable to help himself.

"They probably think we're both nuts."

"Speak for yourself," she said.

He puffed on his pipe and went back to listening to the "remember when" stuff like, "remember when Nikki brought home the injured bird in a shoe box, only forgot to tell us and we opened the door and keeled over from the stench." Brannagh couldn't help nodding along with the rest of them, and every time Zhuk waved the bottle of vodka she held out her shot glass too. After the first try, she was a pro.

"I used to dream I could fly when I was a kid, and I'd be so frustrated when I woke up and realized that I didn't have wings." Nikki, loose-limbed and benevolent, confessed this in an aside.

"What was it like?"

"What?" Nikki paused to look at her, really look at her. His cheeks were flushed, eyes bright.

"Flying?"

His gaze was naked and penetrating, and the drowsy interlude was broken. She felt disoriented, as if the whole room had tilted, and she was gazing into the currents of a fast-flowing river, waiting for the sun to break through a cloud so that she could determine what lay in its depths. Hoping that it would reveal itself, praying that it wouldn't.

"It was," he admitted shyly, "the only thing that mattered."

Brannagh stared at the rug on the floor.

Zhuk passed Brannagh a dish of pastries shaped like bowties that had been dipped in icing sugar.

"Nikki," Valova announced, "I want to show you something." She pulled open a drawer on a refectory table crowded with papers. "Here." She held up a photograph of a little girl standing on a porch. She was dark-haired and fine boned and wore a radiant smile. "I find this of your sister, Marina, in a box in the toolshed."

"The lawyer, years ago, he sent me things. I never looked at them." Zhuk dug a hanky out of his back pocket. He blew his nose loudly, enthusiastically, as if it had taken years of practise to perfect the ritual.

Nikki's jaw tightened. Zhuk laid a hand on his shoulder. Nikki turned away, stretched his arms over his head and yawned.

"I mean notink." Valova said softly. "Just maybe you wantit to have it."

Nikki picked up a *Maclean's* magazine on a nearby table. "What's Trudeau up to now?" He pointed to the Prime Minister's picture on the cover of the magazine. "I've never seen him without a red rose on his lapel. What's the deal?"

Zhuk batted one hand through the air. "Thinks he's a celebrity. Running around with Barbara Streisand and Yoko Loko."

"With all those stirrings in Quebec, he'll have his trial by fire."

"I hear he's going to be married."

"That would do it too."

The men laughed.

Valova pressed her lips together, as she tucked the picture back into the drawer. "Coffee. Who likes coffee?"

Brannagh helped her carry the dirty dishes into the kitchen.

"Marina, that picture, it was good of you to save it." Brannagh couldn't understand why Nikki had been so rude and dismissive when Valova had been so thoughtful saving the photo of his sister for him.

Valova's eyes probed Brannagh's. She pulled a tray down from an overhead cupboard, and pointed toward a shelf that held cups and saucers. Brannagh took down four of each.

"We're exhausted, Nikki, me, it's been a long hard haul." Brannagh flushed. Why was she making excuses for him?

Valova gestured toward the fridge. "Milk."

Brannagh found the sugar bowl and spoons on the kitchen table.

"Nikki look after his sister, just babies when his dad he die. So sad, so young. Then his mom was sick, they takeit children away." Her voice drifted off. "Would be same if Zhuk died and leave me when I come to Canata."

"But, why take the children? You'd think they'd look first to family."

Valova glanced back toward the living room, and then dropped her voice. "Nikki's mom Indian. Nikki's dad's family Russian, rich, own hotel, say want notink to do with her. She was the daughter of the woman they brought in to do the hotel laundry. So Nikki's mom all alone. Wit children. Tries to support hiself, but no one gonna givet her job. No good." Valova scraped plates into the garbage under the sink. "They send Nikki and his sister, Marina, to foster family, then lady say, changet my mind, don't want Nikki, only the girl. Nikki get mad, real mad." Valova paused and stared blankly at the plate in her hands. "Zhuk say Nikki good boy, not hurtit nobody. Talkit of murder make him sick." Valova clutched the plate so tightly her fingers turned white.

Brannagh dropped the sugar bowl onto the tray with a loud clatter. What the hell was Valova talking about? She clasped her hands together.

Valova sighed. "After, he never forgivet himself for dat. Never."

Brannagh rubbed one hand along Valova's arm in a comforting gesture. "Did something happen to Marina?"

But Valova wasn't listening. "I tink her picture make him happy. But no, he don't like dat."

Brannagh lined the spoons on the tray.

"That where Cindy good. Like little Marina. I tink so, yah." Valova nodded.

Brannagh busied herself filling the tray according to Valova's instructions, debating how to question her further without appearing obvious and intrusive.

"Wait. Wait." Valova went to the cupboard and pulled out a small bottle of cherry brandy.

"Brannagh?" Valova put a hand on Brannagh's arm.

"Please consider me a friend, Valova."

"You know when I tellit you we jump in lake and men close hisit eyes?"

"Yes?" Brannagh's mouth turned dry.

Valova put both hands over her lips. Her dark eyes pleaded for understanding, "I fib little bit, to make you to go."

"You mean …" Brannagh closed her eyes. She had known this. Felt a strange, warm, unidentifiable stirring deep down.

Valova grabbed her hand and squeezed. "'S okay. I see right off,

he likes you," she whispered. "Soon as he walking in."
Brannagh wanted to kick her in the shins.
"And now," Valova murmured coyly. " Now he *really* likes you."
Brannagh pushed her out of the way and carried the tray down the hall, chin held high.

After imbibing all that vodka the night before, Brannagh expected to awaken with a wicked hangover, but to her amazement she felt refreshed and clear-headed. She lay sideways across the bed with a pillow tucked under her chin, gazing at the white ridge of light below the green window shade. The sash swayed lightly in the early morning breeze.

Brannagh couldn't quash a sudden curiosity about Nikki. She tried to direct her thoughts elsewhere: the bird count, her drawings, her future options once the expedition ended. But it was useless. Her inquisitiveness had been disturbed like larvae deep in the permafrost, shifted out of hibernation by the thaw, until tough casings cracked with the upheaval of the earth, and the migration began up, up, toward the light.

Brannagh tiptoed out of the bedroom and into the kitchen. The place was deserted. She took a long hot shower and put on clean cords and a T-shirt. She went into the living room and pulled a chair towards the south wall. She climbed it and began to inspect the photographs on the shelf close to the ceiling. There was one of an old native woman standing on a front porch with a bundle of clothes in her arms. Her eyes were sunk like two raisins in a bun above her smile. Beside her stood a young native woman with large doe-like eyes that were almost obscured by a pair of black-rimmed glasses. Her waist-length dark hair fell across her face as she gazed down at a boy, pale-skinned, with two front teeth missing and one arm wrapped around her waist. His other arm was flung protectively around the shoulder of a pig-tailed toddler, a younger version of the picture Valova had shown the night before.

The sound of the door opening reached Brannagh's ears. She jumped off the chair just as Nikki and Zhuk walked in. A hot flush rose up her chest.

"Ready?" Zhuk's face wore a questioning look.

"Did you have a good sleep?" Nikki asked.

She nodded.

"All right then?" Zhuk shifted his feet impatiently.

"The sketches," Nikki clarified. Brannagh tried not to stare. He had shaved off his beard. He had a funny, curved mouth. It didn't belong to him. It was a mouth for singing cantatas in a schoolboy choir. Brannagh pulled out the sketchpad and immediately defended herself. "They're just rough, preliminaries." She paused, gripping the pad tightly in her hands. Zhuk glanced at her, the pad, Nikki.

Nikki smiled. "She's a little bit defensive."

Sternly, Brannagh waved them over to the window where the light was better. "All right." She opened it with a snap and explained to Zhuk from the beginning. A Bufflehead skirting some reeds, a Blue-winged Teal waddling on shore, a lone kestrel. The last set were the turkey vultures that Nikki had shown her. Their wings were dark arcs against a pale blue sky. She had touched them up with watercolour.

Brannagh felt Nikki's warm breath on the back of her neck. She turned. He studied the painting. "This is fantastic, Brannagh. I don't know why you wouldn't show me before."

A well of ridiculous elation rose within her.

Brannagh brusquely resumed explaining to Zhuk how she had tried to capture each individual bird's path of flight, the feather and wing structure—upper tail and outer, under was always tricky—the crown, rump, moustache and wing bars.

Zhuk took the sketchpad to a standing lamp in the corner, turned it on, and flipped pages.

Nikki came and stood beside Brannagh. "You didn't tell me."

"Tell you?"

"That you had *the dream*." His cheeks were flushed.

She eyed him curiously, and then in an instant she remembered the story he had told her about when his father died, how he had dreamed of defying gravity, of growing wings and escaping.

"Of flying." He paused, rubbing his chin nervously. "Do you still?" His eyes filled with curiosity, and a brief glimmering of something else.

You were a boy once, she thought. Goddammit! A heart-welling-up-in-your-eyes, anything's-possible, life-goes-on-forever boy. It was knowledge that she didn't want to have.

"Do you?" he asked. There was an earnestness beneath his words, an edge that revealed a longing, so deep and wide it made her tremble.

"No. Never," she said quickly, and turned away.

※ ※

In the dream the sky was always a pristine cobalt blue.

She ran down the sidewalk towards Simm's Corner, and just as she passed the bulk of the Provincial Asylum it was as if a balmy summer breeze grew invisible arms that picked her up and bore her aloft. She moved her limbs, as if treading water, and felt deliciously free, unbound from the tendrils of shadowy grief holding her captive. She drifted over the house on Argyle with the weathercock slowly turning in the wind, past Annie's house, Tish's, Dianne's. Past the toll bridge, the docks and the ships with their tiny specks moving on board. She followed the water to the Reversing Falls Bridge, heard the growing roar of the rapids. The windows in the Simms building reflected the puffs of smoke jetting from the tall paper mill stacks.

Down below, seals played in the currents, their dog-like snouts jutting through the foam.

The honk of a car horn caught her attention and she noticed for the first time all the cars lining up at the bridge, and her heart froze in her chest. Her mother was running, running, running towards her. Brannagh waved her arms in a motion that should have taken her further away, but that instead betrayed her and resulted in the discovery that she had become a wingless angel.

She experienced the deep gut-wrenching pull of gravity, heard the squawk of the gulls, felt the icy spray of the falls on her shins.

Above the cacophony of impressions her mother's eyes, empty sockets, the bib of her dress soaked crimson with the blood that dripped down her chin. Her mother's terrified cry, "Help me Brannagh! Help me!"

And no matter how many times she dreamed the dream, no matter how heavy the burden of guilt, she continued to carry over into the waking hours, her reaction to her mother's cry was always the same. Uncensored: appalled and furious.

Brannagh turned her back on her mother and flew back home.

Thank God for the day-to-day routines. Annie no longer abhorred the sameness, the entrenched ruts that seemed to mark and mock the days in a small town like Saint John, the long stretches of time that would sneak up between the daily tasks.

Now she clung to the repetitiveness, welcomed the sanity of the familiar, the relative calm that the performance of insignificant rituals brought.

In Sanderson's store, Mrs. Cunningham complained about a group of young hooligans who had snatched someone's purse at the Bingo Hall. They had laughed gleefully at the shocked expressions that followed them up the stairs and out the door.

"Couldn't care less." Mrs. Cunningham hugged the butcher-wrapped thin-sliced bologna to her bosom and sniffed. "Kids today. Pathological liars. Every one of them."

And the word had echoed in Annie's mind all afternoon. Everywhere she went. To the clinic, the market, the hospital.

Pathological liar.

That was what her stepmother had always insisted she was.

Was it true?

She had a good reason to twist the truth now. It was better this way. Fewer people hurt in the long run.

Or was that simply what she needed to believe?

She stopped at the second-hand book store and bought a tattered copy of *The World of Odysseus*. She had always loved Greek mythology.

She left the store and kept walking. Eventually she found herself, unable to recall having walked that far, outside the Catholic church she had come to with Brannagh and Gran and Aunt Thelma years ago, when she stayed at the Nervous Clinic. So different from the church she had attended with her stepmother and father.

At first Annie could see nothing.

Darkness. Gloom. Recrimination.

Then ... a wavering flame from a single taper up front. She

kneeled on a pew. The statue of the Virgin Mary blurred. Became two.

> *Hail Mary, full of Grace*
> *The Lord is with you*
> *Blessed are you among women*
> *And blessed is the fruit of your womb*
> *Jesus.*

On the way home she bought him wool socks because he had been getting cramps in his feet, unused to the bone-chilling Fundy fog.

Sometimes she forgot about him. Sometimes she didn't.

Sometimes she longed to stroke his dark head against her breast.

Sometimes she wanted to shake some sense into him.

Sometimes she thought they could go on this way forever.

Sometimes she wanted an ending like the endings in the ridiculous romance novels she was becoming addicted to.

She didn't know what he wanted. She was afraid to ask.

And now all she could do was wait.

For hearts to turn like spring tulips seeking the sun.

And things to fall into place.

Or not.

Chapter Five

Brannagh stood at the kitchen window in the cottage waiting for the coffee pot to boil. She had not slept well.

No! Please. Don't go.

The sky outside was pearly grey. A veil of mist swept across the face of the river. It was too early to tell what sort of day it would shape up to be.

When the phone rang, it took her a minute to remember that she had shoved it in the pantry because she kept tripping over the cord.

"Hello." Brannagh slid the door shut.

"How long did you think it would take me to track you down?"

Brannagh grimaced. "I called to tell you I was going on vacation, detective. Your co-worker said you weren't in."

The accusatory tone in his voice sharpened. "Is that so?"

"I left my number," Brannagh lied.

"You know what interests me?"

Brannagh sighed and leaned against the cupboard.

"You skipped town in one hell of a hurry."

"Something came up."

"Ah, yes. Vacation." He paused. "Like you said."

"Did the autopsy results come in?" Brannagh rolled her eyes.

"It was the missing hunter."

Brannagh felt her shoulders relax. She hadn't realized how much she needed to hear that. "Thank you," she whispered, and meant it.

"I'm going to find out what happened to your friend." It wasn't a reassurance. It was a challenge.

"Any leads?"

"Talked to the insurance investigators about the murder on your expedition last summer."

"I told you before, it was an accident." Brannagh felt a sting behind her eyes.

A scratching sound was followed by a sharp inhalation of breath. "You ever listen to the Beatle's album 'Sergeant Peppers'?"

"Not a lot, maybe parts."

"Did you ever notice that Paul McCartney is wearing an OPP badge on his uniform on the cover?"

"Detective?"

"Details. I'm a stickler for them, and that's why I have no cold cases. It's why the big city rookies' balls shrivel up north. Cockiness, assumptions, the urban ego. Lulls them into stupidity. You miss Toronto, Miss Maloney?"

"Look, anything you—"

"I've been doing some research and some interesting facts keep rising to the surface over and over. Why, I wonder?"

"Like?"

"Death."

"Death?"

"Yeah, and you always happen to be nearby."

Brannagh closed her eyes, felt a faint headache beginning behind her eyes.

"Why is that Miss Maloney, do you think?"

"I don't know."

"Bad luck, I guess. You Upper Canadians just don't get any breaks in life." She could hear him smile. "Like I said before, if anything important comes up, like you decide to head off on a cruise to Alaska, call me. Will you do that?"

"I'm not—"

"Anything important."

"Yes, yes. Of course." As soon as Brannagh hung up, she pulled the business card for Laurentian Court out of her jean pocket and stared at the writing on the back: Detective Arto Pietila.

Brannagh drank her coffee standing at the window, watching the last tendrils of mist rise toward the sky. She spotted the red roof of the neighbouring cottage in the distance and was filled with a sudden impulse. After snagging a wool sweater off a hook next to the back door, she pulled on rubbers then grabbed a handful of shortbread cookies and tucked them up one sleeve. Like she was heading out on a casual morning stroll, a picnic. Who was she trying to kid?

The road leading to the cottage with the red roof led up a steep hill, filled with large humps of granite. The sides of the road were overgrown with purple-stemmed asters and mugwort. What riveted Brannagh's attention was the fact that the weeds in the centre of the road were bent and broken, as if a vehicle had recently travelled down the road. As she approached the crest of the hill, Brannagh's steps slowed. She recalled that day when the mayor, Tish's father, had finally given in and ordered, Andy Barton, the neighbourhood policeman, to drive them all to the cottage. She recalled the looks on people's faces as they sped past, red light flashing. As they had pulled into the driveway, a group of emergency technicians came trotting down the hill carrying a stretcher. For some reason, the body upon it was covered in a sheet, not encased in a body bag. Blood stains formed odd peony-blossom shapes, and Brannagh had found herself, numbed, studying them the way she studied clouds on blustery summer days. She heard a noise, like a whistling kettle as it gathers steam. The wind picked up and lifted one corner of the sheet, pulling it back. Tish's father threw his jacket over

Brannagh's head and twisted her face into his armpit, cursing the incompetence of the crime-scene invesitagators; barking orders at a detective standing on the road; and commanding the policeman at the wheel to drive on. She didn't see anything, but the horror of what she heard never left her: Gran's high-pitched keening, rising and falling through the bleat of the ambulance siren.

Brannagh stood at the top of the hill, rubbing her cold numb fingers, and surveyed the cottage down below. It was small and resembled nothing more than an upside-down pop crate. The white clapboard had faded silver. Mould had blackened the wood. The front stoop sagged. The windows were shuttered, and the sills were coated with rotting leaves and bird droppings. Only the front window, the one that faced the water, had the shutters unhinged. It shone as if someone had recently taken a rag to it.

Immediately, Brannagh realized that this was as far as she could go. She couldn't help but imagine a body propped on the roof, spine resting on the peak, legs jack-knifed on either side. She had had to sneak up to the attic in the house on Argyle to read all the newspaper accounts of her mother's murder, despite Gran's forbidding it. She had had to know. One overly zealous reporter, carried away with his own self-importance and the flattery of headline-hunting national news editors, painted graphic pictures that Brannagh could not remove from her mind. *The body had been laid out as if on an ancient funeral pyre, and the severed flesh an offering.*

Brannagh stiffened as a hand clutched her right forearm from behind. For a split second she was paralysed with fear, then she choked, and stumbled helter-skelter down the hill. She quickly realized, no, no, don't run towards the cottage. She turned and scrabbled through the weeds toward the water. She saw movement out of the corner of her eye. Someone called her name. Only then did she allow herself a brief glance back up the hill.

Where she had stood seconds ago was a figure, a tall, thin girl wearing a dark trench coat and a pair of boy's black sneakers. Her hands were thrust deep into the pockets of her trench coat. Brannagh put her hands on her knees, hung her head and tried to catch her breath. She could still hear her name being called. Slowly, she walked back towards the hill. As she drew closer, Brannagh realized that the girl was a woman.

Dianne.

Dianne! Oh, for frig sake. Dianne.

Dianne with a new short, bristly haircut and huge blue eyes that could swallow you whole. Dianne, still resembling a newly hatched bird with her long, graceful neck and hungry eyes.

Dianne, all grown up. Not beautiful. Never that. But shining with that unidentifiable quality that was all her own.

When Brannagh was in grade five and the winter of mastering fractions in the kitchen of the house on Argyle was long and hard, Aunt Thelma entertained her with stories of how Gran and Dianne's mother, Jocelyn, had once been best friends. This was a shock to Brannagh. One would never know it now. They never exchanged words, not even in church. "But why did they stop being friends?" Brannagh wanted to know, spreading a bit of raw dough around her tongue like bubble gum.

"Life doesn't always go the way you want it to." Aunt Thelma kneaded a moist ball of bread dough. "Time has a way of changing things."

Brannagh stuck a raisin up her nose. Aunt Thelma snatched it out.

"They were both nurses?" Brannagh felt the heat emanating from Aunt Thelma's torso as she pushed the dough flat then pulled it back towards her and folded it in on itself as if she were diapering an invisible baby.

"B block at the asylum."

Aunt Thelma dug out a picture, buried in a box of stained, yellowed recipes. There was Rye and Jocelyn dressed in long white aprons with funny white caps on their heads, standing on the staircase at the Provincial Asylum, with their arms encircling one another's waists.

In the early days, before the murder, before Hilda Outhouse peppered Brannagh's imagination with grisly images, and long before Brannagh understood the stigma attached to the Provincial Asylum (and by association the Nervous Clinic), Brannagh was hungry for details about the place. Sometimes Mrs. McGillvery would send her across the street if an important letter arrived in the mail for Grandfather. Brannagh was eager to comply. She had heard a radio program on the CBC about how the Great Houdini had once visited the asylum, and that it was there that he developed his most famous trick with the straightjacket. It only took a few visits down dark cold passages, echoing with muted mumblings and whispers, to raise the hair on the back of her neck, and for her interest to wither.

Ironically, Gran would often quiz Brannagh about Dianne. How is her penmanship? Does she have a good singing voice? Did Brannagh play hopscotch with her at recess time?

Brannagh didn't come right out and say so, but she never played hopscotch or jump rope or monkey bars with Dianne, because Dianne didn't play any of those things. At recess time, Dianne pulled on a poop-coloured sweater, and a puke green hat, and headed to the far end of the playground where she leaned against a birch tree, her pale face blending into its bark, until eventually, when Brannagh twirled on the monkey bars, it looked as if Dianne were part of the tree; a sucker shooting up from the trunk with a single brave leaf (her hat) seeking the sun.

Dianne was the sort of person whose arms and hair and eyes wove themselves into the seams and corners and holes. Brannagh forgot she was there. On those rare occasions when Dianne was forced into the spotlight, if for example Sister Mary Margaret asked her to stand up and recite *The Call of the Wild*, Dianne's agony was a miserable sight to behold. If she let herself, Brannagh could actually feel the trembling in Dianne's limbs, the rolling churn of her stomach.

There was only one point of interest in regard to Dianne, the sole fact that made her, on occasion, the centre of attention. It was her father, Raymond. He had thick dark hair, a baby-bum chin and dark eyes ringed with long eyelashes. The schoolgirls forgot his wrinkles when they gazed at his perfect cupid-bow mouth. Their cheeks flushed and words tripped on their tongues. His voice was magnificent, a rich, deep baritone. Mrs. Sanderson claimed that when Raymond was in his youth and performing on the stage, he had been offered a British film contract but turned it down because he didn't want to leave his poor deaf mother's side. There was one other thing about Dianne's father that riveted all the girls' attention. He had no legs.

Dianne's father, a veteran of the Great War, was in a wheelchair. Every Remembrance Day, the class went to King's Square, scarlet poppies pinned to their coats, and, after the opening remarks by the mayor, Jocelyn would wheel Dianne's father to the microphone. He always read "In Flanders Fields," and his voice would crack when he got to "we lived, felt dawn, saw sunset glow, loved and were loved …"

Last fall, after the ceremony, as the grade five class marched down the hill to Market Slip, Brannagh overheard Hilda Outhouse wonder out loud, "How could a man paralysed from the waist down possibly 'do it'?" Heads swivelled to contemplate Dianne. "Musta been old man Gallant next door who shot the elastic in his drawers and stuck his thingy in her thingy." Hilda chortled. "Thought I saw hair growing out of Dianne's ears." High-pitched twitters rose like a flock of sparrows spreading down the line.

First of all, Brannagh, who had yet to discover how babies were made, didn't get the joke. Second of all, Hilda's uppity tone made her tired. Brannagh paused and turned around. Dianne's nose whumped against her chest. Brannagh couldn't look away from Dianne's huge blue eyes, wincing into the horizon at something that only she could see.

What was it like, Brannagh wondered, having a mom and dad old enough to be your grandparents? Brannagh dug an orange out of her pocket and, aiming carefully, zinged it with all her might, smack towards the middle of the braids pinned on the crown of Hilda's fat round head.

Sister Mary Margaret materialized out of thin air, grasped Brannagh by the ear, and marched her double-time to the front of the line.

Brannagh looked back and saw Dianne's pale face breaking into red blotches. Brannagh stood before Hilda, scuffed the dirt with one toe, and muttered, "Sorry. It was an accident." As soon as Sister Mary Margaret turned her back, Brannagh stuck her poppy pin directly into Hilda's jiggly behind.

Shoppers the whole length of King Street puzzled all day over the origin of the God-awful, ear-splitting scream that sent the pigeons, from King's Square clear down to the wharf at Market Slip, scattering into the rafters.

"Come see what I found," Dianne said.

The cottage with the red roof disappeared, as Brannagh followed her through the soggy marsh. "I'm really not in the mood for frog catching. I haven't had breakfast yet."

"I arrived at the cottage about an hour ago." Dianne scratched her ear. "No one answered my knock."

"I was on the phone."

"So I went for a walk."

Brannagh's jeans were damp. She was getting cold. They came to an opening in the brush. Dianne hurried forward and dropped down on all fours.

"Nice runners."

"Uh, thanks." Dianne gazed briefly at the boy's runners on her feet. "Look! This is so, so weird." She pointed.

Brannagh approached hesitantly. "Is it a footprint?" She paused. Dianne was gazing at the surface of a flat black stone that rose out of the soil, the size of a hubcap. It was overgrown with lichen and moss.

"It's a sun dial. Aunt Thelma told us about this. Remember how good she was with us? So patient when she helped us with our homework?"

Brannagh sat down. In the distance a cormorant rose slowly from the surface of the water, dark wings flapping.

"Look!" Dianne pointed to initials scratched into the surface within a heart. B E N   L O V E S   T H E L M A. Beneath it, someone had carved a star.

"They played together as kids." Brannagh shrugged. "He had a huge crush on my mother, but was too shy to talk to her."

"My mom saved all the newspaper articles about your dad and Aunt Thelma. They placed first in the high school oratory etitions three years in a row. You can have them if—"

"No thanks." Brannagh didn't know what to make of the change in Dianne. In her mind, Dianne had always appeared to view people as coat-racks, a place where she could contentedly hang herself for the day, like a hat, and go along for the ride, borne aloft by the sheer energy of another to view the world from a borrowed perspective. But from the moment Dianne had thrown her arms around her, Brannagh had been aware of something foreign, running like a humming energy beneath her friend's shy persona. "How is everything, since your Mom …"

Dianne spit on her sleeve and polished the edge of the rock. "Uh, good, it's good."

"I thought maybe something happened. When you couldn't come last night."

"That has to be ancient. I wonder who put it here. Didn't your great-grandfather own this property too once upon a time?"

"The cottage used to be the boathouse. Whoever bought the property converted it. It's always been empty as long as I can remember."

Dianne's head bobbed. "I had a call from Kate."

"Kate?"

"At SeaWinds Gallery? About Aunt Thelma." Dianne rubbed her nose vigorously, muttering into her fingers. "She'd fallen, broke her ankle, and Kate needed help getting her upstairs to bed."

Brannagh experienced a pang in her chest. Aunt Thelma was the closest thing to a mother she had ever had. She had wondered if she'd be able to come this close to Saint John without visiting her. But she knew how painful it would be.

"I spent the night at SeaWinds. Keeping watch. Anyway, I told Aunt Thelma that you were home."

"Dianne." Brannagh pressed her lips together.

"I told her you were here." Dianne crawled to the other side of the rock and peered at it from that angle. "I wonder if it's lava rock. Didn't Aunt Thelma say that polished, it's a mirror that reflects your soul? Remember?"

"It was a long time ago."

"The stuff you know, and the stuff you don't want to know. Remember? Very interesting, using it to measure time, past and present."

Brannagh stared at the river. "That was brilliant. Why did you tell her?"

"I just thought Aunt Thelma should know you're here, that's all."

"And did she know who I was?"

"I think so."

"You *think* so."

"Well, she didn't exactly come right out and say your name, but her face lit up when I told her."

Brannagh fingered a dandelion. Even though Aunt Thelma hadn't left Saint John, she had disappeared from Brannagh's life just like everyone else.

"It did light up. She does remember you. She knows who you are."

Brannagh sighed. "C'mon." She rose to her feet. "I'm starving."

"Remember how we used to collect rocks with your Gran? She could tell you what every kind was."

Brannagh tugged Dianne's elbow. "I think that one is a little too big to lug home."

On the way back to the cottage, Dianne reminisced, but Brannagh found it impossible to concentrate. While Dianne placed thick ceramic plates and mugs on the table, Brannagh stoked the fire and dropped several slices of bacon into a frying pan. Her hands shook and she had a desperate craving for a cigarette.

Worse than any illness that caused a person to lose physical strength, she concluded, was the sickness that ate away at the mind until they gradually lost all the familiar anchors that tethered their heart securely in place. The woman at SeaWinds Gallery wasn't Aunt Thelma, the tall woman in the faded sundress standing with feet solidly planted on the ladder in the library as she pulled down the books she thought would help the girls with their school essays. The woman Brannagh had come to depend upon had slowly disappeared. Kate had written faithfully to Brannagh over the years, cataloguing the progress of what Dr. Baird called "early dementia." Aunt Thelma had begun to show signs of it when Brannagh was in high school. "Feel brave?" Brannagh asked Dianne. "Want to knock on Tish's door?"

Dianne hesitated in the doorway. "Kate asked if you were still scribbling."

Brannagh drained the grease out of the frying pan into an empty tin can. Kate had influenced Brannagh and Aunt Thelma's lives equally. In grade six, the nuns at Saint Patrick's, in an attempt to compete with private schools, had brought in an art teacher from Toronto. Miss Matthews. Brannagh had been mesmerized by her at first sight. She would stride down the aisles with long scarves fluttering behind her, leaving a trail of exotic perfume. She was one of the first people to pause and digest one of Brannagh's sketches, to deem it worthy of interpretation. She brought the class to view an exhibition of Kate's work. Afterwards she told Brannagh, "Kate's a friend of mine. She's a Jungian therapist and an artist. We grew up together in Stratford. She's a little unconventional, and driven beyond belief, but I adore her. How would you like to visit her studio?"

Brannagh remembered how she spent most of that first day in

the studio covertly watching Aunt Thelma. She seemed so out of place, sitting on the edge of a love seat, smoking with jerky, darting motions. Kate stood at the easel, warming tubes of paint between the palms of her hands, wearing a man's shirt rolled to the elbows and black toreador slacks, giving off a scent of turpentine and oil and sin.

There was a sense of the forbidden about Kate. Brannagh hadn't quite been able to put her finger on it, but what it had boiled down to was that Kate was just having too much darn fun to be a woman and a grownup.

Kate invited them to come back every Thursday night, after her patients had left. Gradually, Aunt Thelma started to relax and ask Kate questions about the places she had lived, Saskatoon and Oil Springs and Espanola, and slowly, slowly they became friends.

One day Kate paused to scrub the bristles of a paint brush with the rag that she kept hanging out of her back pocket. She announced, "I want to paint you."

"Oh." Brannagh's eyes widened.

"Yeah." Kate turned and smiled at them both. "Now."

Then she slipped the combs out of Aunt Thelma's hair and made her take off her silk stockings and sit cross-legged on the deep window sill, where the weak honey-dew light circled her shoulders like a shawl.

Dianne's feet pounded down the stairs. "Tish is in a coma."

Brannagh sipped her coffee. "Been away too long." She sighed.

"You're right. And whose fault is that?" Dianne seemed to have acquired a new definition, as if the lines of her mouth, her hands, her profile had grown a little bolder. She shrugged. "I'm going to get my duffle."

Dianne didn't ask for Brannagh's help, and Brannagh, filled with a growing prickly irritation, the source of which she couldn't pinpoint, didn't offer.

<hr />

When Brannagh and Nikki returned to their base camp in the Lake of the Woods after their stay with Zhuk and Valova, she felt awkward in his company. While he constantly invaded her thoughts, she tried to avoid being alone with him. This was virtually impossible given the casual setup of the small investigation team. Then Nikki imposed what Cindy called "the cone of silence."

It rained for a week straight. Brannagh, Nikki, Cindy, Tom, Gordon and Alex tramped through the bush surveying plots and tying fluorescent markers around tree trunks, not talking all the while, because Nikki wanted all the team members to become accustomed to being utterly silent, to learn to listen, to discern the living data with their Eustachian tubes, in preparation for the census. No verbal conversing was allowed, not a peep, blurb or syllable.

At first Brannagh heard only the faint tippy-tap of rain on the leaves. Once in a while a large leaf overhead would collapse under the weight of the water, flipping a cold rivulet down the neck of her mackinaw, and she would bite her lip. Then, as time passed, she heard, really heard for the first time: the wind soughing through pine needles, branches creaking, the drumming of birds' wings, bugs crawling, rocks crumbling. She imagined the sounds of petals unfurling, cells in ponds dividing, clouds rushing across the face of a pitiless sky. Nothing was silent. Nothing.

Brannagh could not stop replaying the conversation with Velova in the kitchen over in her head: "Nikki's mom Indian. Nikki's dad's family, Russian, rich, own hotel, say, want notink to do with her."

Brannagh noticed, to her horror, a queer phenomenon developing between her and Nikki in the silence. It was as if something in their brains had shifted, as if some inner antennae had quivered onto hyper-alert mode.

"They send Nikki and Marina to foster family, then lady say, changet my mind, don't want Nikki, only the girl. Nikki get mad, real mad. Zhuk say Nikki good boy, not hurtit nobody. Talkit of murder make him sick."

Brannagh had become attuned to an inner unseen aspect of Nikki, and he of her. Sometimes she watched his face and instantly knew what he was thinking.

"After, he never forgivet himself for dat. Never."

She would hand him her canteen and his expression of puzzlement made her shrug and get busy doing something because she did not know, and she did not want to know, how it was that she had discerned without words that he was thirsty.

"What's wrong with Dianne?" Brannagh tucked the phone under her chin, glanced down the hall then slipped into the pantry. Tish and Dianne were upstairs freshening up.

"Didn't I say this would happen?" Annie griped. "Didn't I?"

It was true. Annie had predicted in high school that if Dianne did not follow her advice and "get a life," the consequences would be deadly.

"She's worse than a nun. Been cooped up in that tomb of a house too long."

Just before Dianne had gone upstairs to unpack, she had taken the clock above the wood-stove off the wall. "This is fifteen minutes slow. Why do we have clocks?"

Brannagh swallowed the retort that rose to her lips. "Uh, to tell time?"

Dianne's brow furrowed. "To feel like we have some sort of control over it. Past, present, future. But we really don't."

"Right." Brannagh busied herself at the sink.

"Not in the long run." Dianne unscrewed the clock face with a dime. "I'll bet this loses five minutes every hour. Wound too tight."

"I'm worried," Brannagh confessed now to Annie.

"I tried ever since I moved back home to bring her out of her shell, invite her to a movie, or take her to dinner, but she wasn't interested."

Brannagh felt a pang of guilt. What had she done over the years? A few phone calls, belated birthday greetings.

"She did invite me for a spaghetti dinner on Christmas Eve but I was—"

"Spaghetti?"

"She's so desperate for company, she'll let anyone through her door. The neighbours have taken over her life. Half don't bother to knock."

Brannagh picked up a clouded jar of pickled cucumbers from the pantry shelf. How old was it?

"Another reason I wanted the reunion. Get her out of that house."

Brannagh closed her eyes, set the jar down. "What about you and Tish?"

A long pause followed. "What about me and Tish?"

Brannagh swallowed. "She said you had a falling out. She's worried about you. To be perfectly blunt, she's worried about you and Eddie."

"Really?" Annie's voice hardened.

Brannagh waited. She could hear Annie breathing on the other end of the line. "So?"

"I don't need this right now."

Brannagh stared at the phone in her hand. "I …" She tried to find the words to bring up what she had witnessed, Annie going into the cottage with the red roof. *There was a perfectly logical explanation for it, wasn't there? Annie was controlling, but she always meant well, didn't she? She would never intentionally hurt anyone, would she?*

"I'm leaving in an hour, two tops," Annie continued brusquely.

"Good." They would discuss it face to face.

"And here's the best part. I'm leaving my beeper behind."

Brannagh hung up the phone, stepped out of the pantry and stared thoughtfully at the clock hanging on the wall above the stove.

⁂

One morning Brannagh woke in her tent and instantly discerned the shift. Something had changed. It was quiet. One by one, Cindy, Tom, Alex and Gordon emerged from their tents blinking in the brightness. On the very day that the cone of silence was lifted, the rain had ceased. They decided it was a good omen.

Their first words were monosyllabic and hoarse as if their vocal cords had turned rusty, and if someone spoke louder than a whisper, the others would wince as if no longer accustomed to the timbre of the human voice.

That night they held a celebration over passing the test of silence, replete with a flask of vodka Nikki had dug out of the first aid kit (except for Gordon who smugly disapproved of revelry in any way, shape or form). The night wound down by the fire with a silly game of Confessions that Cindy started. Nikki, pausing in the middle of the laughter, abruptly turned to Brannagh, and queried in a playful undertone, "So what are you afraid of, Brannagh? True confession."

She contemplated the fire.

"In terror of. More than anything else in the world." He tapped his pipe against the side of the log.

She watched the flames dance, yellow-white in the centre, blue around the edges. She drank the dregs of vodka-laced tea. Alex tipped his hat and headed off to his tent. Cindy and Tom wandered down to the water. She followed the path of their torch bobbing in the darkness.

"Nothing? Nothing frightens you?"

She shrugged. There was a marsh nearby, and the late night chorus of peepers rose in volume.

"Name one thing. One thing that you are truly fearful of."

She studied him, perched on an upturned log, shoulders hunched. "Sliding," she said softly.

"Eh?"

"Sliding." Into people, beneath their skins, she clarified silently. Needing them, loving them, sliding into the hole, the darkness left behind when they're gone. Brannagh stood, shoving her hands into her pockets and started to walk to the tent. "Sliding backwards. Not moving forwards. Stagnating. That's it."

He rose to his feet. "All right."

She walked towards the tent.

"Wait, I haven't told you what I'm afraid of."

Only ears tuned to stillness for so many days could detect the minute vibration in his voice. She glanced back at him, and then looked away.

He approached her hesitantly. She thought about going into her tent but didn't.

His trembling fingers, long and cold, circled the back of her neck. She sensed something hard and bright beneath the fear. His thumb traced a rough line from her temple to her jaw, paused. She looked deep into his eyes and awakened to a prism of light and within it, silt filtering, like dust motes, down, down, whirling silver-streaked minnows darting silently toward the bottom of the river.

She knew nothing. Absolutely nothing.

It was like pressing her lips into the heart of a peony, softer than she had ever imagined a man's mouth could be.

⁓⁓

Brannagh stood in the hallway upstairs in the cottage silently observing Tish and Dianne. Dianne sat on the bed. Tish was trying to get her to stay still long enough so she could wrap her one-inch bangs around the curling iron.

Dianne, why didn't you tell me you were so lonely? I would have come home.

But even as Brannagh thought it, she couldn't be absolutely sure that it was true. She looked at Dianne's bowed head. Her ears looked like clean pink shells washed up onto the shore.

Dianne, why didn't you tell me you were so desperately lonely? I would have come.

I would have.

Wouldn't I?

⁓⁓

Loneliness could kill a person.

Brannagh realized this when she gazed into the depths of Nikki's eyes the night they kissed for the first time. Knew it the second she made a choice not to turn away from him and slip safely beneath blind ignorance, but instead chose to wrestle with the darkness, pin it to the ground and demand a moment of reckoning.

There is a language beyond words where spirits meet and weep and entwine fingers and longings in the cold night air.

His mouth on hers; a flood of impressions as souls sparked across synapses; giddy questions cart-wheeled in recognition across the northern lights.

For one brief moment, he allowed her to glimpse, in an unhurried sunrise of awakening, a shedding of his need to hide. It mirrored her own blunted, submerged cowardice. They were like the lost tribes of Israel wandering in the desert searching for a land to claim as home.

The kiss changed everything.

The kiss changed nothing.

There were so many reasons to kiss again.

There were so many reasons not to.

Brannagh looked up P for policeman and D for detective in Nikki's rolodex cards. No luck. She tried A for Arto and L for Laurentian Hotel. Nothing. After she had cursed a few times, she was inspired to try F. There it was: A. Pietila 1-807-492-6345. F for friend or F for foe? Brannagh wondered. She heard a rat-tat-tat on the bedroom door.

"Hey," Dianne said softly. She glanced down the hall, then stepped inside and closed the door behind her. "What's up?"

Brannagh shoved the rolodex under the bed. "Last minute notes before Annie gets here."

Dianne sat cross-legged on the floor. "I remember when Kate gave you this." She picked up a book, *How to Draw*, which had fallen out of Brannagh's knapsack. "I'd come over and you'd be lying on the couch in the parlour with this propped on your knees, crinkled balls of paper all over the floor."

"I still have the pencil bump." Brannagh held up the index finger on her right hand. She must have drawn a hundred pictures of extremities in motion: legs, arms, elbows, toes. It was the musculature beneath the skin, the invisible that needed to be hinted at: the inner life force that must be explored and revealed in order for the visible to become authentic. This is what Kate had written inside the book when she presented it to her on the last day of school in grade six. Brannagh had loved the sound of that phrase on the page. Copied it out. Tacked it onto her bulletin board. But in truth, she had had no clue what it meant. "You coming on the walk to the ferry?"

Brannagh shook her head. "I'll have a cup a tea and wrap up this data. Then it'll be 'Hello, Annie' and party time."

Dianne hesitated, picking at the loose ends of wool on the bed's afghan.

Brannagh jiggled her elbow. "What's up?"

Dianne shrugged, flushing. "Annie." She stood up and walked over to the shelf against the wall. She fingered the war medals hanging around the Virgin Mary. "She was calling me all the time to go out, you know? So one time I said I couldn't, but after she called, I changed my mind. I thought, yeah, I need a change of scene." She paused and glanced at the closed door.

"Good for you."

"I just went over to her house. She said she'd called from home. Well, the thing is," Dianne turned to face Brannagh, "it probably sounds stupid, but see, I know she was there. Only by the time I got out of the car and up to the front door, she had drawn the curtains. I rang the bell, but nobody answered. I heard …"

"What do you think you heard?"

"Voices. So I went around to the back door. I peeked through the split in the curtains on the window, and for a second I caught a glimpse of Annie in the kitchen."

"So a person's not entitled to change her mind?"

Dianne rubbed her nose. "Sure. Only she wasn't alone."

Brannagh rose to her feet, started putting everything back into the knapsack.

"I only saw him for a second before they both ducked down. But from his dark hair, his height, I'm pretty sure …"

Brannagh threw the knapsack onto the bed, dragged her fingers through her hair.

Dianne's shoulders sagged. "I'm positive it was Eddie."

"Absolutely?"

Dianne shook her head. "And there's something else."

Brannagh waited.

"Remember when we were kids, and we vowed to honour, uphold, and protect one another's self-a-steam in the club, at any cost to life and limb, until death do us part, amen?"

"Not really."

"That's just it. We've all forgotten that pledge. But Annie? She hasn't."

"Meaning?"

Dianne blinked. "I just wanted to warn you. Annie can be obsessive about us, about—"

The bedroom door swung open, and they both jumped.

"Why does everyone complain about me being slow?" Tish looked as if she was heading out to the theatre, in a cream skirt and blouse in a mint-green leaf pattern.

"It's just you and me." Dianne leapt up.

"I'll wait for Annie." Brannagh followed Tish downstairs,

ignoring Dianne's attempt to catch her eye.

"You don't mind?"

"No, no." Brannagh stuck her hands in her jean pockets and traced the edge of the rolodex card with her fingertip. She filled the kettle. When she stopped priming the pump, there was a sound overhead, as if a parade of chipmunks tramped across the roof.

"Oh, crumb." Tish gazed upwards. The rain's overhead patter grew louder.

"We can still go." Dianne flitted from one room to the next, pressing her face against the windowpanes. "Bring an umbrella."

"You can still go." Brannagh smiled tightly.

"This is not a sprinkle, it's a soak." Now it was Tish's turn to press her nose against the windows. "Maybe Annie isn't coming back."

Brannagh sighed. "Three teacups it is."

On cue, the old kettle gave a low whistle that stubbornly rose until the lid clattered and the water boiled over, sizzling onto the wood stove below.

⁂

"How old are you?" Cindy asked Brannagh. "If you don't mind me asking." They were sitting in a small clearing, on trampled shrubs and weeds above the river, salvaging the packing ropes that had worn and shredded on the journey to base camp.

"Twenty-eight."

"Ohhhhhh. Almost thirty." Cindy grimaced as if Brannagh had just confessed that she thought Ed Sullivan was sexy. "I never woulda thought. Huh. You don't look it."

Brannagh fought the urge to pinch her. She laid the unravelled end of a rope onto a flat rock, cut it clean across with a filleting knife, and then pinching it tight, held it up.

Cindy scraped a wooden match across the rock and applied it to the end of the rope. They both watched intently as the stray ends sizzled and splayed, then collapsed, surrendering, fusing into one.

"What makes two people fall in love?" Cindy tossed the rope down, and pulled her thick black hair back into a ponytail. "I mean, what really causes two people, two completely different sets of hands, feet, fingers, toes to … to connect?"

Brannagh removed the reef knot she was trying to loosen with her front teeth and spat. "What causes DNA, two different sets of atoms to reach out invisibly through space? Biologically one would deduce that something about that other person affects your senses big time, in a new way—sight, smell, touch, whatever—and all your synapses start firing, causing various new combinations of endocrine reactions in your body, your brain. Over time you equate that chemical reaction, the physiological sensations, with the person." *Cripes she sounded just like Annie.*

Cindy gazed through half-closed eyes past Brannagh. "Uh huh." As she inhaled softly, her body seemed to swell like a piece of ripened fruit.

Brannagh didn't need to glance over her shoulder. She knew Tom was climbing the hill from shore, bearing a cooler filled with freshly scrubbed clothes. She rose to her feet. "Better get this line strung."

Working with Cindy and Tom made Brannagh feel like a hag, as if she were over a hundred years old, as if the blood was petrifying in her veins, as if the wrinkles around her mouth were fanning, the sag beneath her chin wobbling, as if all the energy bubbling within her was flat as week-old ginger ale. What would they say if they found out that she and Nikki had kissed? They would giggle their fool heads off. She herself chalked it up to a momentary spot of bush fever.

"Need a hand?" Nikki, who had come up behind Brannagh unawares, took the rope out of her hands. He began to fasten it around the trunk of a birch. "Clove hitch is a better knot for this."

Tom, standing next to Cindy, wringing out socks, winked.

Brannagh took the free end of the rope and ran it towards an adjacent cedar. "Your beard," she observed.

Nikki's ears reddened. "What about it?" he asked, avoiding her eye.

"It's grown back."

Nikki shrugged.

Brannagh tightened the knot. "I like it better that way." She gathered all the chopped ends of unravelled rope and tossed them into the fire.

She knew Nikki was standing behind her, that she could turn around and begin a conversation, one that would provide an excuse for Cindy and Tom to wander off and leave the two of them alone. She could ask him about what happened to his mother and his sister. Ask him about what it was that he could never forgive himself for. Isn't that how it was done? Two people shared their deepest need to connect by revealing their innermost secrets? The blind misleading the blind? Until somebody decided to leave.

Brannagh silently stared into the fire, watching the messy unravelled rope ends twitch and shrivel and shrink until they were no more.

When she finally turned around, Nikki was gone.

As soon as Brannagh heard the sound of the car engine fading down the cottage driveway, she picked up the telephone and carried it into the pantry. As they drank their tea, she had pretended to suddenly realize that she had forgotten to buy mix. "Annie will kill us if the bar isn't well stocked," she had insisted, sending Tish and Dianne to buy some.

Brannagh closed the pantry door. She hid the bottles of mix that she had bought in the back of the lowest shelf. She pulled the F rolodex card out of her pocket and dialled the number written on it. It rang and rang and rang. Brannagh was about to hang up when she heard an abrupt click.

"Hello?" It was an elderly woman's voice, out of breath. "Ahem. Who's there?" she asked.

"I, may I speak to Arto. Arto Pietila?"

Silence.

"Is this some kind of prank?"

"I'm sorry?"

"There's no Arto Pietila here."

"My apologies. Wrong number."

"Wait." The old woman wavered, coughed. "Arto, my husband, passed away. Last Easter."

"I'm so sorry."

Silence.

"I wanted to talk to him about Nikolai Mirsky." Brannagh held her breath.

"Why?" The old lady wasn't going to let down her guard.

"I'm his sister."

"Oh my. I didn't realize he had another sister. How awful it must have been for you."

"Yes." She'd hit the right note!

"It was such a terrible, terrible time. Arto vowed to do everything he could to keep him from being locked up. Who could blame him? He was just a boy, not violent by nature, under normal circumstances." She paused. The silence grew. "You aren't his sister. You're lying."

"I'm a friend." Brannagh crossed her fingers. "A friend who's worried about him."

"Digging up the past is pain and misery."

"But ..."

"Stop! Before it's too late."

"I'm not trying to—"

But the old woman had already disconnected. The dial tone buzzed like a hornet's nest kicked by a clumsy boot.

Chapter Six

"Who dreams up these clues?" Tish sat in the wing chair in the parlour, chewing her bottom lip, intent on a crossword puzzle. "I need a seven- letter word for mislead. Starts with *d*."

Brannagh sorted scrabble tiles on the floor. She could hear Dianne humming in the kitchen as she potted the shrivelled begonia bulb she'd found amongst a pile of broken garden pots under the sink. "Deceive."

Tish glanced up from the folded newspaper on her lap.

"Seven-letter word for mislead?" Brannagh tossed the dictionary at Tish. "Deceive."

They had supped on a can of chicken noodle soup and crackers, reminiscent of rainy days when Aunt Thelma served hot broth in mugs in the kitchen of the house on Argyle, while wet socks and sweaters sizzled on a line strung above the woodstove.

"It's crazy." Tish's brow furrowed.

"Yes, you are." Brannagh was only half-listening.

"A hospital emergency wouldn't hold Annie up this long." Tish chewed her pencil then began carefully filling the squares. "Unless … she didn't really go back to Saint John because of an emergency."

"Why else would she?" Dianne set a chipped clay pot on the shelf beneath the parlour window.

One corner of Tish's mouth bent downward. "Maybe she wanted to see somebody."

Brannagh scooped the tiles into the lid of the game box and began flipping them over.

"What somebody?" Dianne's back grew rigid.

"So who's ready for a high-stakes game of Scrabble?" Brannagh flipped open the board and laid it flat on the floor.

Tish rose off the chair with the air of a prisoner being led to the torture chamber. "Who wants a drink?"

Once they got rolling, Tish completely forgot that she had ever had a wisp of a reservation. Whether it was the rum or the triple word score with *susurration*, which Tish informed them airily meant murmur, whisper, mumbling (she had read that in the Reader's Digest, thank you very much), she suddenly couldn't get enough of Scrabble and harangued Brannagh and Dianne into playing a third game when it was already past midnight and they were begging to switch to Monopoly or Clue. They had just selected their tiles, and were patiently waiting for slowpoke Dianne to lay the first word on the board, when suddenly the cottage was plunged into darkness.

"Yikes."

"Shit."

"A blown fuse?" Tish rose to her feet.

Brannagh could feel her heart beginning its familiar jitter beneath her ribs. "I think I saw a couple in a drawer by the fridge."

"Creepy."

"Hold on, give me your hand." Dianne muttered. "I'll come with you."

Brannagh rose, but didn't budge. "Maybe it would be better just to stay in one spot?" When she received no answer, her voice rose an octave. "Wait, don't leave me by myself." She scurried forward coming to an abrupt halt when she jostled into a warm body.

"Ouch." Dianne yelped. "Tish, take off your heels."

"Sorry."

They inched down the hallway. "There was a candle on the bookshelf. I could have …"

"Slow down," Brannagh ordered. "I'm spilling my drink."

"Give me some of that."

Tish banged her shin on a trunk. "For God's sake. Will you two …" She glanced up and inhaled sharply. A fleeting apparition passed before the kitchen window.

"Holy sh—did you see? What was that?" Dianne dug her fingernails into Brannagh's shoulder.

"It looked like a face."

"A man's face."

Brannagh's stomach clenched. "It's the reflection of the moon on the window pane." Despite her brave words, her voice quavered.

"Sure it is." Dianne refused to budge.

"Move," Tish ordered. Slowly, the three of them inched toward the kitchen door.

Brannagh's lower limbs trembled. "There is nothing to be afraid of."

"Shhhhhhh!" Tish pinched Brannagh's arm. "I hear something," she hissed.

They huddled together by the kitchen door listening. After a few seconds of silence, Tish whispered, "There is nothing out there. On the count of three, I'm opening the door."

"No!" Brannagh grabbed her arm.

"Not yet," Dianne ordered. She reached for a carving knife in the dish rack and held it over her head.

Tish gripped the doorknob. "One, two, three!" She swung the door open.

They gaped.

There was Annie holding a tall white candle that cast an eerie upward glow upon her facial features. She flashed a grin, and then her face turned sombre. "Ladies, " she announced hoarsely, "I hereby call this meeting of the Tuatha-de-Dananns to order."

A few weeks before summer vacation in grade eight, Brannagh arrived home from school to encounter the surprise of her life. There was no premonition, no warning of what was to come. It was an ordinary day, no different from any other. She had taken the shortcut down the back lane. It was drizzling lightly. She could smell the dust rising from the gardens mingled with the scent of geraniums and chives and tender tomato plants.

Brannagh hopped the fence, and flung open the kitchen door of the house on Argyle. "Gran! I'm home," she called, then froze.

A woman with long legs and dark shiny hair that sat like capital J bookends on each shoulder sat at the kitchen table. She wore a creamy dress made of the softest material that Brannagh had ever seen. It fell in whirls about her thighs, curling like an upside-down tulip. The handles of Brannagh's satchel slipped through her fingers. It fell to the floor with a whump.

The woman was intent on her nails, applying thin lines of crimson polish. Only after she had slowly brushed two strokes across the left thumb did she pause and park the lid back onto the bottle. Her brilliant gold cat's eyes fixed on Brannagh. "Look at you," she murmured, blowing lightly on her fingertips. Her voice was husky, beguiling. "You're late."

"I was ..."

"C'mon, give me a kiss." Pamela tilted her head, offering one cheek. There was a hardness about her, in the penetrating gaze, in the pursing of her lips, that dug deep into Brannagh's belly.

Brannagh pressed her mouth against dry, powdered skin. Her mother was surrounded by a cloud of scent that clutched at the back of Brannagh's throat. A picture rose in her mind's eye of white fringes brushing a hardwood floor, and through the fringes, as though through the thin white bars of a prison cell, her mother sitting on a bench, the delicate knobs of her spine rising above the lace trim on her silk slip as she leaned forward to pat and pinch and press and inspect the image in the three-sided mirror. "Are you …?" Brannagh couldn't quite get the words out.

"Home for a visit." Pamela smiled and the granite melted. All the carefree loveliness that Brannagh had stored in her memory emerged in the sparkle in her mother's eyes and the soft swell of her lower lip. Pamela nodded toward the door to the dining room. "Art had some business to tend to so I said to myself, Pamela, it's time for a vacation."

It was only then that Brannagh noticed a brown fedora hanging on the back of one of the kitchen chairs. She turned and saw a sandy-haired man leaning against the wall next to the phone. He wore baggy cuffed pants and shiny shoes. He loosened the knot in his skinny brown tie and folded short, muscular arms across his chest. He had the receiver tucked under his chin. There was an air of challenge emanating from him, as if he were primed to pounce.

The smile that Brannagh had been slowly working on didn't stand a chance.

"This is my fiancé, Art." Pamela gestured with one hand. There was a thin gold ring on one of her fingers. "Art, this is my niece, Brannagh."

Brannagh stiffened.

Art's hand rose, and the shiny watch on his wrist winked.

"Uh, hi." Brannagh picked up her satchel and walked through the swinging door to the dining room, continued down the sidewalk, past the Provincial Asylum, past the Simms Building, over the Reversing Falls bridge, and down Lookout Lane to Reversing Falls Park where she sat on a crag of rock, batting orbiting mosquitoes, until it grew dark and Andy Barton, the policeman on foot patrol, came and bellowed, "Look ducky, shouldn't youse be making tracks soon?"

After the kiss, it was as if some invisible buttress between Nikki and Brannagh had tumbled, and they were left gazing across the clouds of dust and strewn rubble trying to discern an enemy that they no longer recognized.

They were quiet around one another after the kiss, speaking in either solicitous, shy queries or brusque, curt one-syllable commands that left Cindy and Tom scratching their heads.

Brannagh embraced her work. She had one week to train everyone in mapping and survey methods. She methodically explained how the birds were to be detected by sound: crowing, drumming, cooing (while neglecting to confess that despite the hours she'd spent listening to the Toronto Naturalist's records of bird song she still couldn't tell the difference between a *whit* and a *wheep*.)

Brannagh saved the best bit of information for last, when she informed the team that they would be woken three hours before sunrise to cook, eat, clean up and hike to their stations, in order to be ready to go thirty minutes before the sun came up.

They drew for partners. Brannagh was in the makeshift biffy when she unfolded the scrap that she'd pulled out of the canvas hat and read Nikki's name scrawled across it. She dropped it down the hole.

"Jeesus, Annie," Tish protested. "You scared the crap out of us."

Annie stepped into the kitchen of the cottage, and they all involuntarily stepped back. "That was the whole idea."

"Yeah," Dianne sided with Tish. "That was quite an entrance."

Suddenly the lights turned on. Everyone blinked. Annie stood beside the fuse box, one hand on her hip. "All right you bunch of sookies. All better now?"

Before they had a chance to say one word, the lights went out and Annie sang.

Let the shadows fall behind you
Take my hand in the setting sun
Together we will conquer fear
Loyal forever, we are one.

"Grow up," Tish whinged. "If you're through with the melodrama, we'd like the lights back anytime now."

"Shush, we're having a meeting," Annie admonished.

To my sisters, to my sisters
I remain loyal and true
Our protection at all costs
I pledge forever to you.

"Speaking of sookie," Brannagh muttered.

"I have to go to the bathroom," Dianne announced.

"Too late," Annie said.

"The torch is on the counter." Brannagh gestured towards it.

There was no deterring Annie.

"Does anyone else want a drink?"

"God, yes!"

"I was ready to go to bed."

"Make mine a double."

Let the shadows fall behind you
Take my hand in the setting sun
Together we will conquer fear
Loyal forever, we are one.

"Enough already!"
"Does that sound revolting, or what?"
"Sappy school girls."
"Pass the barf bag."
"You guys are one big unappreciative pain in the ass." Annie strode toward the parlour. "Now, get your sorry butts in here."

For the next few weeks, Brannagh was fascinated by the guests at the house on Argyle. At night, if she stood in the chimney of the fireplace in the spare room on the second floor, she could hear everything Art and Pamela said in their bedroom as clearly as a program tuned on the radio dial.

Aunt Thelma slammed cupboard drawers and rattled cooking pots. She ignored Art altogether despite his, and Pamela's, efforts to impress. Only Grandfather seemed excited, exclaiming, "You're more beautiful now than ever," whenever Pamela entered the room.

"We'll be sitting on easy street one of these days," Pamela boasted to Gran like clockwork every night after supper when they retired to the parlour. She'd kick off her high heels and swing her feet onto Art's lap. Sometimes Pamela took out a white leather case, took Art's hand in hers, and clipped his hangnails, pushing back the cuticles with a pearl-handled tool. She buffed his nails until they shone, and then he chewed them, one by one, while he talked on the telephone.

"Yeah, Art's cooking up a big deal." Pamela would arch her spine as Art picked up one of her feet and massaged the arch with the tips of his fingers. "He gives me wads of money to go clothes shopping. Insists I wear the top of the line, right honey?"

Once in a while Brannagh glanced up and found Art's eyes resting on her. He would smile and she felt as if someone had plopped a cold dishrag onto her crown. She tucked her head into her chest and blushed. For a fleeting moment, she hated them both.

"You're dropping nail clippings on the floor," Aunt Thelma scolded. But Pamela and Art ignored her.

"Advertising. That's where the money is these days. Billboards," Pamela clarified, though no one had asked. "Art's renting space on a string of billboards from Saint John to Moncton."

"Is that right?" Annie, who sat beside Aunt Thelma studying Bulfinch's *Greek and Roman Mythology*, threw out these comments in her fake "ain't that interesting" voice, the same voice she used when the Fuller Brush salesman managed to pull the heart strings and con Gran into letting him past the front door.

One morning Brannagh went out to the porch to get the milk and Art was sitting on the step in his undershirt reading the *Times Globe*. He grunted, "Morning," and reached back to quickly pull on his shirt, but not before she saw the blue tattoo of a serpent that circled his biceps with red flames coming off its tongue. Now, when he wasn't looking, Brannagh's eyes hunted for the faint line of a serpent beneath his shirt sleeve.

Brannagh couldn't figure it out. Was it just a game? How everyone silently agreed to ignore the fact that her mother had suddenly turned up, out of the blue, after disappearing so many years ago, not to mention the fact that she had brought along this strange man? It was as if everyone in the family was encouraging any train of thought that brought them further and further away from the truth. Brannagh felt as if her head was going to burst.

And then she would spot Annie, on her hands and knees behind the couch where no one could see her. Annie held the tip of one finger to her mouth, working it in and out. She made a soft, gagging sound in her throat. *Barf,* she mouthed the word. *Double, triple barf.*

Brannagh, who was lying on the rug, rolled back and pinched Annie's shin.

Annie yelped and grabbed a fistful of Brannagh's hair. They rolled towards the bookcase, knees in crotches, elbows in ribs, noses in stinky "forgot to shower after volleyball" armpits.

Afterwards, Brannagh decided, while the June bugs thumped against the windows and Pamela's voice droned on and the sun fell lower in the sky, that sometimes grownups were downright scary.

Two minutes into their first survey stop, Nikki finally caught on to her. Unless they were solely listening for whippoorwills (who sound just like their name), Brannagh was up the creek.

"You'll have to be our eyes, and I'll be our ears," he concluded, as he gazed off into the horizon through binoculars. "Besides, there'll be times when we have to conduct our survey a little differently from the rest because you have to get the drawings done." He sighed here, and she knew that not confessing about the white lies on her job application had been the right thing to do.

Every day at lunchtime, they settled into a cubby Nikki created in the brush. After a lecture, he ordered her to listen carefully and then he fell asleep; all she heard was faint snoring in the afternoon breeze.

Despite this, Brannagh eventually learned that a musical *queedle, queedle* of the blue jay, was not to be confused with the *zhreek zhreek* of the scrub jay; that a nuthatch crawled down a tree trunk while a creeper crawled up it; that robins were cranky, chickadees fearless.

Sometimes when the deer flies were biting, or there were miles of dense bog to slog through, they argued. Nikki lectured her on the need to concentrate and she yawned in his face while he explained the difference between a bird bobbing, fanning or flicking its tail.

"Thank you for imparting that scintillating information," she'd say, and yawn again.

"It's all in the field guide," he'd continue, losing his patience. "And you better study it tonight, because if you don't know it come morning, I'm fining you two rations of chocolate."

It didn't help that the rain had let up, and that Mother Nature had loosened her stranglehold on summer's blossoming, allowing it to assume full gallop, until the days slowly gave in to an indolence illustrated in still, expectant cobalt skies and warm feathery breezes. The scent of pine sap and peppery wildflowers hung in the air. Brannagh imagined that she could hear the life juices of the surrounding flora flowing from root to stem to leaf. All around her was an unfolding, a lazy rich mellowing.

When Brannagh lay on the bracken in the cubby that Nikki cleared at lunchtime, she could almost feel the earth humming in her belly, could recognize the trembling of it beneath her.

She welcomed the warmth of it, the lushness, the energy of all the creatures of the earth gleaning sustenance from it and reaching up, up towards the sun.

One afternoon, while Nikki snored softly, Brannagh heard a snapping of twigs, a crackling of brush. She turned away from him and watched the leaves of the poplars in the distance flipping lazily in the wind, as if an invisible hand ruffled the nap of the landscape. Further back, the clouds spilled shadows onto the hills.

Into the clearing stepped a creature that at first glance looked like a large dog with a reddish-tan coat and long, thin legs. Brannagh rose on her elbow, noticed the puff of a tail, the over-large ears, the spotted flank. There was a cracking sound. The young doe paused, its ears perked. A buck with large antlers galloped out of the brush, nostrils quivering. The doe stood silently upon his approach. He ran his nose along her flank. There was a thick bald patch on his rump where the fur hung in clumps.

Loosestrife, fireweed and bright yellow sow thistles waved round them in the summer breeze. While horse flies and hornets droned in the heat, the buck attempted to mount the doe. She lowered her head, seemingly oblivious, sniffing at the undergrowth.

The buck reared and with an awkward lumbering grace straddled the doe's flanks, the tip of his swollen shaft rising from the long thick casing. His hind legs stumbled as he pushed against her. The doe's head rose and she stood perfectly still, ears cupped forward, large eyes glistening.

Their thrusting, quivering, staggering dance held Brannagh spellbound.

Suddenly the doe bolted, crashing through the trees.

Brannagh turned around. Nikki stared, unblinking. He ran his fingers through his sweat-slicked brow and plopped his hat back onto his head. "It isn't rutting season."

Brannagh gathered her papers and secured them to the clipboard. "Guess they neglected to study their field guide," she quipped. "So fine them, why don't you?"

Tish took roll call and tried to decipher the minutes from the last meeting of the Tuatha-de-Danaans that had been held so many years ago. "Penmanship was never my strong point."

Annie unearthed a popcorn box covered with cut up bits of candy wrappers and passed it around, insisting everyone had to pay dues. Brannagh cursed as she fumbled around in the dark for her purse. "Who elected you boss?"

"Some things never change." Tish twirled a ringlet between her fingers.

"Wake me up when it's over." Dianne yawned.

There was a rattling sound and Annie set a toffee tin in her lap. She opened it and took out four rocks. She handed one to Brannagh. It was green, round and smooth. Brannagh balanced the familiar weight in her palm.

"I never wanted this one," Tish complained. The rock in her hand resembled a speckled egg.

Dianne licked the roughened surface of her rock and held it in front of the candle flame. "Look, you can still see the cross."

"If you say so," Brannagh mused. The licking of the rocks was a ritual the girls performed in grade school when collecting them on Saints' Rest beach because Gran said you could never tell what sort of promise a rock held unless it was spit on a few times. When Annie decided that they should cut their palms and exchange blood, Brannagh argued that that was too boring.

"Life would be so much simpler if we still believed in faeries and Jesus and magic." Tish gazed sullenly into the candle flame.

"Don't you?" Dianne's face screwed up.

Annie signalled for everyone to set the rocks down. "Tuatha-de-Dananns, are we all in the circle?" She spit on her palm and extended her arm.

Brannagh followed suit. "I am in the circle of Tuatha-de-Dananns in my heart and in my prayers so help me God."

"I can't believe I remember this crap." Tish reluctantly thrust her wet palm beside Brannagh's.

When Dianne had finished reciting, Annie announced, "We are one in the circle." She slapped her palm across Brannagh's, Tish's and Dianne's. They each followed her actions, chanting the phrase with each slap. Then each picked up their stone, rubbed it in the palms of their hands and set it down once again.

Annie folded her arms across her chest. "God, I thank you for, just, life. This week I need courage. Courage to ... to tell the truth." Annie tapped her rock.

"I didn't want to come here. But I did." Brannagh opened her eyes. "Shouldn't I win the door prize?"

"Don't forget to tap your rock."

"I was getting to it. Don't rush me."

"Thank you God for Billy, how funny she is, refreshing, and for Eddie. This week I need strength to do what I need to do."

"Friends. Thank you God for friends," Dianne said, blushing. "I need patience to just be still. Patience to wait and see."

They all picked up their rocks and dropped them into the toffee tin. Annie snapped the lid shut and shook it as they all stood and chanted:

"I am you and you are me, one in the sky and the sun and the hills. I promise to honour, uphold, and protect my sisters' self-a-steam at any cost to life and limb, until death do us part. Amen."

Dianne and Brannagh burst into laughter.

"We used to think that was brilliant."

"Isn't it?"

Tish rolled her eyes.

After the meeting they each took the rocks out of the tin and vowed to carry them on their person, at all times, until the next meeting. Annie, the ascetic, was the only one who insisted on putting hers in her shoe, or back pants pocket, convinced the answer to her prayers would be all the more powerful after having subjected her wicked self to suffering.

Annie dug around in the shopping bag.

"There's more?" Brannagh asked.

"How quickly they forget." Annie unearthed a package of cigarettes.

Dianne blanched. "Export A, no filters, gack, how did we ever smoke those things?"

"From saints to sinners in seconds," Brannagh said.

"We wanted to cover all the bases," Annie insisted.

"Didn't Moses smoke?" Dianne asked.

"Get serious," Annie retorted.

"The burning bush?" Tish put in. "I rest my case."

Annie lit a cigarette from the candle and stuck it in her mouth, puffing. Later Brannagh would recall that it was with the appearance of the cigarettes that the mood in the room began to subtly change. She became aware of the cold draft coming from the open window in the kitchen. Tish took a gulp of rum and coke. The ice cubes in the glass cracked sharply. Dianne peered anxiously into the candle flame.

Annie took a puff of the cigarette and handed it to Brannagh.

Brannagh inhaled and coughed. "Argh, the old airways ain't what they used to be."

"We all made a pledge to uphold one another's self-a-steam," Annie studied her hands.

Brannagh took another puff of the cigarette, attempted a smoke ring.

"When Dianne was so afraid of dogs that she walked miles to avoid one, we walked with her around the block, again and again.

Made her approach the dogs with her hand out."

"Cats are classier," Dianne observed.

"Here, here, " Brannagh raised her glass. Dianne would not meet her eye. Brannagh felt her stomach tighten.

"When Tish was so afraid of writing the driver's test," Annie continued, "we took turns quizzing her from the manual, and then went with her, all three times, until she passed."

Tish gulped the rest of her drink. "That old bat instructor said my skirt was too short. So sue me."

Brannagh's heart beat high in her chest.

"And now the time has come to support another sister."

"Okay, enough hokum pokum for one night." Brannagh started to rise to her feet. Annie reached out with one hand and yanked her back down again.

"And now the time has come."

"This is dumb." Tish glared defiantly at Annie. "I'm not going through with it."

Annie ignored her. "Brannagh we know you always said you'd never go back to Saint John but—"

"She wants you to come back with us." Tish interrupted. "To Saint John, for your own good, apparently."

"Is this some sort of joke?" Brannagh closed her eyes for a moment and gave her head a shake.

"She thinks you and your Grandfather need to see each other." Tish continued.

Annie poked at her glasses. "It's about letting go, learning to trust."

"I thought we were goofing off here. Having a little fun."

"You try to pretend that summer with your mother coming home, her death, all that never happened. It's about acceptance."

"Trust? You are the expert on trust?" Tish sneered.

Annie's jaw muscles twitched.

Brannagh jerked to her feet. The three women sitting on the floor turned strained faces toward her. Brannagh stumbled toward the kitchen. "I don't believe this."

"I tried to warn you." Dianne was close on her heels, with the others trailing behind.

Brannagh opened the fuse box and tightened the loose fuses. The lights in the cottage blazed. She spun round, blinking. "Why can't you ever leave well enough alone?"

Annie held one hand up. "Look, I didn't know how else to bring it up. I thought this way you could treat it like a joke, or not."

"Some joke."

Tish stepped forward brandishing her glass in the air. She was clearly enjoying watching Annie squirm. "Annie has it all figured out. What you need to do to keep from going off the deep end. Accept what happened to your mother that summer, and confront your grandfather once and for all." She daintily picked up the rum bottle on the counter and poured. "Because she cares. She cares about all of us so much." Tish's face hardened. "Don't you Annie?"

Dianne's face was pinched. "It's not like we got together to run you down behind your back. Annie was worried, after Nikki disappeared..."

Brannagh grabbed the rum bottle from Tish's hand. She took a hefty slug. Eyes smarting, she swiped her mouth with shaking fingers. "So when was this little pow-wow to try and figure out how to help poor, pathetic Brannagh pull her life back together?"

Annie shook her head. "It was just a telephone call. I only wanted—"

"How could you Annie? How could you?" Brannagh hurled the bottle into the air. An arc of liquid plumed towards the ceiling. The bottle hit the wall with a klunk and rolled across the floor.

Brannagh yanked her jacket off the hook by the door and picked the torch up off the counter. "You're a godammed bully. There's no other word for it. And you know what they say about bullies." Brannagh fought the urge to smash the torch across Annie's face. "Bullies are just cowards with fangs." Brannagh stepped onto the porch slamming the door in Annie's guilt-flushed face.

After Pamela had been home for two weeks, Aunt Thelma dubbed it "the summer of stupidity." It turned out that Pamela's high school graduating class was having a reunion. They hadn't sent her an invitation claiming they didn't know how to get in touch with her, but she was sure welcome to come, they said, Pam and her fiancé. Of course, Aunt Thelma had known about it all along because, after Pamela had flunked a few grades, she and her older sister had graduated in the same class.

"I don't know why you didn't tell me sooner," Pamela complained every time she came through the kitchen door with shopping bags draped like bangles from wrist to elbow. She bought half a dozen outfits, modeled them for everyone, then took them back to the store the next day. She was developing an ulcer, she insisted, trying to find "just the right thing."

Aunt Thelma looked up from the crackers she was crushing on the counter with a rolling pin. "Yellow makes you look jaundiced."

"Does not." Pamela glanced down at the taffeta cocktail dress, the string from the sales tag dangling off one button. "Art has the final say anyway with all this money he's spending."

Aunt Thelma smiled.

Brannagh sat at the kitchen table doing her homework and watched her mother come in and out in a parade of silk organza blouses, hour-glass skirts, cotton shirtwaists, and occasionally, though it was rare, an evening gown, the very thing she had gone shopping for in the first place. Words trailed in her wake like rose petals drifting in the wind: "I'll have to do something with this hair, a rinse, or Toni, and God I need some silk hose, blast synthetic."

After Pamela exited the kitchen, Aunt Thelma pulled a long face in Brannagh's direction and said, "Welcome to the summer of stupidity."

"Who are you bringing?" Pamela asked Aunt Thelma one night.

Aunt Thelma pretended not to hear. "Think I'll bake a chocolate cake, Brannagh. For your class end of the year party." She sorted through the carrots in the vegetable bin, handing the withered ones to Brannagh, who put them into a paper bag to feed the horses at Rockwood Park on the last outing of the school year.

"Who are you bringing?" Pamela persisted. She ripped off a sheet of wax paper and wrapped it around one arm.

"I could write on the cake *Class of '54* or *Happy Graduation Grade 8* in white icing."

"Nah, don't put nuthin'," Brannagh mumbled.

"You are bringing someone, aren't you?" Pamela patted wax paper around the other arm.

"Yes." Aunt Thelma closed the fridge door.

Pamela wrapped towels around the wax paper.

Brannagh watched nonplussed. She should have been used to these complex rituals by now.

"Well, who?" Pamela demanded impatiently.

"Kate."

"Kate?" Pamela's pencilled brows rose. Her mouth hardened into a straight line. "You can't do that," she dismissed flatly.

"Why?"

"What will people think?"

"Most people don't think, that's the problem."

Brannagh stuck the carrots in her satchel and did up the straps. She avoided looking at either one of them.

"What's gotten into you?" Pamela muttered.

"Hmmmm."

"Kate's idea, I'll bet. You weren't like this before you met her. Started going to those women's meetings."

"Kate's smart. Really really smart." Aunt Thelma pulled the bread tins out of the oven and set them on the counter. "She just bought a Victorian house with a hipped roof. She wants to turn it into an art gallery called SeaWinds."

Brannagh thought it was funny because she had always believed that someone with a name like Kate would be so ordinary. But Kate was delightfully unusual. She had short curly russet hair, freckles, and a wide mouth that was always moving, just like the rest of her. Kate never stayed still, unless she was in front of an easel. Then she was stiller than still can be. But usually she was a ball of energy, words and passions. Kate didn't believe in being lady-like, or in the importance of "being nice" or in holding anything back. She was developing a whole new theory about why people behave the way they do, and writing a book. Kate insisted she'd be famous some day. She came in the door like a whirlwind ("holy terror" Pamela would murmur) and the very air in the house changed, turned electric, charged with possibilities. After losing several arguments over the merits of Freud versus Jung, Grandfather now disappeared when Kate was around.

"I can handle whatever life throws at me," Kate had informed Brannagh, "because I have self-esteem."

Brannagh learned that self-a-steam was like the fuel that ran steam locomotives. If a person stoked their engine with enough, they'd be able to add cars to their engine, first one, then two, then a dozen, and still make it up, up, up to the top of the steepest hills. At least, that's how Kate had explained it.

Self-a-steam, Brannagh had concluded, sounded like it would come in handy. Like it would have a lot to do with the "inner life force" mentioned in the book Kate had given her on how to draw. Only where do you get it? she had wondered.

"Kate's brilliant. Is that why you keep picking on her?" Aunt Thelma demanded, tossing a dishtowel over one shoulder and planting both hands on her hips.

"What on earth are you talking about?" Pamela feigned puzzlement.

"Are you jealous of what you'll never have?"

"Where did having a brain ever get you?"

"We aren't talking about me."

"No, of course not." Pamela primped her hair. "Brannagh, honey, open that bag on the chair. I bought you something."

With a sense of dread, Brannagh pulled out a white garment and unfolded it. It was a pair of latex panties filled with tiny holes. Metal garters dangled off the legs. Brannagh remembered how one day her mother pointed out an ad in a women's magazine of the amazing, new Playtex Magic Controller: With tummy-flattening finger panels that echo the firm support of your own body muscles as Nature intended!

"A girdle?" Aunt Thelma set down a frying pan with a thwunk.

Brannagh blanched at the words: Resilient, firm control that revitalizes your proportions, your posture, your pride! In her mind's eye she saw the lady in the advertisement, dancing across the page in her Magic Controller. More than a girdle … better than a Corset! Maybe this was the kind of advertising Art planned for the billboards clear from Saint John to Moncton. Brannagh imagined a chorus of ladies, with their serene smiles, leaping jauntily across farmer's fields, cows with heavy teats and swollen bellies benignly munching at their feet.

"You've got a bulge, honey. Course if you stopped slouching and threw your shoulders back."

Aunt Thelma snatched the offensive garment out of Brannagh's hand. "You are not wearing this thing!" A vein in Aunt Thelma's forehead had started to throb. Brannagh could scarcely breathe. There was a lull as the women's eyes locked.

Pamela rose slowly to her feet. "She's my daughter. I'll do what I like."

"If she's your damn daughter, then where the hell have you been for the last seven years? I'm the one who's been stuck in this house …" Aunt Thelma glanced at Brannagh. Her voice steadied. "Tending to your responsibilities."

Pamela's jaw flinched. "How dare you."

Aunt Thelma tossed the girdle on the kitchen counter, marched over to the sink, picked up the bread knife, set it down again, took a deep breath, turned back to Pamela. "You are not making her wear this thing."

Pamela wrenched the towels, then the wax paper off her hands. She wiped the goop off and lit a cigarette with shaking fingers. "What business is it of yours?"

Thelma turned to Brannagh, ignoring Pamela. "Welcome to the dark ages. Iron corsets and metal farthingales. Those contraptions caused more deaths than any plague." Pamela furiously puffed the cigarette.

"Just one more insane rule that men hammered out for women."

"What are you, a walking tour guide for the museum of ancient history?" Pamela was calmer now, determined to treat the whole thing with an air of superiority.

"He never loved you." Aunt Thelma breathed heavily. She plucked the girdle up as if it were a dead bird the cat dragged in. "Never." Aunt Thelma swung open the cupboard beneath the sink, opened the trash and dropped the girdle in.

"Quit talking nonsense. I swear you've gone dotty," Pamela scoffed.

"You hated that he was mine. You just had to destroy it, didn't you?"

"I didn't have to do anything. Just look in the mirror."

"You're jealous. Always have been."

"In your dreams. You're a bitter old spinster who has wasted her life. Don't take it out on me."

"You do not want me to start speaking the truth. Do you Pamela? Do you?" Aunt Thelma's hands tightened around the folds of her apron. Pamela stepped back, but her gaze never wavered.

"I have been grounded on the rocks, year after year, forced by a sense of duty, a sense of decency not to abandon …" Aunt Thelma glanced at Brannagh then turned quickly away. She grasped the knife on the counter and sliced the bread in huge jagged hunks. When Aunt Thelma spoke again, her words came out rough and low and wooden. "Brannagh, please escort Pamela out of my kitchen right now before I get a notion to stick her fat head under the kitchen pump and never let it up again."

Brannagh finally managed to pry Pamela out of the chair. Reluctantly, she allowed Brannagh to push her through the swinging door, but not before pausing to turn back and hiss, "Old maid!"

There was no surprise to Brannagh when the falling out came. She had felt the tension building at base camp for days, like dark thunderclouds gathering on the horizon.

Nikki came upon Cindy and Tom in the woods. Only they weren't gathering moss as Nikki had ordered them for cushioning the packing of specimens. No. Cindy's length was pressed up against a tree trunk. She arched her spine. Tom's fingers were entwined in the hem of her T-shirt. One breast popped free and the nipple rumpled in the cool air. Tom briefly pulled his mouth away from Cindy's to gaze at it reverently. Cindy picked up his hand and laid it over her heart.

Nikki bellowed.

There is no other word to describe the eruption that sent the birds of the air, the beasts of the fields and all that swim the depths of the sea, scuttling for cover.

It took Brannagh, who was sitting in the shade of a sumach rewriting notes, a while to figure out what had happened. But then Nikki and Cindy squabbled so loudly, it wasn't hard to deduce.

Nikki dragged Cindy over to the sumach tree. "From now on, Brannagh is your counting partner. I'll look after Tom."

As he strode away, Brannagh shuddered to think of how exactly Nikki would look after Tom.

"Go to hell!" Cindy yelled before a sob caught in her throat and she ran tipsily down to the water.

Brannagh sighed and laid her head against the trunk. A spider, tiny and delicate as thistle seed, dangled from an overhead branch. It descended as if from an invisible pulley and then meticulously, methodically began to weave a web. Its faith in the outcome was excruciatingly pathetic. All that work and the web could disappear in an instant.

With a grunt, Brannagh rose and slowly made her way down to the water. Cindy sat hunched over a rock with her chin in her hands. The back of her jeans rode low. Brannagh could see fly bites and the tiny purple daisies on her cotton underwear.

Brannagh sat down beside her on the shingle. She had grown used to sitting on these rocks. Her cellulite had become tattooed with their imprints. Brannagh pulled a rectangle of foil out of her pocket and unwrapped a bar of milk chocolate. She broke it in half and offered some to Cindy. "I've been saving this for a special occasion. Seems as good as any."

Cindy hesitated for a moment, and then her mouth softened. "Thanks," she said gruffly. She bit into it and closed her eyes. Such an expression of utter rapture Brannagh had rarely witnessed.

Brannagh knew perfectly well that the sexual tension uncoiling between Cindy and Tom like a slow dribble of rope coming unknotted from its moorings was far more tantalizing and satisfying than any bit of melting chocolate on the tastebuds, but it was the only comfort she had to extend. She was an older woman who had been without a man for so long that her bodily juices had slowed and mummified long ago. What did she know? What possible succour could she offer?

As Brannagh bit into the chocolate and felt the sweet liquid satin entwine her tongue, it occurred to her that she needed the chocolate far more than Cindy did. Her senses needed to trace the long forgotten paths of arousal: a voice crying out, the softness of rumpled sheets on sweaty limbs, the weight of heaviness pressing, the sharp scent of a man's corners, the frisson of male skin soothing her own. Memories held suspended in the deep.

Brannagh gobbled the rest of the chocolate bar. She had been young. Once. She knew what it was to wait trembling and suppliant for a man's warm breath to slide down her throat. Or did she?

"I wonder if the jerk ever regrets not seeing her." Cindy picked up a handful of stones and tossed them one by one into the water.

"Who?" No need for Brannagh to ask who the jerk is.

"His mother."

Brannagh hugged her knees to her chest.

"She was a Native Canadian you know."

Brannagh nodded.

"It wasn't until she stopped drinking that she found out they had put Nikki in the residential school, after the trial for the death of his sister Marina. Uncle Zhuk told me all about it."

Cindy tucked one wing of glossy black hair behind her ear.

"What happened to Marina?"

But Cindy wasn't listening. "His mother and one of her friends in twelve-step drove up north, worked in hotels along the way. They settled in Fort William. She sent Nikki letters at school, then to Uncle Zhuk's, after he took Nikki to live at his place. He never answered. Even when she got sick, liver cancer, he never went to see her before she died. Refused."

Brannagh liked the water at this time of day. The afternoon breeze had died down. There wasn't a ripple on the surface. The reflection of the overhead clouds rolling past appeared to meet the real thing somewhere on the horizon.

"Cold-hearted prick." Cindy glowered, scooped up a handful of rocks and flung them at the water. They plucked the surface like furious fingers. "What do you think?" Her face assumed a sudden earnest vulnerability as she tilted it upward. "What do you think about me and Tom?" Her cheeks were luminous as daisy petals.

Brannagh regarded her thoughtfully. "I think … I think I'm so jealous I could scream."

Cindy's smile burst unexpectedly and her laughter when it came echoed the swallows at sunrise, scattering in random beauty across the pale horizon.

The night of the high school reunion was a long one. For Brannagh at least. It began when Pamela sneaked Brannagh away from her duties in the Nervous Clinic, insisting that many hours were needed to get properly attired. When it was time to pour a bath, Brannagh was allowed to drop in the translucent red balls that dissolved and sat like clots of blood on the porcelain after the water had drained.

"How do I look?" Pamela primped in front of the mirror. She wore a black velvet halter top with tiny silk-covered buttons down the front, and a full white taffeta crinolined skirt flocked with delicate black swirls. "It's Art's favorite. He says I outshine Marilyn Munro, wearing this."

"It looks all right." Brannagh lay on the bed, chin in hands.

Pamela sat, pulled off one shoe and tried on another. She flexed a calf and circled one ankle in the air. "Never forget honey, shoes are a woman's secret weapon." She slid a tall, thin silver flask out of a side pouch of a black silk suitcase. "Nectar of the gods," she said, winking, as she tilted her head back. Brannagh realized that all along there had been another smell in the room, mingling with the perfume, powder and bath beads. Metallic and musky and sharp.

Pamela stood in front of the mirror, eyes narrowing. She placed one hand over her bosom. "I know just what you're thinking." She dragged a chair over to the closet and wriggled a dusty box off the top shelf. She opened the lid and took out a white shawl. She shook it. "Save the best for last, right?" Pamela draped the shawl over her shoulders and worked a sultry look.

"Take it off." The voice from the doorway was startling in its abruptness. "It doesn't belong to you. Take it off. Now." Grandfather's face was pale against the dark mahogany doorframe.

Pamela's cheeks flushed. "Well, I don't think this belongs to you, does it?"

"Did you ask Rye?"

"Of course I did."

"You did."

"Well, I meant to, just didn't have a chance before she left." Here Pamela faltered momentarily, then she thrust her shoulders back. "But she'd want me to wear it. It was her mother's."

"Haven't you learned how dangerous it is to mess with things that don't belong to you?" Aunt Thelma stood in the hall in her bathrobe, with a frayed green towel wrapped around her dripping hair.

Grandfather didn't move a muscle. "Take it off."

Aunt Thelma plucked the cigarette out of the corner of her mouth and took a puff. "Maybe you better take it off, Pam." Her voice quavered. "For the sake of—"

"Of what? A miserable old man who can't stand seeing anyone else have any fun?"

It all happened so quickly that Brannagh realized later that she wouldn't have been able to do anything to stop it, even if she had wanted to.

One minute Grandfather was shouting, and the next Pamela was swinging one arm back. When the long thin heel of the shoe in her hand hit Grandfather's cheek he didn't even flinch.

"I'm beautiful, that's all that matters, isn't it? For me to be beautiful?"

A thin thread of crimson sprang below Grandfather's earlobe, then widened until a steady stream of blood turned the white collar of his shirt crimson.

For a brief moment no one moved. Then Aunt Thelma grimaced. "Hold still," she muttered as she moved closer to inspect the damage.

"I'm fine." Grandfather winced.

Aunt Thelma grabbed him by the arm. "Better put something on it."

"I didn't mean to …" Pamela looked like a frightened child. "I was just …"

As Aunt Thelma pulled Grandfather down the hall, he sputtered, "You won't ever leave me will you? You're the only one I can depend on. Just a little peace and quiet, is that too much to ask?"

Brannagh stood by the bed, listening to the voices drift down the hall. There was a vague stirring deep in the back of her mind, and she recalled another day, long, long ago, filled with the same strange smell, only it was Aunt Thelma's hand raised in anger, and it was her mother, oh, poor, poor, Pamela, whose face was crumpled. Her father's, Ben's, picture lay on the floor, a crack through the centre of the glass. And then Pamela was throwing a suitcase onto the bed. Or did Brannagh really remember this? Maybe she was just making it up. Maybe she'd gone a little crazy, like the cuckoos on the third floor, from living in this house too long.

The fringes on the white shawl swayed, like baby fronds of seaweed, in the small of Pamela's back. She turned to Brannagh. "Do I look okay?" Her voice shook and something about the way she stood, with her feet turned slightly inward, and the fingers on her breast trembling, made Brannagh's stomach knot.

"Fine, just fine," she managed and hugged her mother tightly.

"Oh honey," Pamela clung to Brannagh, inhaling her hair. She drew back and pulled the tiny flask out of the black bag. Pamela walked over to the window and, sighing, laid her cheek against the frame. After a while, she tossed her head. "I'm not like other mothers. I never will be. So don't waste time wishing it were so." Her eyes, when she turned them on Brannagh, were brilliant black.

Pamela plopped down on the bench in front of the mirror and

brushed her hair fiercely. "Fifty strokes, twice a day, that's the secret, Brannagh, to gorgeous hair."

Brannagh sat on the bed and tried hard to ignore the white shawl. It had slipped off her mother's shoulders and lay in the doorway barely covering the spotted trail of blood.

After that the house was filled with a funereal air. Doors no longer slammed, but closed methodically. There was no pounding of feet on the stairs, only the light tip-tap of heels, and polite knocks on bathroom doors. Pamela and Art headed off to the tavern to "bolster their spirits" for the reunion. Aunt Thelma gathered her things into a bundle to be carried to Kate's. "I can't do this any more," she kept repeating, eyes bright. She gave Brannagh a quarter to buy pop and potato chips at Sanderson's Store. "I'm sorry," she said, and they both knew she was talking about more than just the fact that Brannagh would be alone with two patients from the Nervous Clinic, Allen and Mrs. Simon. Gran was tending the corner store for Mrs. Sanderson, who was down with influenza. Grandfather had been called to the Provincial Asylum for an emergency.

But Brannagh wasn't worried. She put three bowls of potato chips and three glasses of orange soda on the coffee table. She turned on the radio. Lorne Greene was reading the news. They settled down and listened to Jack Benny and Fred Allen.

Allen fell asleep. Mrs. Simon didn't say one word through the entire broadcast, but each time she ate a potato chip she methodically licked her fingers and dried them with a tissue. When a musical program began, a band broadcasting live from the Palais Royale in Toronto, and a woman sang "Que Sera, Sera," Mrs. Simon hummed off key. Brannagh hid a smile. By the end of the program there was a pile of balled tissue beside Mrs. Simon the size of a snowdrift. The chip bowl was empty.

Allen looked so peaceful with his head tilted back on the arm of the couch, and one arm thrust back over his head, that Brannagh hated the thought of waking him. On closer inspection she noticed that his face was abnormally flushed. Under her touch, he stiffened and turned his head to the right, stretching his neck to its fullest length. A slight froth of saliva formed on his lips. Then his arms and legs began to jerk rhythmically, as if in tune with the slow dull pounding in Brannagh's chest. For a brief moment, Brannagh realized that she was all alone, that there was no one to turn to. Allen rocked against her and she held him and started to shake too. Mrs. Simon sat and stared with a growing horror filling her eyes.

"It's all right," Brannagh's voice trembled. "He's not feeling well. He'll be fine in a minute."

Mrs. Simon jumped up from the chair, walked over to a plant stand, contemplated it briefly, and then toppled it over. She opened the china cabinet and took out a cranberry-coloured platter. She raised it over her head. When the piece of china shattered, she marched to the cupboard and retrieved another one.

"Mrs. Simon," Brannagh begged. "Please sit down. Allen doesn't feel well."

At first Mrs Simon was too busy, too caught up in the magnificence of what she was doing. She threw all the pillows onto the floor, overturned a chair, picked up a magazine, tore its cover in strips and tossed them about like fall leaves in the wind.

"Mrs Simon!"

But it was no use. She couldn't hear Brannagh, or just plain didn't want to. Brannagh, who was forced to sit so still and helpless with Allen in her arms, caught a glimpse of the seductive heady glory Mrs. Simon was experiencing in her act of rebellion. It wasn't until Grandfather came through the door, stopped dead in his tracks and shouted, "Edith!" that Mrs. Simon finally paused. She set down the doily that she had been twirling on one finger, and clasped her hands in front of her.

"It is time to retire. Now!" Grandfather took Allen, who was passive and mute, out of Brannagh's arms, laying his fingers upon his forehead and cheeks. He glared at Brannagh. "What did you do to agitate him?" Brannagh bit her lip, and shook her head.

Grandfather marched up to the third floor with Mrs. Simon trailing behind him. She was humming *que sera, sera*.

Brannagh fell to her knees on the carpet and sobbed with relief.

She was still sweeping up shards of glass when the sky outside the window started to glow pearly pink. There was a rattling of the back door and the sound of Pamela's giggle and Aunt Thelma's groan. Someone turned on the tap to fill the teakettle and the thrum of rattling pipes rose in the walls.

Pamela tiptoed through the swinging door into the parlour. "Holy Doodle!" she said. All the careful touches that she had spent hours perfecting were now skewed. Her right shoulder strap had fallen, the bobby pins in her hair had tumbled round her ears, her belt was crooked. Something about her face was off-kilter too, as if it had been smudged with a thumb.

"Mrs. Simon," Brannagh explained as Pamela glanced around the room.

But her mother didn't seem to care. "What a party," she crowed. Her voice, also, wasn't right. It was lazy, loose, garbled. "Knocked 'em dead. The fuddy duddies."

"Did you dance?" Brannagh put teacups and saucers onto the round tray on the sideboard.

"Never stopped." Pamela extended her arms towards an invisible partner, weaving slightly. "All those gals whose mothers filled the neighbourhood's ears with it for so many years, their husbands lined up at my table."

Brannagh found the sugar bowl, hunted for the creamer. She glanced at the dust bin to see if it had been one of Mrs. Simon's victims.

Pamela plucked errant strands of hair as she stood in front of the mirror. "And the looks on their faces when I walked in with Art. Half their old men have beer bellies and no hair. Only Glenda Outhouse had the guts to ask Art to dance, when I was jitterbugging with someone else, but he told her, 'It wouldn't be gentlemanly of me to leave my sister-in-law and her friend unattended, now would it?' And then, didn't Art get up and dance with Thelma, just to prove a point, and keep winking at Glenda whenever they went past her table."

Brannagh picked up the tray.

Her mother followed her towards the swinging door to the kitchen. "Glenda was one for spreading nasty rumours and …"

Brannagh stood with one foot in the kitchen, one foot in the parlour, hip holding open the swinging door. There was a noise like a bicycle tire makes after running over a nail. Later, when she replayed the scene in her head, she could never be sure if the noise came from her or her mother. It would all become a jumble of images in her head. Her mother's white fingertips pressed against scarlet lips. Her mother's eyes: wide, startled, the pupils growing smaller and smaller. The flick of air that seemed to come from the back of her mother's throat and fall futilely from her mouth.

And Aunt Thelma. Aunt Thelma with her back against the counter, head thrust back, tender, white throat exposed.

Aunt Thelma with her eyes closed and the buttons of her dress loose and hanging.

Aunt Thelma with her dress peeled open to the waist and Art's dark head at her breast.

Aunt Thelma with her jaw slack, and no words coming out of

her mouth. Just a sigh. The expiration of something dark and deep within her.

There was a look in Aunt Thelma's eyes when she first opened them, before the reality of Brannagh's and Pamela's presence hit, a look that Brannagh was unable to define, but she knew it was meant to cut Pamela like a knife. It was a look that for years set off a reverberation of familiar dark faint echoes within her.

It was a look of pure triumph, of raw gloating that Brannagh finally acknowledged long after she had left home. It was a look that would haunt her forever.

Brannagh clambered down the cottage steps and paused to stare at the bush that separated Gran's cottage from the cottage with the red roof.

How could you Annie? How could you?

The torch flickered. Brannagh gave it a shake. She strode down the road toward the lighted highway. What right did Annie have to interfere with her life? What right did any of them have? She was going to make them leave, and once they were gone she would pack up her bags and head back to Northern Ontario. Screw the reunion!

What Annie didn't understand was that Brannagh had tried as hard as she could to forget what happened the night of the graduation party, the summer that her mother had come home. But the scenes refused to stop playing over and over in her head, each as vivid and painful as if it had happened only hours before.

Aunt Thelma had slipped off the kitchen counter, calmly pulling the front of her dress up. Pamela turned and fled out the back door of the kitchen, fingers pressed to her lips, looking as if she were going to be ill.

"Shit!" Art swore before he punched the wall. "Goddammned shitless shit!"

Brannagh set the tea tray carefully onto the kitchen table and followed her mother on foot. When Pamela abandoned her high heels, tossing them into a culvert, and marched down the sidewalk towards Simms Corner at an incredible clip, Brannagh ran back to the house to get her bicycle.

By the time Brannagh caught up with her again, Pamela was standing at Simm's Corner, tapping one foot, waiting for cars to pass. Mill workers, bleary eyed and whiskery, headed to the early shift. Pamela marched across the street and then, in front of the Simm's building, unzipped the back of her skirt, hopped out of it and threw it on the lawn. Brannagh heard the squeal of brakes. A beady-eyed man rolled down his car window and shouted, "How much do you charge?"

The crinoline followed the skirt.

Brannagh pedaled, faster, faster, her heart thumping wildly against her chest.

Pamela marched past the Simm's building. Hopping on one foot, she pulled off one silk stocking then plucked at the other one, which seemed to stubbornly stick to her garters, but she was determined. Pamela twisted and yanked until finally it snapped loose. The expensive hosiery, hand-picked by Art because of the perfect seams, flew behind her shoulder, two airy beige banners. They fell to the ground and rolled down the sidewalk and became snagged in a rose bush.

Pamela tugged at her half slip.

Brannagh was acutely aware of everything happening at the moment that it was happening; the fact that her mother was heading to the Reversing Falls Bridge in her underwear, that people were staring, coming to stand outside in their housecoats.

Nut house whore!

Brannagh caught up with her mother just as they came to the bridge, but she had to wait for the long line of cars to stop before she crossed the street. She could see the mill over the green railing, the tall stacks chugging great plumes of white smoke. Above the idling motors and the honking and the voices rose the sound of the water, the unrelenting, determined wildness and impatience of it. The rapids spurted foam into the air as water whirled first one way then the other, currents mingling, fighting, relenting and giving way to the brutality of the tides.

In the middle of Reversing Falls Bridge, Pamela wriggled out of her girdle. She paused for a moment with one hand on the green railing. She turned, squinted at the cars lined up behind her, turned back then let it drop.

The girdle whirled round and round, a giant pale bat sailing on the wind.

For a moment it looked as if it might land on one of the outcroppings of rock jutting from shore, but a gust of wind lifted it gently and bore it further aloft.

Then came laughter and grumblings and the sound of engines starting.

"Crazy bitch!" someone hollered.

Brannagh hung over the rail, watching the girdle. It floated on the surface, then grew fainter, fainter, yellow, brown, grey, and disappeared beneath the cold black water.

"Brannagh! Brannagh!" Her mother called her, holding her shaking hands to her white pinched face. "Bring me your sweater.

That's what I think of his fancy clothes. Art can dive in after it for all I care. Come help me. Please."

Brannagh's stepped back from the rail. She got onto her bike. She pedaled furiously.

Away from her mother.

"No! Please, don't go!"

As fast as she could.

※ ※

Brannagh rounded the bend in the road that approached the highway. A man hunched over the cottage mailbox. Brannagh froze. The man straightened abruptly. He was large-nosed, ugly. His clumsy hands rose to mid-chest. "Och, you gave me a fright."

"Mrs. McGillvery?" Brannagh approached her.

She straightened, tucked the mail under one arm and brushed at her pants.

Brannagh hugged her. "I'd recognize you anywhere."

She handed Brannagh the mail. "The red flag was up, thought I'd leave it on your porch." She dug into the pocket of her jacket and pulled out a beeper. "I couldn't sleep. Annie forgot this on her desk. She'll need it, in case of an emergency."

Brannagh started to explain that Annie would be leaving soon but stopped herself. "She's probably been fretting about it without saying a word."

Mrs. McGillvery nodded stiffly.

"C'mon back to the cottage. I'll make you a cup of tea. We made you an honorary member of the Tuatha-de-Dannans after all."

Mrs. McGillvery shook her head. "I should turn in."

Brannagh hugged her again.

"Brannagh." There was something in Mrs. McGillvery's voice

that caught her attention. "If a friend of yours wanted to help you, but lied, or withheld information—with the best intentions of course—"

Brannagh nodded encouragingly, but a cold puddle formed in the pit of her stomach.

"Would you be able to forgive her?"

Mrs. McGillvery's question hung in the air between them.

"I ..." Brannagh scuffed at the dirt with her toe. "You mean Annie, right? About tonight?"

But Mrs. McGillvery stared thoughtfully into the distance, mouth pressed into a thin line. When she finally glanced up at Brannagh, her eyes held a message that took a moment to decipher.

Pity. Pity first.

Then, a frisson so minute it was barely visible. Fear.

Panicked, guilt-ridden fear.

"Uh, look, they'll be worried. I better head back." Brannagh smiled weakly before turning on her heel.

Mrs. McGillvery turned toward the brown Volvo parked at the side of the road. "Your Grandfather sends his love," she called out.

Like hell he does. Brannagh blanched inwardly. *Can't these busybodies mind their own bloody business!*

"Don't ..."

But Brannagh couldn't make out the rest of the words as she ran down the road.

This is how it happened.

He sat for hours in the chair. His mind drifted. He was enthralled with long-forgotten scenes, lucid images that had been locked in a trunk in his mind. He ached with the knowledge that he had once been filled with a sheer, airy, fearless joy, the sort of unfathomable, radiant energy that emanates from trees and flowers after a much needed summer rain, and that flourishes in a newborn's soul. And he grieved this, the knowledge that he had forgotten. When he had stomped down the pain, he had unwittingly trampled the joy.

When Nikki's mother got so sick that she could not keep scrambled eggs down, a lady came to visit their house in Toronto. At first Nikki wouldn't let her in the door, but she sat on the front steps and acted like she was never going to leave. She told him that she was a caseworker. Mrs. Wiggins. She was going to help him and his sister, Marina, find a new place to live while his mother went to a special clinic. Nikki didn't want help. The lady said she would take Nikki and Marina on a trip and they would eat hot dogs. Nikki relented.

But Nikki did not really understand.

When he and Marina got off the train in a town by a huge lake, a young couple was waiting at the station. They said their names were Peter and Nan. The town was called Nipigon. Peter worked at a fish hatchery and he liked to eat beans out of a can. Nan made delicate glass animals that hung in people's windows. Five days after their arrival, Nan called Mrs. Wiggins. "We aren't ready for this. We thought we were, but we aren't. We'll keep the girl. But not the boy. If he was younger, maybe."

Nikki panicked. He couldn't leave Marina all alone. He took a butcher knife from the kitchen drawer. "We're leaving, and if you call anyone, I'll hurt Marina." Nan slumped, white-faced, into a chair. Marina protested. She liked the wallpaper with farm animals. Nikki had to cover her mouth and drag her out of the house kicking at two in the morning. When the sun peeped over the hills, Marina finally stopped crying. She complained she was hungry. She peed her pants. Nikki had not thought to bring any food.

Nikki thought if he followed the train tracks, they wouldn't get lost in the bush. He promised Marina that he would buy her a roll of Lifesavers when they got to the next town. They came to a wooden bridge, high over a river. Marina refused to walk across. He got down on his hands and knees and told her to ride piggyback. He sang one of her favourite songs about a monkey who ate too many bananas. Marina tickled Nikki, the same way she did when they played the game on the hill behind their house. Nikki squirmed and cursed. "Stop it! I'm serious. Stop it right now!" Marina giggled. "Bad Horse!" She pulled his ears. He tried not to buck like he usually did when they played the game, forcing Marina to go tumbling off, rolling down the hill. He tried not to buck. He didn't buck. Did he? One moment Nikki could feel Marina's knees pinching his rib cage, the next her weight was sliding off his back. He reached behind him, fingers scrabbling in the night air. He heard a small mewling protest. Nikki yelled, "Wait!" And far, far away, down below, there rose a sploosh of water.

Nikki scrambled down the riverbank and dived in. "Marina! Marina!" For hours he flailed about, screeching her name. When the policeman found Nikki the next morning, lying exhausted in the ditch, he kicked him.

"Where's your sister?"

Nikki told him.

"Where is she? Where's the knife?" he persisted. "I'll make sure you're locked up for the rest of your life." And then a tall man with soft eyes and a bald head came over the hill. He picked up Nikki and asked him if he needed water to drink.

"My name is Detective Arto Pietila," he said.

While Nikki awaited a court hearing in Kenora, he wanted to die. He hoped the judge would sentence him to hanging, or the electric chair. Every day Detective Pietila visited and listened to Nikki's stories of summers spent in the Laurentians at his parents' hotel. Nikki told him how his mom and dad had met there. His mother's mother had worked in the laundry. His father's family disapproved, disowned Nikki's father when he married, and refused to let his name cross their lips; but Nikki's father adored his mother, and didn't care in the least. Detective Pietila always said, "I believe you kid. I won't let you down. You'll see. You and I will go to that hotel some day and eat their homemade strawberry ice-cream." The day before the first court hearing Marina's body was found. Mrs. Wiggins brought Nikki to a brown car and she drove onto a dusty dirt road. They arrived at a building called a "residential school." Nikki took one look around the classroom, at the blank dark eyes of the other students, students with skin in various shades of brown, and straight black shiny hair, and knew he had joined the land of the living dead.

Nikki dozed and when the sun lightened in the sky, he climbed up onto the back of his chair, opening the blind on the window above it. He braced his hands on the sill and studied all that filled the square of glass: the rose-tinted sky, a blooming thistle, an intricate glistening spider's web.

And that was when he knew it was over. The time had come to leave.

Chapter Seven

On Sunday the cottage was quiet. Too quiet. Brannagh packed her suitcases then sat alone, drinking tea, ruminating over the events of the past few days.

When Brannagh had returned to the cottage on Friday night, after running into Mrs. McGillvery, she laid down the law.

"I can't do this right now." Brannagh avoided looking at any of them. "I need some space. I want you all gone in the morning."

No one breathed a word. Brannagh went up to her room, locked the door and quietly, methodically packed.

Long after midnight, Brannagh lurched upright, heart pounding, blinking into the darkness. She had dreamed of being trapped in the cellar, could smell the thick fusty air, hear the groans and creaks.

Brannagh tip-toed down the cottage stairs. In the parlour, she paused, discerning a profile in the shadows beside the window.

"Annie?" She moved closer.

Annie stood so still she appeared not to be breathing. "I'm sorry. I really am."

Brannagh paused and pressed her palm against the window pane. It was cool under her fingers. "You're right," she said softly. It was always Annie who had come to the cellar to set her free. Annie who brazenly snuck the key right out of Grandfather's suitcoat pocket; Annie who was never afraid to defy him. "You're right. I should go back." Brannagh exhaled slowly. "But I won't."

Annie's distant expression didn't change. "I'm not who you think I am." Her voice was thick.

Brannagh said nothing. Annie laid her hand flat on the windowpane next to Brannagh's. "I'm a fraud." Annie's baby finger trembled. She laid her cheek against the window. "If anyone needs saving right now, it's probably me."

Brannagh stared at the blurring moon as the windowpane misted. "It rained."

Annie cleared her throat. "Why did my stepmother hate me so much?"

Brannagh reached out a finger to stem the trickle dripping from Annie's chin down the glass.

"The day my brother went missing, it rained." Annie gave her head a shake and the ends of her hair, wet from the tears, lashed her cheeks. "I woke up, lying by the side of the road. Feeling wetness all down my front and then seeing it … the blood. Why couldn't I remember what happened, Brannagh, why?"

Wilfred Adamson, Annie's young student intern, arrived Saturday morning to pick her up. He looked like he'd grown up on a backyard rink. He was tall and muscular with a ruddy glow and wind-blown, dark good looks.

"I'm so glad to meet you finally," he said, energetically shaking Brannagh's hand. "I've heard so much about you."

He held the car door open for Annie and laid one hand on the small of her back, and the last thing Brannagh saw was Annie's shrug as she shook it off.

On Sunday morning, once Brannagh's bags were packed and she was ready to leave, she took one last walk through the cottage. She dug through the fridge and threw away all leftovers beyond redemption. She noticed a kitchen drawer that wouldn't close. She tossed out a warped egg beater and an antique cheese shredder. Brannagh reached back with her fingers and felt a wad of paper jarred in the catch. It was the mail Mrs. McGillvery had retrieved from the box Friday night. Brannagh had tossed it aside and forgotten all about it.

Brannagh pulled out the rumpled wad of paper and sorted through it. There was a letter from Max, her boss up north, telling her to give him a ring as he had misplaced the files on the Norwegian studies. There was a post card from Glen, the ornithology student. *The Rockies are unreal. Snow in July. Rachel, a masseuse at the Banff Springs Hotel, is taking me hiking.* There was a thin white envelope, unmarked. Brannagh ripped it open.

Inside was a piece of red and blue lined paper, torn out of an old school scribbler, the kind the nuns used to keep under lock and key at Saint Patrick's. Brannagh slowly unfolded the page. Only two sentences had been typed on it.

Don't worry about Nikki. He's being tended to.

And then in the bottom corner, as if an afterthought: In the spirit of the pledge of Tuatha-de-Dananns.

Brannagh awoke shivering in the darkness of the tent with a pain in her side. She had been lying on top of a tree root. She rolled down the flap on the window and tied it shut. The temperature always dropped at night in the northern clime, but tonight it was exceptionally frigid. Brannagh felt around in the dark for the sleeping bag and wormed a pair of long underwear out of the bottom. As she pulled them on, she heard the pitty-pat of raindrops spattering across the canvas. Soon the tempo increased.

Brannagh started when a clap of thunder sounded. The roof of the tent dipped and billowed.

She heard a shout in the distance.

Lightning flashed, illuminating the tent's interior for a few brief seconds.

"Brannagh?"

She hunched forward.

"You awake?"

"Nikki?" She started to breathe again.

"You in there?" he asked hoarsely.

Brannagh got down on her hands and knees and crawled to the door. She opened the zipper just enough to poke her head through. "Where else would I be?" Cold drops splattered her face and she pulled back, holding the tent flaps up for protection.

Rain dripped off the brim of Nikki's canvas hat and ran in streams off his vest. She could not see his eyes, only the curve of his mouth and the blackness of his beard. He was crouched low to the ground.

"Just checking to see if it was you."

"Me?"

"There's a canoe missing. Someone's gone out for a midnight paddle, got themselves caught in this mess." He glanced over his shoulder, then back at her. "Do you have a torch?"

Brannagh groped backwards for her boots. "Just give me a sec and I'll—"

"No." Nikki's head shot up. "Stay here. There's no point."

"But I can help."

"Please." Nikki laid one wet hand on her cheek.

Brannagh watched a rivulet of rain roll down the crease in his cheek and drop off his chin. She nodded reluctantly and watched him melt into the night.

The day Brannagh's mother threw her clothes off Reversing Falls

Bridge stood like a sentinel in her memory. It marked the end of an innocent belief that there was still hope, that there was something redeeming within her, like the answer to a question, the solution to a mystery, that would make all the longing, and confusion, and alienation fall by the wayside.

Brannagh had left her mother on the bridge and cycled up to Fort Howe, as if she didn't know the woman standing in her underwear for everyone to see. When she returned to the house on Argyle, it was silent and empty, the car was gone. By suppertime, Aunt Thelma and Gran had returned, but Pamela and Art had disappeared.

"Where—?" Brannagh began.

"Eat your supper," Aunt Thelma ordered.

The next morning Tish's father, the mayor, knocked on the door. His face was pale and he would not look Brannagh in the eye, but brushed past her and grabbed Grandfather by the elbow.

"The cufflink thief. He's struck again," he announced in a gruff undertone, steering Grandfather toward the study.

"Thief? Nothing's been stolen." Grandfather's eyes narrowed.

They disappeared behind the closed door. By the time they emerged, Mrs. Cunningham had already burst through the kitchen and broken the news in her blunt, cruel way, the necessity of being the first to announce ill tidings overriding any trace of common decency. Pamela had been murdered. Just like the young lad all those years ago. They had found her body in the same spot in the woods, posed in the same macabre fashion.

Then Andy Barton, the policeman, arrived white-lipped and trembling, looking for the mayor. Nobody spoke. Gran took Brannagh by the hand, and led Andy Barton to the study. Once again the door opened then slammed shut, and the women sat outside waiting.

"I can't believe it." Gran buried her face in her hands.

Tish's father tried every trick he could think of to force Gran and Brannagh to stay at home. Finally he swore under his breath, clamped his hat onto his head and ordered Andy Barton to drive them all up river. "Against my better judgement."

When they crossed the Reversing Falls Bridge, Brannagh pulled her sweater up over her ears and welcomed the distraction of Gran's bony fingers grasping her arm tighter and tighter; but already the guilt over abandoning her mother was building; already there was a premonition that the haunting would last forever.

Brannagh had been away from home so long she was no longer accustomed to the fickle temperament of fog. When the car entered the hilly outskirts of Saint John the temperature dropped and beads of moisture formed on the windshield. In the distance it looked as if a dense ashen curtain had been lowered from invisible pulleys in the sky. The car descended an incline and the bank of grey loomed ahead, appearing as solid and impenetrable as a cement wall. But the car slipped through like a ghostly spectre.

Brannagh drove slowly, chewing her lip, hunting for the correct exit number. The old landmarks were burned into her memory: the gold brick General Hospital on the hill, the craggy cliffs of Fort Howe, the Harbour Bridge arcing over the decks of barges and trawlers. This was a land fierce in its determination to survive: the rush of the tides flogging the mainland, the corrosive brine, the raging gales capable of washing a road clean into the sea.

Brannagh's first view of the city was blurred. There were great blank stretches of nothingness, then in an instant the curtain of fog parted to reveal a glimpse of the past: cracker box houses (either as drab as an undertaker's coat or as flamboyant as a clown's tie) upended in rows, creating the illusion that they were growing out of the craggy cliffs, followed by waves of low-lying scrub, a scraggly tree or two, then a large old-fashioned manor, dating back to the heyday of wooden ship building, with its fancy hipped roof and gingerbread trim.

Brannagh drove across the bridge over Reversing Falls, ignoring the dark froth churning below. On the left was the Provincial Asylum, a tall maroon-brick building that resembled the setting of a Gothic novel. Brannagh fully expected to see a man dressed in a black topcoat and cape running down one of the winding paths along the cliff adjacent to it, a pack of sleek dark hounds frothing at his heels.

Brannagh turned down a wide street, shaded with enormous birch and oak. She passed a fire hydrant and a corner store. She stopped in front of a three-story Victorian-style old English cottage with Tudor flower-trimmed eaves, and tall, crooked chimneys. On the roof was a weathered cock turning in the Fundy breeze.

In the middle of that cold unforgettable northern Ontario night, Brannagh leaned over the fire, cupping her hands around the nest of twigs. She blew gently upon it, and then stared intently at the spiral of rising smoke.

"C'mon." *Shit. Shit, shit.*

She wanted to see a spark, just one fragile twig bursting into flames. The smoke coiled into the damp and dissipated.

Rain drummed on the canvas overhead. Brannagh straightened and tucked her numb fingers into her armpits. She stepped out of the camp kitchen shelter and stared through the downpour toward the open water. She could barely make out any of her surroundings, but still she continued peering over the water every ten minutes. Nikki and Alex have been gone for over two hours. She had been trying her damnedest to get a fire going. Brannagh could practically wring out the wood that Tom had gathered yesterday.

Brannagh caught a flicker of something on the horizon. She squinted. A glimpse of yellow in the darkness? A cape? She heard a shout.

"Hey!"

"Over here!" She waved the lantern back and forth. As the canoe drew closer to shore, she made out Alex sitting in front and Nikki in the rear. Nikki jumped into the water and Alex followed suit. The canoe made a slow grinding upon the rocks as they pulled it to shore. Brannagh stared at the hunched form braced in the middle. Tom? Using the fisherman's hold, Alex and Nikki hoisted him upward.

Brannagh hurried toward them, holding the lantern high. "Where's—?" Brannagh hesitated as Alex's hood fell back and his eyes flashed a warning. She glanced toward Nikki, but saw only his mouth set in a grim line below the brim of his hat.

The men scuttled up the incline, and she scrambled after them. They dropped to their knees outside Tom's tent and clumsily eased him inside.

"First aid kit!" Nikki ordered. Alex ran. As Brannagh fumbled in the dark, he barked further instructions to peel off Tom's clothes, pile on sleeping bags, check his airway, keep him talking. As she spoonfed him sugar water, he mumbled. "I'm good, I'm good, gotta find Cindy."

After Alex had restrained Tom, Brannagh woke up Gordon. "Hey, hey. Wake up, you asshole! Alex needs you."

She crawled out in time to see Nikki heading down towards the canoe.

"Wait! I'll come with you."

Nikki shook her off. "Keep the fire going." He tore a tarp off the beached canoes and threw it into the bottom of the one he and Alex had pulled to shore.

Brannagh unconsciously wrung her hands.

Nikki waded into the water and climbed aboard. Brannagh pushed the canoe away from shore then stood and watched the upside-down triangle of its retreating back end grow smaller and smaller still.

※ ※

Nobody talked about it the rest of the summer of '54. Nobody in the house on Argyle ever mentioned Pamela's murder.

Outside the house, Brannagh discovered, it was another matter entirely. That summer, the nature of the neighbourhood gossip changed. Any hesitancy or shame the kinder souls felt over the airing of another's private affairs in public vanished. Nobody bothered to whisper anymore. Talk wasn't reserved solely for the aisles of Sanderson's store. Tongues flapped faster than shutters in a hurricane. And then someone found a dead cat in the empty lot at the end of the street; and then another and another. Dozens of carcasses deep in the undergrowth, stiff with rigor mortis as if they'd been posed and stuffed for a museum. The newspaper said they'd been poisoned. The police were investigating. Kids avoided the field. Instead they roosted on the sidewalks where it was impossible for Brannagh to ignore them.

Kids playing marbles or hopscotch wouldn't look up when Brannagh walked down the street, but they would sing:

Lady on the bridge
She don't care
Let everybody see
Her underwear.

Lady on the bridge
Underwear is red
Cut out your eyes.
And make you dead.

None of the family living in the house on Argyle talked about it, but it was there, haunting them nevertheless.

Grandfather simply upped the number of clients in the Nervous Clinic and was even more short-tempered than usual when it came to interruptions. In one fit of rage he not only locked Brannagh in the cellar, but also took away her pencils and sketchpads and threw them into the garden compost. Mrs. McGillvery would stop for a brief moment to prop her tired feet on a stool and complain, "Och, he'll be sorry when they cart me off to the emergency ward." Aunt Thelma complained, but her objections were half-hearted. She seemed to embrace his curses, welcome them even; taking over all the work in the clinic, holing up with grandfather in the old nursery for days. She became dedicated to wearing brown: brown shoes, brown skirt, brown blouse, brown sweater. The only hint of brightness was the star necklace around her neck. It was as if she longed to be miserable. Brannagh stopped doing her homework in the kitchen, stopped seeking Aunt Thelma out when she had a problem to solve.

Gran sat in the parlour in the rocking chair, crocheting, which was something she would normally never do during the day in the summer. Whenever she was almost finished a square she frowned, muttered and, quick as a blink, she unraveled the whole thing and started again from scratch. The gardens outside sprouted dandelions and thistles. Once when Brannagh was sitting in the oak tree, she gazed into the parlour through the window and for a heart-wrenching moment thought her Gran was just another one of the patient's next to the radio.

Only Annie, who still stayed at the Nervous Clinic, seemed immune to it all. That summer Annie had been transformed, growing tall and thin and curvy, all at the same time. She started dressing up and rinsing her hair with squeezed lemons, like Aunt Thelma did, to make it shine. She secretly got a job waitressing at a restaurant in an abandoned trolley car on Union Street for the longshoremen. The tips were great, she claimed, and the customers entertaining, "specially Eddie Tippet." She had a way of tilting her head now and smiling and lowering her eyes that enthralled Brannagh and terrified her at the same time. Annie said she was saving her tip money, because she was going to run away before school started, run away to Halifax.

"Have you ever been kissed?" Annie asked matter-of-factly one day. She was sitting on her bed, heating mascara in a candle flame.

Brannagh grimaced.

"You gotta practise." Annie tilted her head to one side and approached her own lips in the full-length mirror on the back of the door. "C'mere."

Brannagh stood dutifully. She peered at her reflection, so skinny and flat next to Annie. She smirked.

Annie elbowed her in the ribs. "This is serious. Okay, approach your lips, that's it, slowly, slowly, tilt your head, no, not that much, part your lips, nah, now you look like someone just ran over your foot, okay, open your mouth just enough to slip a quarter in, yeah,

yeah, yeah."

By then the mirror was so steamed up Brannagh couldn't see a thing, and she dropped to the floor sniggering, hands cupped over her lips.

Thank God for Annie and her newest experiment, or the neighbours' predictions would have come true. Brannagh would have gone stark raving mad that summer.

Of course it had to come to an end sooner or later.

One night a patient had an attack of tonsillitis. Grandfather was in the kitchen after midnight stirring sugar into a hot lemon drink when Annie snuck through the back door.

Brannagh awoke to the sound of Annie's sobs and feet pounding up the stairs. Brannagh opened her bedroom door a crack. She saw Annie running down the hall, then sprawling as her ankle twisted. She got to her feet, just as Grandfather swung around the corner. He was muttering, "Running away to Halifax, of all the idiotic ..." He caught up with her and shook her by the shoulders. "Is this your way of teaching your stepmother a lesson? By whoring around? She'd love to get rid of you, eliminate the competition. You're proving you're every bit the numbskull she always claimed you were."

Annie ran up the stairs.

Grandfather turned to Brannagh and thundered, "As for you, you will never leave this house without my permission. Do you understand?"

"That's what you think. As soon as I turn eighteen, I'm escaping. And I'm never coming back!"

Brannagh closed her door and flung herself onto the bed.

"You will never leave this house without my permission," Grandfather yelled through the door.

Says who? You gonna nail an anchor to my butt?

That summer Annie went back to live with her family full-time. She burned the waitress uniforms and spent all her spare time holed up in her father's medical library. Brannagh didn't think it was possible to miss someone so much.

※ ※

The old-fashioned mortise lock with its porcelain mountings was still on the front door of the house on Argyle; the key was still on top of the frame.

Thank God, Brannagh thought, the old fart was spending the summer up in Fredericton teaching at St. Thomas University. She could have it out with Annie without having to deal with him.

Brannagh entered the front hall, which had once appeared so imposing with its lofty walls and spacious ceiling. Now the embossed wallpaper and worn dado seemed to yawn vacantly. She pulled a switch on the wall. The light fixture hanging from the centre of the velum ceiling glowed dimly.

Brannagh climbed the great staircase to the second floor, running one hand along each mahogany newel and the cherry rail above. Eddies of dust rose in the air. The dark wood still gave off the faint sweet, mellow scent of Gran's polishing wax, as familiar and timeworn as rich tobacco.

At the top of the staircase, Brannagh gazed down the hallway to the tall windows at either end of the second floor. Gran's bedroom was above the front entrance with a gabled window and widow's walk. Brannagh's was down at the end of the hall. She entered it and flicked on the light. The room had a large dormer window with a bright blue sash and a deep sill upon which Brannagh had spent many hours doing homework and daydreaming. The bookshelves were empty, as were the dresser drawers and closet. Brannagh had taken everything with her when she left for university.

"I'm never coming back here, ever again," she had told Grandfather coldy and calmly before boarding the train. During Brannagh's last year of high school, Aunt Thelma had started forgetting people's names, sleeping all day or staring out the window making strange grimaces. Out of the blue, she had moved in with Kate, and Brannagh had lost the one person she felt she could depend on to protect her. The fights with Grandfather had escalated.

"One less problem for me. Good riddance!" Grandfather had shouted as the train pulled out of the station.

Brannagh pulled back the quilt on the old brass bed. The sheets were clean. She ran her hand over the highboy. It had been dusted. Brannagh kicked off her shoes, crawled into the bed and pulled the quilt up to her chin.

Don't worry about Nikki. He's being tended to.

Brannagh pulled the quilt over her head. She would confront Annie, no holds barred, in the morning.

"What about Tom?" Brannagh pushed back her hood and swiped her face with her sleeve.

Alex bounced on the balls of his feet in front of the fire. "He's stopped shaking. The codeine pills helped. Do you think, will he …?"

Brannagh ignored him. She had become frantic about the progress of the fire. When it sizzled and dwindled, she crawled into the brush on her hands and knees, rooting underneath scrub for dry twigs. She threw a handful onto the smouldering pile, dribbled on fuel from the camp stove, and dropped on a match. She and Alex watched the poof of rising flame, hypnotized, and momentarily distracted. As of yet, Gordon had not emerged from his tent.

"Of all the asshole stunts." Alex spun and paced. "If they hadn't drunk the rum they might have realized the storm was coming."

Brannagh peered at the sky. Slushy crystals now mixed with the rain. She handed Alex a cup of lukewarm tea.

"Snow?" He grimaced.

Brannagh shrugged.

There was a pale line of lemony light, thin as a slice of paper, on the horizon when Brannagh first spotted Nikki's canoe. Initially, she believed he had been unsuccessful, that it was the cold that made him sit so rigidly and gave his face (he was hatless) its stunned, washed-out blur. But then he drunkenly staggered out and pulled the canoe to shore. He bent down to pick up the tarp, now as thick as the trunk of a tree. Alex fell to his knees and Brannagh took a step back, crooking one elbow and raising it to shield her eyes.

But she could not block out the march. Nikki's slow lurch up the ridge, his arms outstretched, the lower half of his body bent, seeming to move in discordant rhythm to the stiff top half, while the tarp with its heavy weight within seemed to throw his balance off-centre and keep him from ever cresting the ridge. He seemed to struggle without gaining any ground and became a surreal cinematic image, moving yet frozen forever on the black and barren ridge.

On the last day of grade eight, Sister Mary Margaret marched into the classroom. The pupils could tell by the way she snapped open the shades on the windows that something of immense importance was about to be imparted. She tapped the yardstick on Brannagh's desk for silence.

"Boys and girls," she announced primly. "For the first time ever, the school will be holding a graduating dance for the grade eights in the gymnasium, but because they are putting in new lights, we will not be holding the dance until the middle of July." This was an experiment, she stressed, something they had never done before. If it worked out well, they would start holding it every year. Therefore this class, the class of '54, had an obligation, a responsibility to do it right.

After Pamela was murdered, Brannagh forgot about the dance. But when July rolled around, and the mayor announced the case had hit a dead end, her friends would not let her come up with an excuse not to go. For ten nights straight, Brannagh, Dianne, Annie, and Tish practised dancing to a "How to Waltz, Cha-Cha and Tango in 10 easy lessons" record that they had borrowed from the library. Dianne squirmed because her Mom had found a black bengaline skirt and organza blouse that she was making over and actually expected Dianne to wear. Annie said she couldn't care less what she wore, but was eager to partake in a ritual that would mark the passing of another milestone that would bring her one step closer to her newest goal: medical school. Tish was reading *The Teenage Manual* by Edith Heal and kept giving them pointers on how to get a boyfriend: Never fuss, never frown, never fret.

"Never fart, " Annie put in, letting a loud one rip. They erupted in hysterics. Tish threw the book at her.

Aunt Thelma found a mauve cocktail dress in Gran's closet with a sweetheart neckline trimmed with beads and sequins. She pulled it over Brannagh's head and tacked the sides with a row of safety pins. Brannagh twirled in front of the mirror.

Aunt Thelma hugged Brannagh. "Something's missing."

Brannagh felt the cool pendant slide across her throat, before she saw the glint of gold. Her hand flew to the star pendant around her neck. "Oh ..." She was speechless.

"Might as well go all out." Aunt Thelma gulped and scolded when Brannagh crashed into her with a hug, but there were unmistakable tears in her eyes.

When Brannagh walked into the gym, she felt airborne and dizzy. It was transformed. Decorations and streamers hung from the ceiling. The band on the stage was decked in shiny black tuxedos. The hanging glass ball sent swirls of light drifting like snowflakes onto the polished wooden floor. An air of expectation and limitless possibilities glowed from the shiny eyes and flushed cheeks of her classmates.

Brannagh found Dianne, Tish and Annie sitting on steel chairs against the far wall, surreptitiously studying the boys who were lined up opposite. The boys made burping sounds with their armpits. It wasn't until the band's second set, when they opened with "Tennessee Waltz," that Ivan Hilroy strode boldly across the floor and took Mary Pritchard's hand. Then one boy, two, a trickle, a stream suddenly found their way to the girls' side of the room. Soon the dance floor was so crowded and hot that boys tossed off their good Sunday jackets and rolled up their sleeves. Girls kicked off the new shoes that no one had remembered to break in beforehand, wiggled red pinched toes and unfastened the wilted corsages their fathers had bought for them.

To Brannagh's amazement, boys asked her to dance, though after several stumbles and yelps, she realized that not a one was going to dance the way the record had taught. It didn't matter, in the end. When the band broke for their second intermission, she went looking for Annie. She was in the cafeteria when Hilda Outhouse informed her with a sly grin that she'd seen Annie going to the grade eight cloakroom with Eddie Tippet.

As Brannagh walked the length of the school building, the noises of the dance began to fade and she heard only the tap, tap, tap of her shoes on the tiled floor. Mrs. Brickland, the janitor, shuffled past pushing a bucket and a mop. "Well, well, well," she said, giving Brannagh an appreciative once over. "You look grand, m'dear. Just grand."

The classroom was dark. Brannagh entered the cloakroom, groping with one hand for the light switch.

"Annie?" She grasped a coat hook.

Suddenly hands—two, half a dozen, then what felt like a hundred— lunged at her and pushed her down. Fingers groped, pinched and poked. She tried to yell, but a sweaty hand covered her mouth. She heard snickers, muffled taunts, beads ping-ping-pinging. Something in Brannagh snapped. She kicked, bucked, scratched, spat. She broke free and ran out of the cloakroom wild-eyed. Laughter and taunts followed her:

> *Bitch on the bridge*
> *She don't care*
> *Lets the whole world see*
> *A whore's underwear.*

A tall woman, one of the half dozen parents who had volunteered to chaperone, stood wavering at the end of the hall. "What's going on down there?"

"Nothing," Brannagh choked. "Nothing."

Brannagh hid in the girls' washroom until the dance was over. Eventually, Annie drifted in. "Where ya' been?"

"I was looking for you. Hilda said you went to the cloakroom."

"Like I'd give her the time of day." Annie leaned against the wall and slid downward until she squatted with her gown billowed around her waist like a powder puff.

After a while she said, "Shitty dance." She pulled out a cigarette, lit it.

"Yeah." Brannagh scrubbed her nose.

"David Corkum puked all over Wanda Markles' shoes. Mrs. Bank bent over to clean it up and her dress ripped right up the—" Annie paused with the cigarette in mid air. For the first time she really looked at Brannagh. Her eyes took in the torn sleeve, swollen lip, red eyes. "Shit. The cloakroom?"

Brannagh nodded.

Annie stuck the cigarette in her mouth and took a deep puff, staring up at the ceiling. "We're too good for these mush heads." She exhaled and glanced at Brannagh. "We gotta start our own club, that's what we gotta do. Band together, protect ourselves from these low lifes."

Brannagh took the cigarette from her. Her hands shook. Tears smarted, threatened to spill. "Yeah," she said gruffly, and took a deep pull. For once she didn't choke, welcomed the searing burn deep within her chest.

"And we'll have our very own pledge."

Brannagh handed the cigarette to Annie.

"We the members of the Annie-Brannagh Club hereby do solemnly swear to make any jerks, doorknobs, or dweebs who try to mess up any members, feel miserable for the rest of their lives." She glanced at Brannagh, waiting for a reaction.

Brannagh got to her feet, wet some paper towel with cold water and held it to her lip. She met Annie's dark eyes in the mirror then looked away.

"What I'm saying is, " Annie inhaled, then blew smoke rings at the ceiling, "when push comes to shove, bite."

When Brannagh awoke it was dark inside the house on Argyle. She wandered downstairs, flicking on lights, and hunted in the kitchen cupboards for tea. She opened a round silver tin that smelt gross before noticing the tiny skull and crossbones on the label. Rat poison? Aunt Thelma had always complained that mice skittering between the walls at night drove her around the bend. Not that Brannagh had ever heard them, thank God.

Brannagh found the Earl Grey in a soda cracker bin. She carried a steaming cup to Gran's rocker by the window in the parlour and sat and watched the knurled oak tree thrashing in the wind.

She recalled Father Angus once telling Gran that the oak should be cut down because, while it looked lovely, it was a disaster waiting to happen being positioned so close to the house. Why, once he had heard tell of a woman in Hampton who had gone down below and found the entire winter shelf of preserves toppled to the floor, every jar of chokeberry and blackberry jelly smashed. Why? Because the roots of the tree had worked their way right through the foundation of the house, clear down to the cellar. She had the tree cut down, but it made no difference. Every spring a sucker sprang from its stump, and continued to send roots crumbling through the potato cellar.

Brannagh rinsed out her teacup and set it on the drain board. She paused at the top of the wooden stairs that descended to the cellar, then quickly shut the door and headed back up to the second floor.

Brannagh opened her grandmother's bedroom door and flicked on the light. It was furnished with an old-fashioned wardrobe with built-in hand basin, an iron bedstead with ivy scroll work entwining the rails, and the steamer trunk that had functioned in turn as a boat when playing ocean liner, and a coffin when playing funeral with Annie.

Gran's needlepoint of a pale stone cottage on a cliff overlooking the sea hung next to the bed, below a plain gold cross.

Brannagh lay on the bed and tried to fall back asleep. Eventually, she gave up. She opened the trunk. A waft of dry, stale air arose. On top lay Great-Grandmother Brigid's white shawl. Brannagh held it to her face. It smelt of mothballs. She felt something cold against her cheek, then noticed a gold chain entwined in the wool. Carefully, so as not to tear the fringes, Brannagh pulled Aunt Thelma's star necklace free. Glancing back into the trunk, she saw Grandmother Brigid's old letterbox. She found the key taped beneath it and opened the lid. On top lay a copy of Bulfinch's *Greek and Roman Mythology*, but it was different than the one Grandfather had in the library; different from the one Aunt Thelma had read to her and Annie when they both came down with chicken pox. This one had a gold-embossed maroon leather cover and the pages were gilt edged. She opened the book. Inside the cover was an inscription written in black India ink:

> *We are not born of the beautiful, and so we are free of the curse that awaits Narcissus. We are born of the wise, destined for the blessings of Apollo and Athena. May this book and necklace always be a reminder of our love, and how someday we will rule together in our castle with the red roof in our kingdom by the sea.*
> *Love always, Ben.*

A picture drawn beneath his name resembled the star on Aunt Thelma's necklace. Brannagh closed the book. In the bottom of the letterbox was a bundle of letters tied with black ribbon. Brannagh pulled one out, opened the envelope and removed the folded sepia-tinged papers within:

Dear Ben,

I am still waiting for word from you. I know you will return for Brannagh and me, that your leaving the house on Argyle was necessary, a well-acted play, necessary because of how life had turned. We had no choice, had we? No other way of fleeing this horrible house, of being set free from his cold dark clutches. Beloved, know that no matter what he tried to do, he will never separate us. I will always wait for you. Nothing can destroy our destiny. Set free from the curse, the blessing will come to pass.

Brannagh stared at the yellowed paper in her hands, turning it over woodenly. Was this some sort of joke? She re-read the page. It made no sense. She picked up the box and pulled out another envelope. Suddenly, she stiffened. A peculiar noise rose from downstairs, a prolonged creak, a thin wail. Slowly, Brannagh rose to her feet. She caught a glimpse of her face reflected in the mirror: pale, thin-lipped.

Brannagh turned on the hall light. It flickered, as old light fixtures often do at the most inopportune times. The hall was enveloped in darkness. The wailing continued, a mournful pitiful sound. Carefully, heart beating high in her throat, Brannagh descended the stairs.

A faint glow shone beneath the parlour door. She tried to remember if she'd inadvertently left the light on. She heard a pounding in her ears and beneath that the unearthly wail, and something else.

Thump, thump, thump.

Holding her breath, she slowly edged open the parlour door.

His feet were what she saw first, shuffling in the dim light across the wooden floor, then the rest of his long, lean form. His whiskered cheek was pressed against the cushion that he held tightly to his chest.

Grandfather.

His old-fashioned brogues thumped across the floor. The screeching came from the record player; a wailing cornet.

He waltzed gracefully round the room.

Brannagh's first instinct was to sneak back upstairs, grab her things, and scoot out the front door.

Suddenly, Grandfather glanced up and instantly looked as if he'd bitten a lime. "I—" he began. Then his foot caught on the rolled up rug, and he tumbled back over the coffee table.

※ ※

Brannagh awoke to the sound of giant marbles landing on the roof of the tent. Hail? She heard the zzzzzzzz of the zipper being opened on the entrance of the tent. She rose on one elbow. A gust of ragged, wet wind blew in through the door while a dark form crawled through. Her fingers tapped circles around the floor of the tent seeking the torch.

"Nikki?"

No response. After he had carried the tarp and deposited it inside Cindy's tent, he had walked off into the woods. Brannagh and Alex tried to follow him for a while. Eventually, Alex convinced Brannagh it was fruitless and dangerous. They would all get lost. She went back to her tent to change into dry clothes, with the intention of continuing the search on her own, but she huddled into the sleeping bag to warm up for a minute and drifted off.

"Nikki?"

Brannagh inched closer.

He was on his hands and knees, chin in chest.

She grabbed his hand. It was frozen. Bits of white filled his hair and the creases of his clothing. His flannel shirt and khakis were soaked. He was panting as if he couldn't get enough air into his lungs.

"We tried to find you."

His teeth chattered.

Brannagh fumbled with the buttons of his shirt with one hand and groped blindly towards the corner of the tent where she kept a wool blanket.

He kept trying to pull away. "I'm sorry."

She worked as fast as she could, cursing uncooperative buttons, soaked fabric and resistant limbs. Her fingers grew numb and she too began to shake. She rubbed his skin furiously with the towel, then zipped open the down filled sleeping bag.

"I'm sorry, Brannagh."

"Get in," Brannagh ordered through gritted teeth. She pounded her fists on his back when he refused to budge.

"I fucked up."

Brannagh lunged at him with all her might, slamming his torso with her shoulder, as if he were a door and she a human battering ram. He didn't budge. He stared at her then slowly collapsed like a card table with a broken leg. Brannagh rolled him onto the sleeping bag, crawled in beside him and zipped it up, tugging it high over their heads. She swiftly rubbed his back and arms and chest with her hands.

"Fuck." He trembled violently from head to toe. "I killed her. Just like my sister, Marina. I killed Cindy."

"Here." Brannagh handed Grandfather a steaming cup of tea. He was half-sitting, half-lying on the couch with one leg outstretched. A bag of frozen peas rested on his right ankle, and another within arm's reach to lay over the goose egg on his head.

For so many years, Grandfather had lived on in Brannagh's mind, untouched from a child's vulnerable perspective, tall and looming and forbidding. It was startling to have this villainous myth shattered. He had shrunk. Brannagh was astonished by the sallow, scaly skin hanging off his shins and forearms, by the sunken hollow of his chest, the grizzled neck, the way his spine seemed to have started curling in on itself. Only his hair remained timeless; a thick swath of white, standing on end, with eyebrows following suit. His cheeks were blazing.

"You'll have to see a doctor."

"No need."

Brannagh leaned against the doorway. "I thought you were in Fredericton, otherwise I would never have come."

"Had a tussle with the guest lecturer, an illiterate opportunist."

Brannagh picked up the ice pack and poked Grandfather's ankle where it was rapidly swelling. He pulled back involuntarily, sloshing tea on his chest. "Leave me be," he grumbled.

She picked up her cup of tea, popped a lump of sugar into her cheek, and sat in the chair across from him. It occurred to her that this was the first time she had ever seen him in such a helpless state, unable to wield control. She was astounded by the rush of pleasure it brought her.

Brannagh awoke slowly, with a vague sense of disorientation. The air in the tent was stuffy and close. The sun brightened the roof of the tent. "Brannagh?" She recognized Alex's voice, and detected the shadowed outline of his face, pressed against the door panel.

Brannagh tried to sit up but couldn't. The right side of her body was numb. She became aware of Nikki's head, knee, and left arm pinning her down.

"Yeah?"

"I've radioed for a plane to take Tom to the hospital, and uh, the body back." He coughed. "The thing is, I still can't find Nikki. I'm sure he's okay, that it's just the, finding Cindy and all that."

Nikki's eyelash twitched against her collarbone. She tried to lift herself off the cot.

She did not want this. She did not.

"The thing is Brannagh," Alex's voice drifted into the tent, "I don't know if Nikki would want me to go ahead and make these decisions without him."

Brannagh tried to shift Nikki's weight off her right arm. The smell of his skin was damp ferns and crushed yarrow and the evening breeze in the pine boughs.

"He's here, with me," she confessed grimly. "Do whatever needs to be done."

<hr />

Brannagh plopped the bundle of letters that she had found in Great Grandmother Brigid's letterbox onto Grandfather's lap.

"I thought you'd have crossed the border into Quebec by now."

"No such luck."

He had just woken up and bits of yellow crust were embedded in the corner of one eye. He ground it free with a red knuckle.

Brannagh opened the curtains wide, letting in the morning light. He flinched, holding one hand across his eyes.

"Not a moment's peace." He made a sweeping gesture with one hand and knocked the letters to the floor.

Brannagh grabbed him by the scruff of the neck. He looked as shocked by the action as she was. The anger suddenly fell away. He was, she discovered, surprisingly light. She let go of his shirt and he fell back against the cushions. Brannagh took a deep breath. "I'm going to make some toast and tea, and then we shall have our breakfast."

"I'm not hungry."

"Explain these letters." She paused, a lump suddenly swelling in her throat. "Why you drove my father away."

He shot her a black look.

"I'll fry up some eggs and we'll get started." Brannagh headed into the kitchen.

"Sunny side up, but none of that damned runny muck in the middle." His orders followed her through the swinging door. "And don't burn the toast. You always burnt the damn toast."

<hr />

Brannagh and Nikki didn't talk about the night of the hailstorm and the way he had come to her tent. Sometimes she awakened in her sleeping bag and imagined he was still there inside it with her. Once again she felt his icy goose-pimpled skin, and the hot bouquet of hardness at his centre, pressing against her hip. And she denigrated herself, in this time of grief, for the smallness within her that allowed her to be reduced to a preoccupation over whether or not he remembered the way she had clutched his head to her breast when he had cried out in exultation.

Nikki was not a man who parted with secrets. The fact that he had come to her as a drowning man to a life preserver left Brannagh, in turns, feeling blessed and cursed, elated and forlorn, chosen and cheap. She did not want this.

Nikki flew back to town with the body. He returned four days later ashen-faced and haggard. He called everyone to a meeting and talked about the inevitability of tragedies in the bush when people let down their guard and did not follow orders and proper emergency procedures.

"And you, Gordon." Nikki's mouth had tightened. "Frankly I'm deeply disappointed by your refusal to pitch in and help. When the plane leaves tomorrow afternoon, I want you packed up and on it."

Gordon sniffed and dug his chin into his chest as his cheeks flushed a deep crimson. His hands clenched into fists at his sides, as Nikki proceeded to go over the same lecture about safety they had received months ago, word for word.

Eventually, Nikki wound down. The hard furrows lining his face softened. "Tom asked me if we could hold a service of our own." He gazed off at the horizon. "I don't see any harm in it."

At sunrise the following morning they canoed into the middle of the bay. Gordon opened his mouth and in two seconds redeemed himself when his honeyed alto rose and carried the words of *Amazing Grace* across the water.

That night Nikki stood outside Brannagh's tent. "May I come in for a minute?"

"Of course." She put aside her notes, ran her fingers through her hair. She remained seated cross-legged on the sleeping bag as he crawled through the door.

"I wanted to thank you," he said, removing his hat and clutching it in his hands as he squatted beside her.

"Thank me?" Her face grew warm. She glanced away.

"Yes. You ... I must have seemed like a raving idiot, ranting on."

Brannagh shrugged. "It's understandable."

"I don't remember all I said."

"Nothing. Really."

Nikki nodded towards her papers. "How is the work going?"

Brannagh cleared her throat. "Good."

"Well, then." Nikki turned the brim of his hat round and round between his fingers, the way Gran used to flute a pie crust. "I'll leave you to it then."

"Yes."

He made no move to rise.

"The funeral …"

"Yes?"

"It was …"

"Difficult?"

He nodded. "Valova's sister, she trusted Cindy's care to me. She will never forgive me for what happened. Her daughter is gone. She can't accept it."

"No. Who could?"

"No one."

"No."

"I'll let you get back to your letter writing then."

Still, he made no move to leave.

"Brannagh?"

"Yes."

"I …"

"Yes?"

"It was—waking up with you like that—it was …" He squeezed his eyes shut for a moment, thumbs whitening on the hat brim. He inhaled deeply.

But Brannagh had already fallen on her knees to press her hot face into the cool hollow of his neck.

Grandfather lay on the couch.

Brannagh held a photograph in her hands. "I don't understand. What's this got to do with the letters?"

"You asked. I'm telling. This is where I start."

Brannagh stared at the sunny young woman wearing a round fur hat, and a long-waisted jacket over a wool skirt. She stood beside a handsome dark-haired gentleman. The couple posed kissing, beneath a pair of linked hands, held high over their heads in an arch. Gran. Brannagh had seen the man somewhere before. She held the picture closer to the lamp and understanding dawned. She was not as surprised as she should have been. The man skating on the ice with Gran was Raymond. Dianne's father.

"They were engaged to be married. Raymond and Rye. Dianne's mother, Jocelyn? She and I were dating back then."

"But what happened?"

"The Great War. The Empire's needs. That's what happened." Threads of red swam across his eyes. "And nothing was the same after that." He yanked a hanky out of the pocket of his shirt and snorted into it. "Nothing." He turned his face into the pillow.

Brannagh waited. The ticking of the clock grew louder.

"When the fighting ended, I was offered a job at the Provincial Asylum." He coughed and snagged a hunk of phlegm into the hanky. "That was how I found out that Raymond had lost his legs at Vimy Ridge. Mrs. Sanderson told me. I remember standing there, staring at the Black Cat sign hanging on the wall behind her head, and she asked me, 'Are you all right? How tactless of me. I forgot you were mates.'"

"It was a shock."

"Of course it wasn't! How could it be after that? There were so many, a bombardment of deaths, and every one brought back the brutal grotesqueness, the wave of inadequacy, watching life slip right through your fingers, having men's guts and sinew explode before your eyes, their limbs shattered sticks flung high in the air."

Brannagh went to the sideboard, poured a glass of brandy and drank it down.

"So Raymond and Rye would marry. Jocelyn would be the maid of honour. Raymond asked me to be his best man. It was all set for Valentine's Day."

"And?"

He turned to her briefly, then flung his head back. "She eloped with me instead."

※ ※

Annie arrived to take a look at Grandfather's ankle. She came into the kitchen, eyebrows raised. "When Mrs. McGillvery gave me your message, I thought I was hearing things. I mean, you ordered us to leave the cottage because you were so insulted that I would even suggest you come back to Saint John, and now—"

"It's a long story," Brannagh snapped. She thought about the note in the mailbox, and a tumble of emotions somersaulted through her. "We need to get together tonight. What time can I drop by?"

"I won't be home." Annie flipped her black bag closed. "He should get an x-ray done when he's back on his feet. Make sure I haven't missed anything." Annie looked exhausted. There were shadows under her eyes. She wrote a prescription for a painkiller and handed it to Brannagh with shaking fingers. Brannagh studied the writing style then folded it carefully in half.

"Is there anything you want to tell me, Annie?" she asked coldly.

"What do you mean?"

"About the note?"

"The scrip?" Annie nodded towards the prescription in Brannagh's hand. "It's three times a day, preferably with meals. Or milk will do. It can irritate the stomach. I have a sample I can give you to get him started."

"No, no." Brannagh felt her tongue tangling, the rush of words halting suddenly. Why was confronting Annie so bloody difficult? "I mean—I *know* Annie."

"You know?" She blushed.

"I know what you've been up to." Because Annie was the only one who had ever really truly understood her, the only one who had truly understood the loneliness and alienation she had always felt, if it turned out Annie had betrayed her then …

"What *I've* been up to?" Annie's brow furrowed. "Pardon me if I'm confused, but aren't you the one who has pulled a one-eighty by coming here? And you want to know what I've been up to?"

Brannagh folded her arms across her chest. "I don't know the how or the why but I know."

"Look, I don't have time to play 'let's solve the cryptic puzzles of the world' right now, okay?" Annie shook her head, chewing her lip. "Do you trust me?"

Brannagh hesitated.

Annie grimaced and picked up her bag. "Never mind."

Brannagh grabbed her arm. "Yes. Yes I do trust you. That's the problem. That's why I'm so confused."

Before Annie reached the door, she halted. Brannagh watched her shoulders rise and fall. "All right. Then give me twenty-four hours. That's all I ask. Okay?"

Brannagh nodded reluctantly. She stood at the window and watched Annie walk down the path.

Brannagh jiggled Grandfather's arm. "No, you can't sleep yet. You have to take your medicine."

"Then give it to me."

"Not until you tell me the rest of the story."

"What story?"

"The one Annie interrupted."

"And then you'll leave?"

"Gone."

Grandfather sat up, scrubbed his face with knobby fingers. "I had been driving over Reversing Falls bridge and saw a figure down below, leaning over the railing. There was something about the hat that caught my eye. I realized immediately that it was Rye. A week before the wedding. You see she had a habit of hanging around Reversing Falls, even then. She had a fascination with it."

"Go on."

He paused, as if calculating how much to reveal.

Brannagh cleared her throat. "Straight up. That's the deal."

"Rye's mother, your great-grandmother Brigid, suffered from melancholia. Nerves. Missed her family, Ireland, something brutal. She had a stillbirth when Rye was seven years old. A boy. Carried him full-term. Going through the labour and then … She could not deal with it. Just shut down. Tried to take her life. Rye's father, not being an educated man, did what his family physician urged him to do, for the sake of his wife, for the sake of the remaining child." He hesitated and motioned toward an empty glass on the coffee table. "Could you?"

Brannagh jumped up, snatched the brandy bottle off the sideboard and set it on the table next to the glass. Grandfather undid the cap and filled it. His right eye twitched.

"They put Rye's mother in the Lunatic Asylum. That's what

they called it then, back in the days when it was overcrowded and poorly heated. When the grounds were a cesspool of cow dung with overgrown gardens and the walkways a crumbling mess. Back when they didn't hesitate to use the iron cot restraints, and the camisole de force."

Brannagh picked up the bottle of brandy and held it cradled in her hands.

He drained his glass. "You look like her. Pamela too. The same hair, large lovely eyes. Gran used to say her heart would turn over sometimes running into either one of you in the hallway late at night." He paused and flexed his fingers.

They sat in silence.

"They found her white shawl below one of the walkways at the Lunatic Asylum, snagged in a bush. She hung herself with a stocking from a tree."

Brannagh looked out the parlour window at the high branches of the oak.

"I realized that Rye was upset, so I got out of the car."

Brannagh poured a dollop of brandy into the glass. Took a gulp.

"'You'll despise me', Rye said. I protested, but she held out one hand. 'I think I'm going mad. I think about my mother, and I think this is how she must have felt. I can't stand the thought of seeing Raymond day after day. That hideous chair. I want to take a sledge hammer to it.' I sat down and waited. 'They expect me to be stoic,' she stumbled. 'I'm a nurse. I'm supposed to come by this inner strength naturally. But I don't feel kind and compassionate and accepting and brave. I'm terrified and sad and I'm so afraid of this darkness. I can't shake it, I can't.' Her face crumpled and she buried it in my coat. 'I'm growing to hate him. I can't help myself.'

"Finally, I managed to calm her down and we strolled by the

water. It was an overcast night. Her hands in mine were blocks of ice.

" 'All I've ever wanted in life was peace of mind,' she said. 'Knowing I have a safe harbour to escape to. I can't stand the thought of being trapped. I don't know if I'm strong enough to pull this off. I can't stand these awful feelings. And then I worry. What if I'm like my mother? What if it leads to that? Being locked in the asylum. It's too late to back out. What reason could I give?'"

Grandfather's gaze softened as he gazed unseeingly at the wallpaper above Brannagh's head. After a moment, he continued in a low voice. "Raymond's moodiness was predictable. I had seen it already in many patients myself, a delayed reaction to the war, to the hard times and shocks we all had witnessed. It would pass with time." He stared. "I could have told her that." He paused. "But I didn't."

"No."

Grandfather roused himself. "She broke down. I drew her clumsily into my arms. 'I'll protect you,' I said. 'Nothing can harm you, no one can lock you up if I'm by your side.' 'And how can you do that?' she asked. 'Marry me' I said. And she laughed, wiping away her tears. And then she stared at me. 'But then people really will think I'm crazy,' she said. 'All the better reason to marry a psychiatrist,' I said. 'Besides if I'm the villain who stole you out from under his nose, you will remain blameless.'"

He paused. "So we made a deal without so many words. I could have her, at a price. Protection. That's what I offered her. Peace of mind. Whether she was conscious of it or not, she believed that the psychiatrist in me had the skills and training to keep her from succumbing to her mother's fate. If all else failed, I held the key. No one could ever be locked into that hell hole without my authorization." He turned to face Brannagh, a look of calm resignation on his face. "She never loved me, you see. That's the truth. Though I had always loved her. From the first time I saw her, bathing at Saints' Rest Beach when I was only fifteen." He sighed.

"Gran was eccentric, but never mentally unstable. That's ridiculous."

"It's amazing the power fear holds over the mind."

"But she was simply distraught. Why didn't you tell her the truth?"

He appeared not to hear her. "Upsets. I tried to avoid them with her. Tried to always keep everything running on an even keel. Rein in the impulsiveness, runaway emotionalism, crazy notions that would strike. Stress, you see, is the number one contributing factor escalating a case of bad nerves into something worse. You all made that so difficult, Pamela, Aunt Thelma, you." He shook his head. "I tried my best, but you, all of you, had a way of messing the works every time."

Brannagh studied him with bewilderment.

He smiled, for the first time all day, a warm, self-satisfied, beaming smile. "But she stayed," he breathed with an air of wonder as if he still couldn't quite believe his good luck. "Didn't she?"

❦

At first, life with Nikki, post-research gathering, in the cabin near Ignace, was fun. Brannagh tried not to think about the future. She tried to pretend that she would be able to walk away from him when it was finished; that she wanted to. Then Nikki began to change. At first his withdrawal was subtle; he stopped sharing his dessert with her or the crossword puzzle. When summer ended he announced he was going to a conference in Winnipeg. Brannagh waited for an invitation, but it never came. She was hurt. With the added stress of the insurance investigation over Cindy's death that Gordon had instigated, seeking his revenge right to the bitter end, he began disappearing at night and coming home hollow-eyed and sullen. Nikki and Brannagh argued over trivialities until every day they drove to the trailer and holed up in the office in opposite corners. Nikki started getting phone calls that were private, the kind of phone calls that would make him pause as soon as he said, "Hello" and give her a long look before proceeding, as if he were choosing his words carefully, oh so carefully, so as not to give anything away. Or so she imagined. "Yes," he would mutter. "I see." Then, "Well thanks for the information. Good-bye."

"Who was that?" she'd ask with forced casualness, coming round his chair to massage his back.

He'd pick up a sheaf of papers and hunch forward on the desk, intently studying them. Her hands would drop. "The Met Library in Toronto. Tracking down periodicals."

As he finalized plans for the conference, Brannagh kept waiting for the olive leaf to be extended.

Disappearances.

It was all Brannagh had known, all she had lived and breathed her whole life. She came from a race of giants and priests and kings renowned in legend for having evaporated off the face of the earth. Even Great Grandfather O'Kelly had packed everything he owned and left the emerald isle in a coffin ship. There one day, gone the next.

Only their ghosts remained
Lingering in the song of the sea
The wind on the waves
The clatter of stones
The rush of the tide
The flow of the Atlantic from one side to the other.

On Nikki and Brannagh's last night together before the conference, she had a fierce yearning to make love, but she was afraid of letting her hunger be unleashed, afraid that he would read the depth of the naked longing for love in her eyes. Instead, long after Nikki fell asleep, Brannagh lay wide-eyed, listening to the rustle of pioneer insulation falling from between the timbers, and waited for the night to end.

❧ ☙

Brannagh stood on the top of the cellar stairs gazing down. Outside, the sun was lowering in the sky. It was the time of day on Argyle when children's laughter grew muted and burr-covered cats trundled home from the fields to curl up on the front porch and lick their wounds.

Slowly she climbed down the stairs. Pausing midway, she sat.

She was sure that her grandfather viewed himself as a hero. He had done the utmost to fulfil his duty in life, to uphold the promise he had made to the woman who had met him at the altar so many years ago. He did not want Rye to disappear. It was that simple.

And it seemed to Brannagh, looking back, that her grandfather had become all the more impatient and short-tempered after Raymond had had his stroke and Gran had begun spending so much time at Dianne's house helping her mother, Jocelyn, cope.

Brannagh remembered once how Jocelyn had asked her to carry the record player upstairs to Raymond's room. Raymond had been sitting up in bed, pillows propped behind his back. He offered Brannagh a chocolate from a large red box. The black vinyl disc spun on the turntable and a husky voice filled the air. Marlene Dietrich. The words were French. Brannagh didn't understand them, but the agony beneath each note was more than she could bear. She excused herself and left the bedroom. She paused in the hallway, did a double take. There was Gran behind the open bedroom door, face pressed to the crack below the hinges. She lifted the collar of her dress to her nose, and swiped at her eyes. Then, saying not one word, she followed Brannagh down the stairs.

Brannagh rose to her feet, climbed the stairs and closed the cellar door. She stepped into the parlour. Grandfather lay on the couch with his eyes closed. Outside the window, the wind rustled the leaves in the oak tree. She contemplated a knot, resembling an old woman's eye, and below it the dip where she used to sit, the wood worn as smooth as a hipbone.

Grandfather snored softly.

She opened the window and sat on the sill, hugging her knees to her chest. The air was filled with the oniony scent of new mown grass.

It seemed wrong that there could have ever been a moment when Gran had feared her wildness, had felt the need to question where it might lead. She would never forgive Grandfather for preying on Gran's fears.

"I do believe God can't resist filling the black holes in children's souls with something good," Gran had mused, many years ago, while warming gnarled fingers over the woodstove, as the wind rattled the cottage windows. Brannagh had been preoccupied with filling out applications for a biology degree at university. "Stop fiddling with that nonsense," Gran had grumbled. "Draw me a picture and show me the heartfelt goodness in those fingers."

Brannagh pressed her nose to the window and tilted her head back until she could see the topmost part of the tree umbrellaed against the sky. As the leaves rustled dryly in the wind, a sound rose, like the cackle of an old woman, and floated down through its boughs. It whirled up the season's decaying detritus that collected around its roots and sent it scattering.

~~~ ~~~

Grandfather stirred in his sleep. "No, no." He flung out one arm and knocked the empty brandy glass to the floor.

Brannagh laid a blanket over him. Suddenly, Grandfather's eyes popped open; the whites of his eyes glistened.

Brannagh laid a hand on his arm. "Your blanket fell on the floor. You dosed off for a bit."

He frowned. Scrubbed his nose with one finger.

He looked so pathetic, this emaciated, pale old man lying on the couch with one gnarled foot propped on pillows, yellowing toenails curling over mottled flesh. It struck her, as she gazed at him, that this is how he would look when he died, when they laid his body to rest in a casket dressed in his best Sunday suit.

Brannagh set the bundle of letters upon his chest.

He squeezed his eyes closed and shook his head vehemently. "All lies. Fairy tales. The fabrication of a sick mind getting sicker. I could have done something. I should have done something. But Tish's father, Chief Eden, he argued we had to bury it. It would ruin any chance of putting one of our boys, a god-fearing Protestant, in the mayor's office."

"What on earth?"

"It really was best for the family, it was. Rye couldn't have coped with that, on top of everything else. You see that, don't you?"

"Gran already knew about Aunt Thelma's childhood crush on my father. What are you talking about? I just want to know the truth, why you sent my father away."

He flinched. "The truth? You want the truth?"

"Yes, old man. Are you deaf?"

"Then I'll tell you the truth." The whites of his eyes grew large and round as if an image had materialized in mid-air, too grotesque to contemplate. "Aunt Thelma murdered your mother. Grant, oh Lord, rest to your servant, that she is in a place where there is neither sorrow nor sighing nor pain." He choked. "Annie's little brother. She did that. She did that awful thing too."

Chapter Eight

The Victorian clapboard was painted sea green with pale blue fretwork and finials that rose like icing trimming a cake. One side of the house had been painted with a mural of Saints' Rest Beach. Eel grass swayed before a rolling succession of white caps crashing onto the rocky shore, as gulls circled overhead. The sign hanging above the door read: SeaWinds Gallery.

Brannagh rang the bell. There was no response. She rapped on the window then paused, contemplating her next move.

"Can I help you?"

She turned to see an elderly woman standing next to the street holding a bag of groceries.

"Yes, thank you, do you know if …?" Brannagh paused and stared hard at the woman. The curly head of russet hair was grey streaked, but the impish grin, freckles and bright eyes were undeniable.

"Look at you." Kate's grin widened as she rushed up the steps and grasped Brannagh's hand. "Just when I gave up begging you to visit. You shocked the hell out of me!" She fished a tarnished key out of the bottom of her pocket bag. "I just stepped out to the market for pork chops. You're staying for dinner, no arguments." She swung open the door and ushered Brannagh inside. "You can christen the new bed in the guest room. I'm still mad about auctions." She tossed her coat onto a deacon's bench at the bottom of the staircase. Then, as she bent to pick up the grocery bag she suddenly halted. Slowly, she straightened. Her gaze penetrated Brannagh's, and the colour rose in her cheeks. "Oh." It was a cry of pain. "Of course." Kate pursed her lips. "That explains it then." She turned round and scooped up the grocery bag. "Let's go up." Her shoes made a sharp clacking sound as the heels smacked each stair runner.

Brannagh stood for a moment in the landing, hesitating. Then slowly she followed Kate up the stairs.

⁂

Kate polished her glasses and held them to the light from the adjacent window. "Inevitably you will blame me."

"Just tell me." A clock chimed in the distance.

Kate donned her glasses. She closed the window blinds. "She loved your father Ben. He was the only man she ever loved." Kate handed Brannagh a cup of tea. They sat in the former butler's room. Kate had calmly illustrated how she had knocked down an entire wall to make the kitchen bigger.

"But Ben secretly loved my mother." Brannagh needed something to do with her hands. Every bone in her body quivered with a frenetic energy. She grasped the teacup. The scalding liquid burned her tongue.

Kate poured sugar and stirred. "Thelma and Ben were in competitions—spelling bees, science fairs, oratory. She was the smartest girl in the class, he the smartest boy through grade school and high school. They naturally came together. Even though they were so intelligent, they shared an emotional immaturity that can often be the downside of such a gift; an inability to relate with others. And, of course, they were teased, ostracized because of their high IQs. They developed an understanding with one another, created a place, a fantasy where they could be comfortable, set free from the burden of being different. They were safe in the old boathouse with the red roof next to your Gran's cottage. Nobody bothered them there. Ben liked to read Bulfinch's *Mythology*. They would role-play fantasies where they were gods and ruled the earth. Ben declared it was their castle, their kingdom. They didn't need the beautiful people. In fact, they should pity them because they, like Narcissus, would be cursed. On the flip side of the coin, he and Thelma would be blessed by Apollo and Athena for their wisdom."

Brannagh glanced around the room. The two doors along the hallway to the kitchen had been closed. There was a staircase to the right.

"She's upstairs." Kate set down her cup and passed a plate of date squares. "Converted the attic to a library. She likes to sit, stroking the covers between her hands."

Brannagh ignored the proferred sweets. "My mother …"

Kate shrugged. "Pamela never paid any attention to Ben until …"

"They were opposites."

"Your Grandfather made her see that Ben was her ticket out. Your father wanted to be a lawyer. When he was home on leave from the Navy, he called. Your grandfather took the message. He sent Thelma to the cottage with Gran on a trumped-up errand. He manipulated Pamela into feeling competitive, playing on fears that her younger sister would be married before her to an enviable catch. When Thelma came back mid-week, Ben was suddenly besotted with Pamela, and she was left out in the cold. Your grandfather did everything he could to encourage the match because he was afraid of losing Thelma, the only person he could depend on to keep the house running. It was your grandfather who helped Pamela and Ben marry secretly before Ben returned to duty. He also broke the news to Thelma. He told her that she didn't have to worry about being the smart one, didn't have to regret not being the beautiful daughter, because she would always have a place in his home, that he, in his generosity, would never turn her out in the street."

Brannagh closed her eyes. Keep the house running smoothly at all costs. No upsets, no fussing.

"After the war Ben bought them a small house of their own, started working on the docks, trying to save money so he could go to law school, but Pamela kept demanding more and more."

Brannagh opened her eyes, and wondered, *Where am I? Who is this woman sitting across from me?*

Kate sighed and brushed crumbs off her lap. "A line of creditors started banging on their door. By the time Pamela was pregnant with you they were forced to move back into the house on Argyle."

Brannagh felt a pricking behind her eyes. "But why did my father leave?"

Kate shook her head. "No idea. I'm sorry. I only know what Thelma told me. What she believed."

Brannagh rubbed her hand across her eyes.

"Thelma had to deduce, in the heat of rejection, that she was undeserving of any option other than life imprisoned in that house. Your Grandfather's praise of her high intellect, her organizational skills, her competence in running things, was both soothing balm and curse. I do know that for the rest of her life she truly believed that the real reason Ben came back to Argyle with Pamela was because he'd realized his mistake, that he had never stopped loving her, that he needed to be closer to her."

"But that's absurd. Then, why did he end up leaving?"

"She convinced herself that he had escaped so that he could prepare a new life, one they could share together. That he would contact her when he was ready to help her run away too."

Kate rose and flicked a switch on the wall. The wicker blades on the overhead fan slowly turned. "Remember when we first met? When you used to visit my apartment on Princess Street and watch me paint?"

"I kept the book you gave me on how to draw under my pillow."

"There was something in her face that I saw, buried deep down, that held me spellbound, that I had to capture on canvas. Behind the eyes, a flashing, roiling light. I suspected even then it was a psychosis." She pursed her lips and sat. "Thelma hated the painting."

"I'd really like to leave now."

"Then go."

Brannagh didn't budge.

"Therapists are like detectives. We view people as puzzles. We want to take them apart and figure out how they are put together." She grimaced. "It's a curse."

Brannagh's mouth thinned. "You were treating her. When she was out two, three times a week. And all that time, we thought you were painting or going to your women's group or renovating."

"We did that too." Kate traced the needlepoint on the tablecloth with one finger. "Mental illness is a disease. With the right treatment and medication, people lead routine lives; they never hurt anyone but themselves."

Brannagh took a sip of cold tea, spat it back into the cup. "Bullshit."

"Your aunt's illness was exacerbated by the need to keep it in denial, just like all her other emotional needs. Very young she knew something was wrong, the manic episodes, the anxiety. She thought if she could just get rid of the mice between the walls, she'd get some sleep, if she could just train the cats to hunt them down. It became an obsession."

Brannagh paled as a recollection flashed through her mind. Aunt Thelma pouring cream into the cat's saucer on the porch and shaking something into it from a silver tin.

"What upsets me most, Brannagh, is that your grandfather knew she was ill. Yet he turned a blind eye, remained in denial himself, because she brought him what he needed. It was that enormous ego. He thought he could cure her. He was treating her. All those times she was supposed to be doing secretarial work for him. But after your mother's death, he finally realized he'd lost. Why do you think he allowed her to move in with me? He knew that I knew. Alzheimer's my ass. Anyone taking massive doses of antipsychotics can't remember how to put one foot in front of the other."

Brannagh recalled how Grandfather would close down the old nursery room and he and Aunt Thelma would hole up in there for days. She gritted her teeth. "There's no excuse. Annie's brother, my mother, how could she? Why did you take her in? She belongs in jail."

Kate wrapped her arms around her waist and hugged herself tightly. "Logic doesn't work here. Don't even try."

"It makes no sense, there's no justification."

"Of course there isn't!" Kate rocked.

Brannagh jumped to her feet and her chair made a harsh scraping noise along the hardwood. "Annie's brother was an innocent child. My mother, for all her self-centredness, was too. How could she hurt helpless creatures? How could she do something so horrible?" Brannagh choked.

Kate reached out a hand and squeezed Brannagh's arm. "You have every reason to be outraged. Every reason."

The dam of self-control deep within Brannagh finally broke. She sank into the chair, curling in on herself, sobbing, moaning into her hands. How long it lasted she did not know. Eventually she became aware of a hand on her crown, fingertips kneading her skull. Brannagh swiped the napkin over her face. "You're covering for her. You know what really happened."

Kate's eyes shone with a cold, hard anger. She blinked. "I know some. What really happened, no one will ever know."

Brannagh waited.

"I don't understand it either. Does that surprise you? For all the time I've spent reading and studying and trying to unlock the wherefore and the why? I still don't know."

"I don't give a damn about your confusion or intellectual fascination. How many papers have you published on this case? Or are you writing that bloody book you were always boasting about. Are you going to go on all the talk shows to discuss your earth-shattering theories and how you saved a psychotic killer from the darkness within?"

Kate inhaled sharply. "Thelma read about Annie's brother in the newspaper. He was a musical prodigy. A short while later a lawyer showed up at Argyle with a suitcase. It was Ben's. It held all of Thelma's letters; unopened. The lawyer wanted to inform Pamela that Ben had died in a tragic accident at sea. Thelma took the suitcase upstairs, and did not say a word to anyone, not that night or the next day or the day after that. One week later, she bundled up the letters, got in the car, and drove to the corner where she had seen Annie's brother waiting on Wednesday nights after his piano lessons. She told the boy that she was a friend of his mother's, and that she had sent the car because they had a surprise for him."

"But what was the point, what warped reasoning?"

"There is no point. Sickness has no point." Kate took a deep breath. "I always wondered how different it would have been if Annie had remembered, if she hadn't developed amnesia."

"What on earth are you going on about?"

Kate froze. "Annie saw her brother get into Thelma's car. Annie followed them on her bike. Thelma couldn't shake her. Outside the city, traffic petered out, and on a deserted stretch of road, she ran Annie into the ditch."

Brannagh willed her tongue to form words, but none would come.

"It's my speculation that Thelma believed the voices that spoke to her; the voices of the gods. Maybe she thought she was saving this little boy from the pain his intelligence would bring."

"Bullshit. She's a psychopath and she has you wrapped around her little finger. Do you actually watch her take the medication you give her? Do you?"

"You tell yourself what you need to so you can sleep at night."

"You actually charge a fee to come up with this claptrap?"

They sat in silence listening to the clock tick. Brannagh closed her eyes and pictured Aunt Thelma standing in the backyard with her feet planted firmly on the landing, clothes pins parked between her lips, as she shook out a wet pillow case, shouting orders to Annie, Diane, Tish and Brannagh.

"At first I told myself it was Mayor Eden's fault," Kate murmured. "He was the chief of police when Annie's brother died. Thelma's necklace was tangled in the boy's shirt. The necklace Ben had given her with the engraving of the flower."

"Flower?"

"Narcissus."

Brannagh pictured it in her mind's eye and recognized instantly that the star was a daffodil. Narcissus. Was the gift a reminder of where obsessive self-love could lead, that it was far better to be gifted with intellect than beauty? How cruel then that Ben had fallen in love with Pamela after all. Brannagh recalled Chief Eden storming into the house on Argyle the day they found Annie's little brother, and the glimpse she had caught of gold as he had pressed something into her grandfather's hand, talking all the while of gold cufflinks that had been stolen and found. Was this what Tish had been trying to tell her? Had she overheard the truth, eavesdropping all those years ago on her father's telephone calls for enough information to please Hilda Outhouse?

"Chief Eden and your grandfather covered it up. Eden was running for mayor and, eventually, premier. The good ol' boys had to keep the Catholic candidate from getting ahead at all costs. Eden couldn't have a scandalous murder, one that would attract the national media, to have happened on his watch, to say nothing of the repercussions that would follow when it was learned that the daughter of such a prominent Protestant, a campaign supporter and a lifelong friend, was a cold-blooded killer. Maybe he really believed your grandfather could cure her, who knows?"

Brannagh wet her lips. And of course Chief Eden and her grandfather had encouraged Dr. Baird to put Annie in the Nervous Clinic where they could keep a close eye on her. They must have been relieved when they realized her amnesia was permanent.

"In time, though, I realized I was just as culpable as they are, while I know the right thing to do, I can't do it. I just can't see what good it would do." She dipped her chin into her chest.

"You must do something."

Kate shook her head. Tears rolled down her cheeks.

Brannagh stood and smoothed her hair, wrung her hands. "Are you ever afraid?"

Kate lifted her head quickly. "No. Never. She wouldn't hurt a fly."

"That's a stupid thing to say. She murdered two people."

Kate's mouth trembled. "Would you … would you like to see her?"

Brannagh felt something sour rise in her throat. "No." Her hand rose in the air. She wanted to slap Kate silly, as if somehow all of this was her fault. But when she lifted her hand, Kate grabbed it.

"What would you have done? In my place. Tell me. Tell me what you would have done."

Later Brannagh could never be sure how long they stood, a frozen tableau by the table. She only knew that all the emotion had drained out of her, and she felt suddenly glacial and weary, so bone-tired exhausted that if she lay her head down she would probably never lift it again. What would she have done, if she had known? Would she have gone to the police? Would she go to the police now?

Brannagh put one hand on Kate's shoulder. She felt the old woman's clavicle through the thin cotton of her dress, could trace the fine line of it beneath her fingers, measure the rise and fall of Kate's breathing, fierce and steady as waves upon the shore.

The tragedy was that everyone in the family had a story to tell. Brannagh could see that now. The leaver and the left behind. And each person's version would probably leave the impression that the teller of the tale was neither all sinner nor all saint, but simply human, with all the struggle that being so entailed. But they were stories that sometimes hid a dark truth she had no way of knowing completely. Ever. She could only guess, take a blind leap, then let go.

And it seemed to her that the echoes of a family's feeble attempts at love were at the heart of the anguish passed down from one generation to the next, an invisible inheritance undetectable to the naked eye, but skewered through the soul; a legacy of mistakes, fears, mistrust, disappearances, vulnerability, sickness, calluses formed around hearts, all these miserly clutchings threaded through one huge lump that a person blindly inherited with no say in the matter, that the universe left them on their own to sort out.

Some managed.

Some didn't.

Brannagh took a deep breath. "I don't know. I don't know what I would have done." *I don't know what I'm going to do.*

Kate swallowed, not bothering to shield the anguish in her eyes. "You will not see her?"

Brannagh shook her head.

"Can I come with you to the graveyard?"

Brannagh didn't bother asking how Kate had known that that was where she needed to go. She simply picked up her bag and headed down the stairs.

⁓◎ ◎⁓

One day, not long after Pamela died and Art had disappeared, and not long after Brannagh, Annie, Tish and Dianne had snuck up to the attic and officially initiated the Tuatha-de-Dananns, a fierce gale blew into town. Within twenty-four hours it would develop into what would become known as Baby Hazel, the forerunner of Hurricane Hazel.

In the meantime, all the girls knew, as they sat on the wide ledge of the window in the parlour, was that trees danced like hula girls, and shirts off people's clotheslines rolled through the streets. Even Gran, who had been sitting in the rocker crocheting, put her hook aside and came to stand by the window.

"Look at her blow," Annie exclaimed.

Gran almost pressed her nose against the glass. "Girls, get your jackets on."

"You can't go out in this? It isn't safe," Grandfather bellowed from behind an upraised newspaper.

Gran ignored him and airily ushered the girls into the hall.

"We're going for a car ride."

Gran didn't have to ask Brannagh twice. But of all the days for Gran to snap out of the glum drums, she wondered, why did she have to pick this one?

The girls meekly climbed into the Packard, already seduced by a sense of adventure. Saint John was always getting the tail end of hurricanes that travelled up from the Florida coast. Some were worse than others. Occasionally there were warnings to bring everything indoors and tie objects that remained down. Dying trees would topple or a dog house would fly.

Gran drove to Saints' Rest beach, and pulled into the parking lot facing the ocean. They sat quietly studying the rollers. They were unlike anything Brannagh had ever seen, ferociously flinging onto shore. When a man appeared on the beach, and they were able to compare the height of the waves to his stature, they realized how truly huge they were. Miss Sanderson's nephew, who had once worked on a cod ship off Newfoundland, had told her he saw waves that rose as high as the Admiral Beatty Hotel. She had thought he was exaggerating.

The man stood on the beach with his pants rolled to the knees. Then one roller, reluctant to unfurl, curled like a fist and knocked him flat, before it loosened and held him pinned to the ground. He clung to a rock as the water swirled round him and pulled back, retreating to the sea. He scrambled to his feet and ran like the dickens, tripping and scrabbling in the wet sand.

"God," Gran said, as if she hoped to start a prayer but couldn't find the words to say.

At first Dianne was afraid, and Annie, Tish and Brannagh too, though they pretended otherwise. They rolled their windows down a crack and heard the moan and whine and hiss of the wind, felt it buffeting the car, and felt the floor wobble under their feet.

Brannagh had no idea how much time had passed before the waves swept clear up to the parking lot. The froth and spume were a foot thick. When each wave crashed, the foam flew and scattered in whirls and eddies until it looked as if it were snowing. Soon everything was covered with suds: the rocks, the car windshields, and the wooden fence around the parking lot. The car felt cosy and warm. Gran turned the engine on every once in a while to run the heater and flick the wipers. Then she pulled a paper bag out from under the seat, unpacked a thermos of tea, and some boxty cakes with jam.

The girls sang with their mouths full:

> *Boxty in the griddle, boxty in the pan,*
> *If you don't eat boxty, you'll never get a man.*

Then they spotted a dark blob being carried by the wind, a log, or part of a car tire, or a ball of seaweed. The blob rolled across the sand into the foam and suddenly sprouted legs, four of them, and scurried, faster, faster and faster to the open door of a station wagon and jumped in.

Annie, Tish, Dianne and Brannagh were almost giddy with relief. Dumb, goofy, loveable dog. Gran remained quiet, leaning against the steering wheel, staring straight ahead. When the girls eventually quieted and started to grow sleepy, she swept one hand at the panorama outside. "I think she's out there."

She opened the car door. Instantly her blouse flapped against her arm, and the serviettes flew out the door.

"Don't!" The girls leaned forward. The wind whined and clamoured.

Gran stepped outside. "She is. She is out there." She slammed the door shut.

By the now the waves washed clear up to the front tires. Gran stood there for a long time, facing the sea, while the wind and water whipped round her. Her grey hair was plastered to her scalp, as if pressed by an invisible hand; her dress flattened against her thighs.

Slowly, she slid one foot forward a few inches. Then, after a time, she slid the other one forward. When Gran had moved about six feet, which seemed from the girls' viewpoint inside the car to be much too far, she put her hands on her hips and turned towards them. Her mouth moved.

"What did she say?" Annie asked.

"Dunno." Brannagh shrugged. But she did now. *Pamela,* her grandmother had mouthed. *Pamela.*

And then Gran smiled a huge smile, a smile that neither of the girls had seen in a long, long time.

Brannagh wiped her nose on her sleeve, Dianne stopped clutching the front seat, Tish sighed and Annie whistled through her teeth. Because they knew, they really knew, in the deepest nooks and crannies of their beings, where it truly counts, that there was no doubt, no question as to just how indestructible a human being could be.

Chapter Nine

As Brannagh drove down the highway heading east towards Sussex, she kept glancing out the partly open car window at the Kennebecasis River. It meandered through the valley between banks that were a patchwork of farmers' fields, ripe with tender shoots of corn and oats rippling in the breeze, and sun-spangled meadows thick with wild clover, over which the heads of contented cows nodded. Unadorned clapboard farmhouses and slanting barns slipped past. The air was filled with the nose-tickling scent of newly cut hay mingled with the sucker-punch of fresh manure.

After putting flowers on her mother's and Annie's brother's graves, Brannagh returned to the house on Argyle with take-out chicken for supper, but Grandfather only gnawed on a bun, and after taking his medication, fell asleep. Exhausted, Brannagh didn't have much of an appetite either. She barely managed to drag herself to bed after a hot soak in the old-fashioned tub.

Brannagh instantly fell into a deep, refreshing slumber, only to be startled awake at two AM by the sharp rat-tat-tat of pebbles being thrown against the second floor bedroom window. For a moment she traveled back in time, back to the days when she, Annie, Tish and Dianne would sneak out for a midnight meeting of the Tuatha-de-Dananns. She pulled on her housecoat with one hand and parted the curtain on the window with the other. Cupping her hands against the pane she could make out a figure in the darkness below.

Later, after she had hurried upstairs to throw some things into a bag, and to pull on a pair of blue jeans, and to write Grandfather a note, she had to keep pausing to go over it again and again in her mind.

If Gran were alive she would say that it was proof that they lived in a world where blind grace still reigned; a world that allowed a knotted lump, worked ragged by clumsy fingers, to be transformed.

Grandfather would harrumph and call it luck. Pure and simple. Nothing more, nothing less.

Brannagh watched the sun on the Kennebecasis River transforming the rippling water into a field of dancing light. She had made early morning rounds in Saint John before she left and had said her good-byes to everyone. Now she was headed north on the highway toward Moncton and the Miramichi.

Brannagh pressed her foot down harder on the accelerator. It had all taken longer than she had anticipated. For once in her life she would not be late.

Please God, not today.

⇜ ⇝

"What's going on?" Annie came to the door of Baker House in her nightgown, half asleep. When she spotted Brannagh, her eyes widened. "I know I promised to talk." Her voice shook. "But now isn't a good time."

"I've come to say goodbye," Brannagh explained calmly. "I have to take a little trip. But I'll be back."

Annie held the door open with one hand, but made no move to invite Brannagh inside. "The cottage, the reunion, we'd only just begun to …"

"We'll talk." Brannagh rose on tiptoe as if she were trying to see over Annie's shoulder.

Annie squirmed. "Just a minute. I don't really have things ship shape, without a housekeeper, I've been so busy."

Brannagh nudged past her and walked into the living room. There were two wine glasses on the coffee table. A pair of man's boots sat next to the fireplace, and a pipe lay in the ash try. Annie edged by her, snatching up the wine glasses.

"You see Brannagh, I …"

"Don't bother." Brannagh paused, giving her a long, searching look. "I already know."

"I don't think you do." Annie's eyes flicked about the room. She poked at the bridge of her glasses.

Suddenly, a voice was heard from downstairs. Deep, gravelly. "You can start the dishwasher! Annie?"

"I do know." Brannagh folded her arms across her chest. "I figured it out. The lipstick, romance novels, you calling yourself a fraud."

Feet pounded on the stairs, and then he stepped into the living room, wearing only a white towel tied around his waist, hair dripping from the shower. He grimaced when he saw Brannagh.

"Hello."

"Hi." He smiled tightly. "Er, Ms. Maloney. Dr. Baird and I, we were just, uh …"

Brannagh couldn't decide whose face was redder. Wilfred Adamson's or Annie Baird's. So Dr. Baird was teaching her young med student a few lessons in her free time was she? Had Annie Baird, who'd always touted the uselessness of men, and had professed bafflement in women's craving for romance, turned over a new leaf?

Annie quickly hustled her into the kitchen. "Look, it's not what you think. He fell asleep in the chair last night when we were going over patient charts. I couldn't turn him out on the street, now could I?"

"I suppose not."

"You understand. I knew you would."

"Oh Annie, do you have any idea how silly you sound?"

"What do you mean?"

"Why did you rent the cabin with the red roof next to Gran's?"

"I never did any such thing."

"Don't deny it."

Annie pursed her lips. "All right. My Medicare and compensation files are a mess, and I've got some nut trying to sue me for malpractice. And I didn't want to put a damper on your visit by dragging the books out every night." Annie plunked onto a kitchen chair and fixed Brannagh with a pleading look. "And, yes, I wanted to keep a close eye on you. I was worried about you being all by yourself."

"Really?"

"Really."

"And of course Wilfred missed you so he drove up."

Annie's expression softened. "He knew I felt weird about it because of my brother. He slept there, yes. How did you know?"

"I saw him. Peeking in the parlour window. Never mind. It's doesn't matter now, does it?" Brannagh sat too, leaned back, crossed her legs. "Imagine. Annie Baird in love."

Annie gulped. "We didn't mean for it to happen. At first it was platonic, business as usual. And then, well, when we started to feel things, we had to hide it. What would people say? My dad would roll over in his grave if I caused a scandal and lost all his patients."

"Scandal. What scandal?"

"Boy you have been away a long time. You've forgotten what an old-fashioned backwater this is. Unmarried people don't shack up! For one, I'm the older woman. For another, I'm in a position of authority and trust, supposed to be taking him under my wing. Do you know how many boards I sit on?"

She rose, opened a kitchen drawer and pulled out a pack of cigarettes. She lit one and inhaled deeply. "I was going to tell you, but I had to talk it over with Wilfred first. Make sure he was ready to be outed, face the music."

"Quit acting so tough, Annie. It has nothing to do with the neighbourhood gossip, does it? It has everything to do with you not being able to admit to everyone that you're just like every other woman on the planet. No one's going to think less of you because you've proved yourself to be as human as the rest of us."

"It'll certainly make my stepmother gloat. My true screw-up colours coming through."

"What screw-up? Your father's patients will be tickled. No one who matters is going to think anything about you and Wilfred." Brannagh rose and hugged her. "Give yourself a break, will ya?"

Annie lit another cigarette.

"I am not in love." Annie tossed her head, puffing vigorously.

"Liar."

"I'm fond of him, very, very fond of him."

"Oh really?"

"I'm embarrassed, after all my years of lecturing you all about love being a weakness; a panacea for the lower classes." Annie closed her eyes, swallowed. "And then, he's so young."

"How many years younger than you?"

Annie poked at her glasses. "Not that much, actually."

"I'm yanking your chain, Annie."

Annie's mouth looked like it couldn't make up its mind whether to smile or frown. The latter won out. "Honestly, what do you think?" The fingers holding the cigarette shook.

Brannagh smiled and rose off the chair. "I think it's terribly sweet. I'm thrilled for you, Annie. I also think you're a royal pain in the arse. I've thought that ever since you came to the Nervous Clinic that day and pulled the sliver out of my arm." She glanced at the closed door, behind which she was certain Wilfred stood listening and dripping onto the tiled floor. "What I really think is that it's time for me to go."

Brannagh passed the statue of the cow that marked the entrance to the town of Sussex. She glanced at the piece of paper with the directions Mrs. McGillvery had written on it.

Pass exit to Sussex. Gas station on the left.

Brannagh drove past a motel, a campground, an apple store, and a petting zoo. Clear to the horizon, on either side of the highway that wound like a black ribbon through the brush, there was no sign of a gas station.

But then, around the bend, tucked into the brush, there it was.

She didn't have butterflies in her stomach.

She had wombats.

"It never ends you know. Wash the diapers, dirty the diapers, then do it all over again," Tish stood on the clothesline stand, still managing in the midst of the most mundane domestic chore to look as if she was about to strut down a catwalk. A pair of boxer shorts and four wet diapers flapped in the early morning breeze.

She shook out a sleeper. "So you're off, just like that?"

Brannagh glanced away. "I already stopped by Annie's to say

good-bye."

"Did she tell you?" It came out muffled through the clothespin between Tish's teeth. Tish concentrated on pinning a pink and yellow striped receiving blanket to the line. "After we left the cottage, she telephoned Eddie and told him he had to talk to me about what was going on or she would."

"Going on?"

"Between the two of them."

Brannagh glanced at the lawn, the purple hollyhocks climbing one wall of the house.

"I guess it's been bothering them both."

Brannagh waited.

"Too much on his mind. Ever since Billy was born. He just, you know, he said from the first time he held her he thought, okay buddy, that's enough of this pretending you know it all, cock of the walk, when you haven't a friggin clue. As of this minute, Billy's counting on you. It killed him to think that when she grows up and goes to school and the teacher asks, 'What does your daddy do?' she'll say, 'Oh, he's a high school flunky.'"

"That doesn't matter."

Tish shook her head. "Nah, well, he doesn't miss school, but he can't stand the thought of cleaning dip sticks for Irving for the rest of his life, know what I mean?"

"So, he doesn't have to."

"Money. Can't do anything without money. I'm no help, being home with the baby." She picked up a diaper, held it suspended in mid-air for a moment. "So, he hasn't been himself. Anxious about it all. He was getting pains in his chest. Didn't want to scare me. Made an appointment with Annie and she sent him for a complete workup." Tish flushed. "And then a few days later he bought Annie breakfast at Reggie's to celebrate because she told him all the tests came back fine. Told him it was perfectly normal for new fathers to feel pressured, that anxiety can cause indigestion which mimics chest pains."

"Annie would know."

"But then who comes walking into the coffee shop but me? Sees him and Annie. Puts two and two together and comes up with five."

As long as Brannagh had known Tish, Tish had never once won an arm wrestle with the green-eyed monster. "But now you know?"

Tish sighed. "Men are such a pain. I mean, being so macho, why not tell me?"

"So now you know."

"Now I know." She smiled sheepishly. "Am I a dunce?"

"Tish?"

"Yeah?"

"I know about my Grandfather, your father, the truth, the secret they were trying to hide."

Tish pressed a wet baby blanket to her mouth. "I'm sorry, so sorry. I wanted to tell you. I didn't know how. And then sometimes I'd think it was all in my head, that I hadn't really heard it right. I didn't want to cause trouble if I was wrong. I kept going back and forth, back and forth. It was so easy to forget about it after you left Saint John and just pretend I'd imagined it all. And then you came back."

"You heard it right."

"Shit, I shoulda told you. I shoulda done something." Tish twisted a ringlet with one finger. "I'm sorry. But, my father, my mother ... I'm so sorry."

"It's not your fault, Tish. You were just a kid."

"Not anymore!" she protested. "Now what do I do? Now what

happens?"

"I don't know. I haven't figured that out yet."

Tish frowned. "Okay. Okay." She picked up a sock, and twisted it in her hands. "So you're coming back, after your trip, right?"

"Dunno."

"But you have to come back, don't you?"

"Do I?"

For a moment Tish looked relieved, but the she shook her head solemnly, "I'll be here, waiting for you."

Brannagh pulled into the rear of the parking lot. The sign hanging over the gas station read Sally's Restaurant.

She glanced at her watch. She was late.

Still she took the time to inspect herself in the rearview mirror. The wind and humidity had wreaked havoc with her hair so that now it stood on end. It looked as if it had been styled with a blender. She dug a compact out of her purse and put on fresh lipstick, but it only seemed to make her skin look sallow, the circles under her eyes more pronounced.

She got out of the car, took a deep breath, and stepped into the restaurant.

"Hello there," said the pudgy, bright-eyed brunette who was wiping down the serviette holders with a grey rag.

The door thwumped closed behind Brannagh. Aside from two houseflies, a fat black and white mongrel, Sally and herself, the restaurant was deserted.

Brannagh glanced down at the directions written on the piece of paper in her hand. Was it possible that Mrs. McGillvery had lied to her again?

Brannagh had found Dianne up on the second floor of her house, hunched over a battered wooden door that rested on two saw horses. She wore gold-rimmed glasses with a set of magnification lenses flipped over the lenses. She had a telephone receiver tucked under her chin, tweezers in one hand, and the minute inner workings of a clock spread on the table before her.

"One sec," she mouthed, then did a double take. She covered the mouth piece with one hand, and whispered, "You? What?"

Brannagh shrugged. She glanced around the room. There were tables and shelves upon which sat clocks; hundreds of clocks. The sound of ticking, whirring, tocking, and humming rose round her.

Dianne hung up the phone and stood up. Suddenly she turned shy. "Oh, I know. Clocks. It's weird, all right. But no two are the same." She walked over to a shelf built into the far wall. "Spring clocks are a challenge, but weight driven clocks operate in a world of their own." She picked up the back of a wooden clock and flicked a wheel, which caught onto a pallet and rocked another wheel, which caused the pendulum to swing. "If the pendulum is properly timed, the escape wheel should move one notch every second." She tapped the bob at the end of the pendulum, watching it intently. "But everybody knows that."

"Sure, everybody knows that," Brannagh said wryly. "When did this happen?"

Dianne flushed. "Remember how my mom used to organize all the jumble sales at the church, and people dropped all their donations off here? My Dad used to fix the broken clocks, and I used to help him. Well, after a while, our neighbours started dropping off their clocks for repair, jumble sale or not, wanting to give Dad a chance to feel useful. He had a knack, and they spread the word when the antique store opened and before you know it

..." Dianne glanced up grinning. Her eyes met Brannagh's and grew puzzled. "Are you going somewhere?"

"Yep." Brannagh leaned on the windowsill, looking down at the houses sliding toward the sea. The world was huge, but it wasn't as foreign as it appeared to be. It was made up of countries, and countries were made up of cities, and cities were made up of neighbourhoods, and neighbourhoods were made up of streets, and the streets were filled with people: noisy, joyful, nagging, caring, hopeful, intrusive, determined, messy people, just like the people who lived outside Dianne's door.

Dianne got off the stool. "You seem different," she said simply.

Brannagh wrapped her arms around her. "I envy you."

Dianne stepped back, face radiant. "Oh."

Brannagh turned back to the window. A boy, just out of diapers, rode a rusty two-wheeler with training wheels on the back. The look on his face as he wobbled down the street was one of pure dogged determination.

"See ya around," Dianne said.

"Sure. See ya around."

Sally the waitress explained chummily that two miles down the road there was another gas station with a restaurant. Well, she wouldn't really call it a restaurant exactly, more like a chip stand, as all they had was a hot plate and a deep fryer, but still, maybe that's where Brannagh was supposed to meet her friend.

Brannagh went back outside and got into the car. As she drove down the highway her limbs trembled. She had to pull over to the side of the road. She took the lid off the cardboard cup of coffee that Sally had given her. "On the house," she'd said. "You look like you need it somethin' desperate, honey."

Brannagh pictured the look on Mrs. McGillvery's face when she had opened the kitchen door in the house on Argyle last night to find her standing there. She held a handful of pebbles in her cupped hands. "Oh Brannagh," she had whispered shakily.

Brannagh led her into the kitchen. While the kettle boiled she set cups and saucers on the table, poured cream, filled the sugar bowl.

"First of all," Mrs. McGillvery began in a wobbly voice, "I want you to know that I'm sorry for lying. I'm sorry for meddling and making such a mess of things. " She pinched her nose with the hanky, took a deep breath, and then stared at the ceiling. "Annie was so het up about your reunion. Och, the plans she had for you and the girls. She said she knew just how to convince you to return to Saint John, to settle all the old business with your mother, your grandfather, once and for all. That this stubborn notion you had of never setting foot here again was just ridiculous and had to stop. I agreed." She paused, took a deep breath and contemplated Brannagh. "And so when Nikki telephoned—"

"Nikki called? When?"

"You had just arrived." Mrs. McGillvery patted her breast. "He called the office looking for Annie, said it was the only Saint John telephone number he could find in your files. Said he'd done something incomprehensible, even to himself. Just up and left without a word to anyone. Had been staying at his Uncle Zhuk's cabin all winter. His Aunt Valova kept an eye on him, bringing food and books. But he had sent you a letter, and only found out recently from Alex that you had received it, but had not opened it. Alex found it, along with a pile of unopened mail, in the port-a-potty. Nikki told me he was mailing the letter to our clinic and asked me to please give it to you as soon as it came." Mrs. McGillvery flushed.

"But you didn't."

"I just thought, since he was fine, it wouldn't do any harm to wait a bit longer. I was worried you'd go running off to him, and then there'd never be any hope that Annie'd talk you into coming to Saint John, really coming home to us." Mrs. McGillvery drew a piece of paper out of her pocket and handed it to Brannagh. "I lost the envelope."

Brannagh unfolded the paper and read:

> *Dear Brannagh,*
>
> *I wasn't sure I was actually going to go through with this until I got in the truck and drove away, watching you standing on the porch in the rearview mirror. I've abandoned it all: the work, the students, the birds and, yes, you. The truth is, after we returned from the count, I started seeing a doctor, a therapist in Ignace, after Cindy died. I never dealt with my sister's death. I didn't want anyone to know about the shrink. He convinced me that I needed to get away. I didn't know how to do it. If I had told you all, it would have been so easy to let you talk me out of it and let the work come first. I've gone to Uncle Zhuk's cabin. You can reach me there if you need to.*
> *Love Nikki*

Brannagh swallowed, turned the paper over, read it again. "Where is he?"

Mrs. McGillvery hesitated. "He called this morning. He's at the camping grounds in Sussex."

Brannagh knew she should feel something. She rubbed her hands together. Her fingertips were numb.

Mrs. McGillvery glanced up, glowered. "Och, I know it seems

ridiculous, arrogant, really, doesn't it, now? After all these years of everyone coming to me for help, looking to me for answers, relying on me to patch things up." Mrs. McGillvery hesitated, and then reached for Brannagh's hand. "I had not really thought it through."

Brannagh wrapped both her hands around Mrs. McGillvery's and squeezed. "If it had been anyone else in the whole wide world."

Mrs. McGillvery's shoulders shook. "I'm such a fool," she blubbered. "Such an impulsive, idiotic fool."

"Aren't we all," Brannagh murmured. "Sooner or later."

※ ※

After breakfast on the Saturday morning of their reunion at the cottage, as Annie parked her suitcase by the kitchen door, she had turned to Brannagh and asked, "Is there anything we can do for you before we leave?"

Brannagh had automatically shaken her head. She had fleetingly noted how pretty Annie looked. She had put her hair up into a bun, and she was wearing lipstick.

"Wilfred won't be here for an hour yet." Annie hooked a kitchen chair with one foot and pulled it out from the table before sitting down.

"Actually," Brannagh said, "there is something I'd like you to do."

Dianne and Tish turned around from the sink where they were washing dishes.

"Yeah?" Dianne dried her hands on a dishtowel.

"To finish the meeting of the Tuatha-de-Dananns."

They all paused, then glanced at one another.

"Maybe it would be better to just drop it." Dianne scrubbed her nose.

Brannagh picked up the candles on the table and strode into the parlour. "We have to finish what we started."

The others followed reluctantly. As Brannagh lit the candle, they looked at one another questioningly, then slowly sat down. Annie retrieved the shopping bag from under the couch. She opened the toffee tin, took out the rocks and handed them to the girls. They all stared at the candle flame, waiting.

Annie cleared her throat. "I want you to chair the meeting, Brannagh."

"What?"

Tish's eyes narrowed. "But you've always chaired the meeting."

"Yeah," Annie said despondently. "That's the whole point."

They waited.

"I'm not sure why." Annie glanced around the circle at each of them.

"Well, you just did it," Dianne ventured.

"Exactly." Annie folded her hands with an air of finality. "You let me, because you wanted someone to be the leader, to tell you what to do." She paused and glanced away. "Someone you could blame."

"Blame?" Tish blinked.

"Someone to be the scapegoat when it all goes wrong. Let you off the hook." She poked at her glasses. "I accepted the mantle because, well, if I wasn't the leader, what was I?"

"Okay. So you don't want to lead. Fine." Brannagh glanced around the circle. The others watched her curiously. Brannagh picked up the Gaelic cross and handed it to Dianne.

"Me?" Dianne's chin retracted into her chest.

"Sure," Tish put in forcefully, frowning at Annie. "Go ahead Dianne."

"If you're sure, I mean, Annie said ..."

Brannagh nodded. "Go ahead."

Dianne's fingers trembled as she picked up the cross. Her face looked white and pinched in the flickering candlelight and for a moment Brannagh was brought back to Saint Patrick's School and the days when Sister Mary Margaret would summon a quaking Dianne to stand up in front of the whole class to recite Dickens.

Dianne glanced around the circle, her dark eyes huge on her pale face. "All right," she began, then paused to cough. "All right." A faint glow warmed her cheeks. "I'll do it," she said firmly. "I'll chair the meeting."

A sense of unravelling loosened the tension round the circle, as if they had all been released form a silent, invisible tether. Despite how angry she had been at the girls' meddling in her life the day before, Brannagh felt a sudden wave of tenderness for them all, so deep and sweet and clear it brought a lump to her throat.

Whatever heaven was, she decided, wherever that place was that you went to when you died, she knew that this moment would be there waiting like a cosmic seed to sprout in their hearts upon the first moment of recognition. She was certain that all that they had been—children, girls, teenagers, women—the loss, the hope, the reaching and stumbling and getting back up again would all be there too. And she was convinced that all the exuberant, shining expectations not yet fulfilled, the dreams and yearnings that had been too painful not to discard over the years, that they had simply given up on, or locked away, would be there too, unsullied and expectant, ready to be claimed, like goods stored in a locker at the bus depot.

"Ladies, "Dianne said with a dignified lowering of her voice, "I now officially open this meeting of the Tuatha-de-Dananns."

I am you and you are me, one in the sky and the sun and the hills.

Pete's was set back off the highway, and was the ubiquitous if-you- blinked-you'd-miss-it establishment that sprang up on the shoulder of the road in July and August from coast to coast. The gas pumps were rusting. Someone had given the wooden building a fresh coat of brown paint. Brannagh got out of the car, but she didn't even have to open the screen door to Pete's.

She could see through the window that the place was deserted. The tall, wiry man standing behind the counter nodded his head and went back to stacking cigarettes.

She turned around and headed back to the car.

How many gas stations were there between Saint John and Sussex? She opened the car door and picked up the paper that Mrs. McGillvery had hastily written the directions on.

And then she saw the wooden park bench. The sun glinted on its freshly painted surface. It was in the dappled shade of a mountain ash. Upon it sat a man with broad shoulders and dark greying hair. His head was flung back. His mouth hung open.

She walked along the dirt road towards him slowly, a myriad of emotions rushing through her.

He wore the same clothes that he had worn the day he had left: cotton pants with a faded flannel shirt and L.L. Bean boots.

She paused in front of him.

Why didn't you tell the truth before you left, Nikki? Why?

She concluded that she could easily slide her fingers around his neck at this very moment and squeeze. It was no less than what he deserved.

She stared at his face. She had always been a sucker for a face in repose; even as a child when she was most furious at Annie for having committed some inexplicable sin, Brannagh would awaken in the night and see her flushed, unguarded, vacant face against the pillow and her heart would soften.

Brannagh reached out a hand and laid her fingers on Nikki's cheek. Perhaps she was not the only one who was confused? Brannagh pulled her hand back and tucked it into her pocket.

Maybe love is supposed to be confusing. Maybe there is no tacking it down. Maybe it is as ambiguous as the bumbling humans who are dense enough to leave its barbed hook snarled in their contracting hearts.

Brannagh took her hand out of her pocket. Her fingers clutched two green stones. She rubbed them idly, and then threw them with every bit of strength she had left in her.

They sailed in a clean arc and landed in the field with a muffled *fwump*. A flock of starlings burst from the tall grasses like a handful of ashes flung heavenward.

Chapter Ten

It was odd. Nikki and Brannagh reuniting in a greasy spoon on a pothole-filled curve of highway. On the surface they acted like old friends who hadn't seen each other in ages. Friends who had bumped into one another accidentally and were pleasantly surprised.

They ordered chicken soup and laughed remembering the game of calling the soup de jour at the EverGreen restaurant in Upsula "Soup de Sewer."

Brannagh found herself chattering non-stop, glutted suddenly with a compulsive need to fill Nikki in on everything that had happened since last September: Max, her new boss, and how he had a habit of paper-clipping everything, which drove her crazy; the funding for the new boat motors, which they didn't get; the fire at the gas station in Ignace; the devious racoons in the cabin. As if Nikki had merely been away on a vacation.

But underneath her brittle, sparkling ebullience, she was perfectly aware of the taut wire of tension running through her. Brannagh didn't know if she was ready to hear Nikki tell her why he had to disappear; didn't know if she was strong enough to handle raw honesty just yet.

In her mind, during the drive to Sussex, she had imagined Nikki looking different, like a man who had returned from a sojourn, survived a rugged quest to a foreign land; wiser, stronger, awestruck.

But Nikki looked no different than the day she first laid eyes on him at the Esso Voyageur in Ignace. His eyes were red-rimmed, his hair knotted and in need of a good cut. His beard was unruly and wild.

After the waitress arrived with their soup, Nikki took Brannagh's fingers and pressed them against his cheek. The skin was warm. Brannagh took her hand out of his. She opensed the cracker package with her teeth, crushed them with one hand and plopped them into the soup. She picked up her spoon then dropped it and leaned back in the booth with a sigh.

"Why didn't you tell me?"

Nikki laid his hands flat on the tabletop, glanced out the window.

"Why did you just disappear?"

A fly circled the sugar, landed on the saltshaker.

It felt as if a long time passed before Nikki answered.

He spoke so softly she had to lean forward and strain to catch the words. "It had nothing to do with you."

"Me? What?" Brannagh's umbrage faltered as quickly as it flared. She was hit with a pain behind her eyes, as if she had just been clobbered. "But I thought I, that you ..." she began feebly, then glanced at him.

Nikki's face turned gentle, serene as a newborn babe's, and his eyes developed the soft blur of one who gazes upon the world as if it were an unexpected, colourfully wrapped box presented at the end of a spot dance. He laid his hand on hers and nodded slightly.

"Nothing to do with you," he said, and his tone was an exact replica of Father Angus's in the confession box: firm, absolving, final.

"Well." Brannagh stared at her soup. The crackers were soggy and swollen and unfamiliar. Slowly they sank to the bottom of the bowl.

None of us is guiltless, she thought. Not one.

We are all conspirators, aiders and abetters, schemers, plotters, traitors. We fall short and recoil in horror then secretly relish a tantalizing familiar corner of the personal drama that unfolds.

You had your absolution to hunt down and I had mine.

"Well." she said. There were details she could ask him to clarify about the hotel, the detective, the trial. But in the end the only real mystery she had to solve was herself.

Brannagh picked up her spoon and dipped it into the soup. It was lumpy with hunks of celery, shrivelled peas, unidentifiable brown specks, and swollen noodles. A mess or a work of art, depending on your point of view.

Nikki shook out his napkin.

Brannagh blew on her spoon then sipped. She instantly pulled a face and clamped a napkin over her mouth.

Nikki handed her a glass of ice water. He quipped, "Soup de Sewer."

Brannagh drank. "Soup de Spew-er."

"Soup de Glue-er."

"Soup de Shoe-er."

"Soup de Poo-er."

"Soup de Boo-er."

"Soup de Flu-er."

"Can I get you anything else?" The waitress asked chirpily.

Brannagh and Nikki sniggered, cupping their hands over their mouths like a couple of grade-schoolers caught pinging eraser bits. Try as hard as they might, neither could emit one coherent word in reply.

When they slid clear out of their seats, heads dipping below the table, the waitress huffed, "Well, just let me know if you need anything else," and walked away.

"I'm glad you're back," Brannagh said.

"Me too."

"I have to go back to Saint John."

"Oh?"

"I have to talk to the police. It's a long story."

"I'm not going anywhere." Nikki's brown eyes warmed Brannagh clear down to the tips of her toes.

Beneath the table, she reached for his outstretched hand.

Kathy-Diane Leveille

Kathy-Diane Leveille is a former broadcast journalist with the Canadian Broadcasting Corporation. Her short story collection *Roads Unraveling* was published to critical acclaim. Kathy-Diane's prose has been published in a number of literary journals including *The Oklahoma Review*, *Pottersfield Portfolio* and *The Cormorant*. Her poetry received Honorable Mention in the Stephen Leacock International Poetry Competition. She is a member of the Writers' Union of Canada and Canadian Crime Writers. When she isn't writing, Kathy-Diane spends her time daydreaming in the garden and watching the birds on the East Coast where she lives with her husband and two sons.

KÜNATI

Kunati Book Titles
Provocative. Bold. Controversial.

Cooked in LA ■ Paul Cook

How does a successful young man from a "good" home hit bottom and risk losing it all? *Cooked In La* shows how a popular, middle-class young man with a bright future in radio and television is nearly destroyed by a voracious appetite for drugs and alcohol.

Non Fiction/Self-Help & Recovery | US$ 24.95
Pages 304 | Cloth 5.5" x 8.5"
ISBN 978-1-60164-193-9

Against Destiny
■ Alexander Dolinin

A story of courage and determination in the face of the impossible. The dilemma of the unjustly condemned: Die in slavery or die fighting for your freedom.

Fiction | US$ 24.95
Pages 448 | Cloth 5.5" x 8.5"
ISBN 978-1-60164-173-1

Let the Shadows Fall Behind You
■ Kathy-Diane Leveille

The disappearance of her lover turns a young woman's world upside down and leads to shocking revelations of her past. This enigmatic novel is about connections and relationships, memory and reality.

Fiction | US$ 22.95
Pages 288 | Cloth 5.5" x 8.5"
ISBN 978-1-60164-167-0

Ruby's Humans
■ Tom Adrahtas

No other book tells a story of abuse, neglect, escape, recovery and love with such humor and poignancy, in the uniquely perceptive words of a dog. Anyone who's ever loved a dog will love Ruby's sassy take on human foibles and manners.

Non Fiction | US$ 19.95
Pages 192 | Cloth 5.5" x 8.5"
ISBN 978-1-60164-188-5

KÜNATI

Kunati Book Titles
•••••••••••••••••••••••••••
Provocative. Bold. Controversial.

The Unbreakable Child ■ Kim Richardson

Starved, beaten and abused for nearly a decade, orphan Kimmi learned that evil can wear a nun's habit. A story not just of a survivor but of a rare spirit who simply would not be broken.

Non Fiction/True Crime | US$ 24.95
Pages 256 | Cloth 5.5" x 8.5"
ISBN 978-1-60164-163-2

Save the Whales Please
■ Konrad Karl Gatien & Sreescanda

Japanese threats and backroom deals cause the slaughter of more whales than ever. The first lady risks everything—her life, her position, her marriage—to save the whales.

Fiction | US$ 24.95
Pages 448 | Cloth 5.5" x 8.5"
ISBN 978-1-60164-165-6

Screenshot
■ John Darrin

Could you resist the lure of evil that lurks in the anonymous power of the Internet? Every week, a mad entrepreneur presents an execution, the live, realtime murder of someone who probably deserves it. *Screenshot*: a techno-thriller with a provocative premise.

Fiction | US$ 24.95
Pages 416 | Cloth 5.5" x 8.5"
ISBN 978-1-60164-168-7

KÜNATI

Kunati Book Titles
Provocative. Bold. Controversial.

Touchstone Tarot ■ Kat Black

Internationally renowned tarot designer Kat Black, whose *Golden Tarot* remains one of the most popular and critically acclaimed tarot decks on the market, has created this unique new deck. In *Touchstone Tarot*, Kat Black uses Baroque masterpieces as the basis for her sumptuous and sensual collaged portraits. Intuitive and easy to read, this deck is for readers at every level of experience. This deluxe set, with gold gilt edges and sturdy hinged box includes a straightforward companion book with card explanations and sample readings.

Non Fiction/New Age | US$ 32.95 | Tarot box set with 200-pages booklet | Cards and booklet 3.5" x 5"
ISBN 978-1-60164-190-8

Sleepers Awake
■ Patrick McNulty

Monstrous creatures invade our world in this dark fantasy in which death is but a door to another room of one's life.

Fiction | US$ 22.95
Pages 320 | Cloth 5.5" x 8.5"
ISBN 978-1-60164-166-3

The Nation's Highest Honor
■ James Gaitis

Like Kosinski's classic *Being There*, *The Nation's Highest Honor* demonstrates the dangerous truth that incompetence is no obstacle to making a profound difference in the world.

Fiction | US$ 22.95
Pages 288 | Cloth 5.5" x 8.5"
ISBN 978-1-60164-172-4

The Woman Who Would Be Pharaoh
■ William Klein

Shadowy figures from Egypt's fabulous past glow with color and authenticity. Tragic love story weaves a rich tapestry of history, mystery, regicide and incest.

Fiction/Historic | US$ 24.95
Pages 320 | Cloth 5.5" x 8.5"
ISBN 978-1-60164-189-2

KÜNATI

Kunati Book Titles
Provocative. Bold. Controversial.

The Short Course in Beer
■ Lynn Hoffman

A book for the legions of people who are discovering that beer is a delicious, highly affordable drink that's available in an almost infinite variety. Hoffman presents a portrait of beer as fascinating as it is broad, from ancient times to the present.

Non Fiction/Food/Beverages | US$ 24.95
Pages 224 | Cloth 5.5" x 8.5"
ISBN 978-1-60164-191-5

Under Paris Skies
■ Enrique von Kiguel

A unique portrait of the glamorous life of well-to-do Parisians and aristocratic expatriates in the fifties. Behind the elegant facades and gracious manners lie dark, deadly secrets

Fiction | US$ 24.95
Pages 320 | Cloth 5.5" x 8.5"
ISBN 978-1-60164-171-7

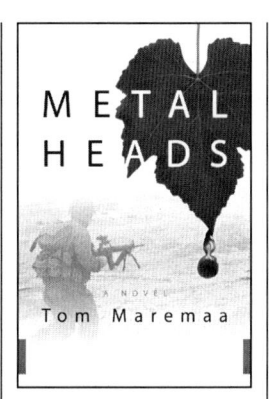

Metal Heads
■ Tom Maremaa

A controversial novel about wounded Iraq war vets and their "*Clockwork Orange*" experiences in a California hospital.

Fiction | US$ 22.95
Pages 288 | Cloth 5.5" x 8.5"
ISBN 978-1-60164-170-0

Lead Babies
■ Joanna Cerazy & Sandra Cottingham

Lead-related Autism, ADHD, lowered IQ and behavior disorders are epidemic. *Lead Babies* gives detailed information to help readers leadproof their homes and protect their children from the beginning of pregnancy through rearing.

Non Fiction/ Health/Fitness & Beauty | US$ 24.95
Pages 256 | Cloth 5.5" x 8.5"
ISBN 978-1-60164-192-2